SPELLBREAKER

FIRST ORDINANCE SERIES, BOOK FOUR

CONNIE SUTTLE

subtledemon.com

Print Second Edition (2018)
Print ISBN: 1-63478-074-4
Print ISBN-13: 978-1-63478-074-2
eBook ISBN: 1-93975-935-8
eBook ISBN-13: 978-1-93975-935-1

Published by:
SubtleDemon Publishing, LLC
PO Box 95696
Oklahoma City, OK 73143

Cover art by Renee Barratt @ The Cover Counts

To Walter, Joe, Larry, Lee, Dianne, Sarah and Mark.
Thank you.

ACKNOWLEDGMENTS

As always, this book is the result of collaboration. If it weren't for the support of my editor, my cover artist and my beta readers, it would be less than it is. All mistakes, as usual, are mine and no other's.

About the Author:
Connie Suttle lives in Oklahoma with her husband and a conglomerate of cats. They have finally banded together to make their demands, which has proven disconcerting to all humans involved.

You may find Connie in the following ways:
Facebook: Connie Suttle Author
Twitter: @subtledemon
Website and Blog: subtledemon.com

ALSO BY CONNIE SUTTLE

Blood Destiny Series:

Blood Wager

Blood Passage

Blood Sense

Blood Domination

Blood Royal

Blood Queen

Blood Rebellion

Blood War

Blood Redemption

Blood Reunion

Blood Destiny Series Boxed Set (Books 1-10)

Blood Recall

Blood Alliance*

Legend of the Ir'Indicti Series:

Bumble

Shadowed

Target

Vendetta

Destroyer

Legend of the Ir'Inditi Boxed Set

~

Rose and Thorn

Black Rose Queen

Queen of Thorns and Roses

Future Wars Series

Buffer Zone

Black Zone*

Other Titles from SubtleDemon Publishing:

Malefactor

Transgressor

Underhanded*

by Joe Scholes

*Forthcoming

CHAPTER 1

*A**vii Castle*
   Quin

There is a song the fierce winds sing as they whip and curve about Avii Castle. I heard its music as I stood on the terrace outside Gurnil's Library, while rain blew into my face and dripped from my hair.

I watched as Commander Ardis drilled his troops in swift, aerial eddies while tourists on three boats observed from the waters below.

Even to someone who'd witnessed the drills many times, the synchronized flight of the Black Wing army was still a marvel to see.

"Quin, why are you standing here in the rain?" Gurnil stopped beside me. I wore no coat or cloak; he was wrapped in heavy wool against the weather, his blue wings covered by damp, gray cloth.

My hesitation to answer made him breathe a troubled sigh. The past six months on Le-Ath Veronis were a gift. Nothing had demanded my attention, other than my training sessions and those who'd chosen me as their mate. I'd spent the previous night with Bel Erland, who'd had to leave quite early to attend court with his father, the King of Karathia.

If Justis knew I stood on the Library terrace with only Gurnil to accompany me, he'd demand that I have breakfast with him. It would be a sly way to inform me that I shouldn't go about without a guard nearby. For that reason, I hesitated to tell him that something seemed amiss—that those who'd taken Vardil Cayetes' body now troubled my dreams and waking thoughts.

~

Le-Ath Veronis
Lissa

Erland was correct—I needed wine and his steady hand around mine to hear my grandfather's story.

Wylend Arden, King of Karathia for more than twenty-thousand years, had quite a story to tell.

"It began like this," he said, his smile slightly crooked as he lifted his cup of wine to me. "I had an older brother, born to one of my father's legitimate mates. His name was Wellend and he was heir to the Karathian throne. On his sixteenth birthday, my father gifted him with the Heir's ring, as was proper. For nearly six thousand years, he stood beside my father as an advisor. He was with Father the day the coup was launched, but managed to get away. Some say he ran at the first sign of violence, but I wasn't there and can't verify anything."

"Where were you?" I asked.

"I was second-in-line to the throne, so I was at the summer palace," my grandfather shrugged. "It's where I was most of the time, unless Father summoned me. Erland was with me," he nodded to Erland.

"So the coup happened and Wellend got away. Then what?" I asked.

"Erland and I spent several days looking for Wellend. We wanted to attack those who'd killed my parents, but Wellend was the reigning King at that point. We had to find him first."

"Did you find him?"

"He was cowering in the library of the Queen's Palace, where his mother lived," Erland muttered.

"So your mother—my great-grandmother, died with my great-grandfather, then?" I turned back to Wylend.

"Yes. Helsa, Wellend's mother, seldom stayed at the palace—by her choice. When we arrived at the Queen's Palace, we asked Wellend to join us in our attempt to take back the throne. He wanted no part of it, but didn't stand in our way, either. I told him he wasn't safe where he was—if we could find him, so could the enemy. Still, he refused to fight with us. We left him there, gathered those about us still loyal to my father and attacked the palace. Eventually we took it back, but there were devastating losses on both sides."

"What about Wellend?"

"The enemies of the throne found him," Erland explained. "Before we could send some of ours to protect him, he died. The Heir's ring was taken from his finger and nobody knew what happened to it. I always assumed the enemy took it and destroyed the thing."

"Why is it so important?" I asked.

"Because if it is placed on the hand of one who isn't the heir, it disappears and finds its way to the real heir. It did not find its way to me or to our younger brother, Wallend."

"What happened to Wallend?" I was surprised to hear that I had great-uncles to begin with.

"Got drunk and died in a fight with another warlock, after claiming he was the rightful heir to the throne."

"Are there any other family members you haven't told me about?"

"Other than Wallend's line, including Daris and Deris, that's it."

"So Wallend was married? What about Wellend?"

"Wellend's two wives had no children by him," Wylend shrugged. "Wallend's wife became pregnant right away—with his twins. Why they consider themselves heirs instead of me, I'll never know."

"Did Wellend and Wallend have the same mother?" I asked.

"Bingo," Erland tapped his nose. "Helsa was quite the shrew, too."

"I can't believe they wouldn't fight beside you," I huffed. "What kind of warlocks were they?"

"Weak ones," Erland sipped his wine. "Wellend was barely Third-level. Wallend much the same. Warlend, their father, ignored it when Wylend surpassed both."

"What is Deris and Daris' level, then?" I asked.

"Deris, a low Five. Daris, a strong Four. Both surpass their sire," my grandfather said. "I imagine they received their talent from their mother—Valia's line contained many powerful warlocks and witches."

"Strong enough to cause a lot of trouble, then."

"More than strong enough," Erland agreed.

"Is their mother still alive? What about Welend's wife?" I asked.

"Valia, the twins' mother and Wallend's only wife, died protecting her husband and children from an attack, if reports are correct," Erland said. "Wellend's first wife, Palia, died in the attack that killed her husband. His second wife, Titia, remarried into another line and has great-grandchildren now. She is no threat to us. Helsa, Wallend and Wellend's mother, survived, only to die a short time later."

"What happened to her, then?" I asked.

"She perished in an unusual accident—according to rumor. I never saw the body. Those who found her say it was a spell gone wrong. It destroyed her." Wylend shook his head. "If she were alive, I'd be talking to her, now, asking what put it in her twin grandchildren's heads that they're heirs to the throne of Karathia."

King's Palace
Karathia
Bel Erland

"Glad that's over," I said, flopping onto a sofa in Dad's suite. Court had taken twice as long as it should have, which was actually a good thing—most court days took three or four times as long as they should.

"It was a short docket," Dad grinned before *Pulling* in a bottle of wine and popping the cork. "Want some?"

"Yeah."

He poured two glasses after *Pulling* those in as well. The kitchen staff was used to things appearing and disappearing—the place was spelled not to allow anything off the shelf if the taker weren't authorized.

It worked very well—for the most part. Occasionally we'd hear from the head cook if we'd taken something he needed to prepare a meal, but after a while, he'd calm down again. Usually after Dad sent him his favorite sparkling wine and a basket of gishi fruit.

"My King," Corolan poked his head in the door. "We have the prospective guards outside, and after that, the assistant cooks the head cook sent for your consideration."

"Prospective guards?" I lifted an eyebrow at Dad.

"Yes," he shrugged. "You know very well that you and Quin are in need of guards."

"Quin won't like it," I said. "She likes her alone time." I felt the same and didn't appreciate being broadsided like this, but managed to keep my complaints in check.

"She can have her alone time, as long as there's a guard or two within shouting distance. This is my future daughter-in-law," Dad argued. "She'll be a target for our not-so-law-abiding relatives, since they're still out there, somewhere. We've seen already that they're not opposed to black wizardry to get what they want. We can't say what they'll cook up next, either. Quin—I don't want her hurt."

"Or me, either," I said. I could see it in his eyes—he worried they'd come after me. If they eliminated all others in line for the throne—I realized I didn't want to consider what could happen after that. Still, I didn't like being cornered and forced to accept someone Dad chose for us.

"That's why I had to exert so much pressure to bring one of these guards to the palace," Dad added. His eyes twinkled for a moment.

"You didn't," I said, squeezing my wineglass so hard it snapped in my hand. Dad waved his free hand and put it back together before a single drop of wine hit the carpet at my feet.

Feeling embarrassed, I gripped the wineglass as it hung in the air before me.

"I did," Dad said, continuing his conversation. "I had to wave the royal arm to do it, but he's here."

"You know—this could work," I said after thinking about it for a moment. "Ilya Ironsmith is just as private and closed-mouthed as Quin ever was."

"Falchani-trained—with blades and hand-to-hand, in addition to being a strong, Fifth-level warlock. I doubt many could stand against him," Dad said. "I want you to choose one more guard—one you think Quin will accept."

"That may be tougher than you think," I snorted. "Corolan, send them in. I'll take a look and ask questions. Lots of questions."

~

King's Palace—Karathia
Zaria

I waited in line with the rest of the prospective assistant cooks. I'd been wandering aimlessly about for more than six moon-turns, but as most planets had a variation in the number of days that actually was, I didn't bother making an attempt to sort out exactly how much time had passed.

It was time to take a job and settle myself. I could cook and this was a good way to get to the palace. With forged paperwork in hand, proclaiming me a strong Third-level witch, I imagined that I'd have just as good a chance as any other.

After all, the head cook had been pleased with my cooking skills in the kitchen; I merely had to pass the inspection of King Rylend Morphis and his son, Prince Bel Erland.

That's when I saw him, waiting in a separate line ahead of mine. He never looked back, either, standing solid and patient until called into the King's presence.

By the time I could get my breath back, he'd disappeared into the King's private study.

WhatshouldIdo? WhatshouldIdo?

With my heart squeezing in my chest, I worked desperately to calm down before my group of assistant cooks was called in to see the King.

~

Bel Erland

"Ironsmith. That's the only one I'll accept," I said. "The rest—completely unsuitable," I added after Dad dismissed the last of the prospective guards. I didn't like any of them, and Quin certainly wouldn't like any of them.

"Then I expect you to find another guard—one *I* find suitable, before you go back to Avii Castle," Dad snapped. "Corolan, bring in the assistant cooks."

I wanted to argue with my father, but he'd outmaneuvered me by calling in the next round of potential servants. Silently fuming, I stood beside Dad's desk as seven walked in. Four witches, three warlocks. I scanned the paper list that lay on Dad's desk and noticed there was nothing there above Third-level. Most were Ones and Twos.

A glass paperweight held the list down on the desk. It was clear—the glass—and contained a real dragonfly, its body an unusual, deep red, its wings perfect and outspread. The paperweight was a gift from Uncles Drake and Drew, when Dad took the Karathian throne.

Dad was quite fond of the bauble. I lifted it off the paper and hefted it in my palm. Heavy, too, I noticed.

"Heads up," I shouted and threw the paperweight as hard as I could toward the waiting seven. Yes, I admit I was pissed at Dad, and fully intended to halt the paperweight before it actually hit anything—or anybody.

Before I could produce the spell (which only took a fraction of a second), the paperweight was halted in midair by one of the assistant cooks while the others cringed. She stepped forward, plucked the paperweight out of the air and brought it to me.

It was set on Dad's desk with a firm thump.

"That was unnecessary," she hissed at me. "A Fifth-level, tossing shit at his underlings? Really?"

I gazed into bright-blue eyes that blazed with anger. She shoved a swath of black hair away from her face as she continued to glare at me.

"You're hired," I blurted. "As a bodyguard for my intended."

~

Ilya

"Ironsmith, this is Zaria Keppler," the Prince introduced the woman to me. "She will be the second guard," he added.

I looked her up and down before coming back to the Prince.

Had he hired her for her looks? That was my first concern. She wasn't even dressed as a guard. She wore black, loose pants and a white, double-breasted, long-sleeved shirt, which would look better in a kitchen.

It hit me, then. The cook's assistants had lined up behind the guards. This woman was one of them. The Prince *did* hire her for her looks. I refused to acknowledge her and turned my gaze away from both.

"Well, you'll get to know one another after a while," the Prince said uncomfortably. "You're both going with me tomorrow morning to Le-Ath Veronis. I'll arrange for you to meet Quin at my grandmother's palace. Pack your things tonight and be ready to go at six bells."

~

Avii Castle

Quin

Justis went with me to Queen Lissa's palace; Bel Erland said he wanted to meet us there for breakfast with his grandmother. I imagined there was more information coming, but I didn't say it when he sent mindspeech.

Whatever it was, he wanted it to remain secret until he could tell me when we were alone. I understood that. Drake and Drew arrived in Justis' suite to transport us; Justis ran a hand down my feathers, which were still as black as his once were, then nodded to the Falchani twins that we were ready to go.

Bel Erland and Queen Lissa were there to greet us, but standing behind Bel were two others. I read the first one—the man. He was trained extensively as a bodyguard. The other? I couldn't read her.

8

That made me blink stupidly for a moment. I turned back to the man and read in him that he thought her weak and ineffective as a bodyguard, as she'd been a prospective cook's assistant before Bel hired her.

I then turned to Bel and saw what he'd seen—that he'd launched a heavy paperweight at her and the other cook's assistants, and she'd stopped it in midair before he could. The other six had cowered away from Bel's anger.

I wanted to laugh at what she did next, thumping the paperweight on the King's desk and scolding Bel Erland—a Prince—in front of his father.

"These are your new guards," Bel announced. "Because Dad insisted."

"I think they should join us for breakfast," I said, surprised that I'd spoken out of turn.

"That's fine," Queen Lissa smiled at me. "Shall we?"

"You applied as a cook's helper?" Queen Lissa turned to Zaria—that was her name—as we sat eating breakfast.

"Yes. I thought I'd be whipping up omelets for the King, the Prince and anybody else who came along," Zaria shrugged. "Until I jumped on the Prince in front of his father. I imagined I'd see the door shortly after that."

"It was funny," Bel Erland admitted. "I don't think anybody outside the family has ever told me off like that."

"You deserved it," Queen Lissa rounded on him.

"I know. I was pissed at Dad and worried about Quin at the same time. It was stupid."

"Worried about me, or what I'd think?" I asked.

"Sweetheart," Bel held up a hand.

"I think the scolding Zaria handed you was sufficient punishment," I said. "She has my permission to do it again, if you deserve it again."

Bel and Lissa burst into laughter. Justis smiled; Zaria, sitting opposite us and next to Ilya, ducked her head. I noticed then that he was right-handed, and she was left-handed. She likely had to work to keep their elbows from knocking during the meal.

I was beginning to accept the idea that they'd be my bodyguards; they felt as if they belonged in a way I couldn't explain.

Ilya

I was invited to spar with Caylon Black when we returned to Avii Castle. I'd offered to transport the five of us, but Prince Bel Erland performed that duty.

I imagined that Caylon wanted to feel us out—to determine how skilled Zaria and I were. I had no doubts about my skills.

Zaria's? I had many.

Bel Erland informed us that we'd begin our duties the following day, before allowing servants to lead us toward our quarters. As expected, those quarters were on either side of Quin's, where the Prince would also be staying when he visited Avii Castle.

Dena, a talkative yellow-winged servant, took us through the castle until we arrived at our suites. I merely wanted to change into sparring clothes in order to meet Caylon.

Zaria, on the other hand, wanted to explore everything. I almost laughed at the prospect of her lifting a blade—I doubted she'd held anything more dangerous than a filleting knife in all her years.

I still hadn't spoken to her; I'd gleaned my information from the conversation she had with Dena. Dena was quite excited and offered to take her about. Zaria accepted. I held back a snort at life's inequities.

I imagined that Caylon Black would find her unsuitable immediately and Bel Erland would be forced to admit the mistake he'd made in hiring her.

Zaria

Yes, asshole Ironsmith had stuck around to see how long it took Caylon Black to wipe the grass with my remains. If he'd been the least bit polite, I might have assigned a less judgmental name to him.

He insisted on being an asshole, which not only upset me greatly, it made me question—again—why I was and where I was.

"I have not trained with blade or bow, Sursee Black," I said, bowing properly to him in the Falchani way. "All I have is the power granted to me by my race and a sharp tongue, if the Prince is to be believed."

Caylon Black stood, unmoving, on the grass within Avii Castle's great, glass bowl. He studied me carefully. When he moved, he moved swiftly, throwing the knife so it would graze my ribs.

It would have left a shallow, bloody cut behind—if it had hit me.

It didn't.

The knife stopped halfway between us; I'd left it hanging in midair. With hooded eyes, Caylon stepped forward to retrieve the knife, only to yelp and drop it to the ground—I'd heated it, handle included, hot enough to burn skin.

I could have done so much more, including a poison that would have rendered his hand useless from now on, but that I held in reserve.

"What the bloody hell?" Ilya thought to intervene. I slapped a bubble shield about him—one meant to rotate as he attempted to walk closer. Like a hamster in a ball, he walked in place until he realized the trap. I had no intention to hurt him; I only wanted to stop him in his tracks.

"Sursee Black, is there anything else you'd like to see?" I asked.

"You see this?" he held up his burned hand.

"Aww, I can fix that," I declared. Walking forward, I took his hand in mine and healed the burn, leaving pink, healthy flesh behind. He blinked as he flexed his hand—the pain had disappeared.

"Karathian Witches who can heal are extremely rare," he breathed.

"Yeah. I get that," I said. "It's just a sideline."

"I believe Ilya is shouting," Caylon pointed out. I turned toward

Ilya, who was still inside his bubble and fighting to get out. "And he's a Fifth-level," I muttered, removing the bubble with a thought.

"When in the bloody history of Karathia were you last tested for talent?" he shouted, once the shield was down.

"Not since I was a child," I snapped. "My mother died in Didge when I was seven. She used the last of her power to send me to safety. I never saw her again, and as I grew up on Tulgalan with an aunt, there wasn't anybody willing to take me back to Karathia for reassessment."

"So Third-level is your assessment after the power was awakened?" Ilya's voice went quiet.

"Yes. It's on my application; that I haven't been tested since."

"There is no need to have this argument where the entire castle can hear you," Caylon warned.

"Shall we sort this out over dinner?" Ilya demanded.

"Not without a referee," I snapped back.

"Ardis has arrived," Caylon announced, breaking up the argument.

"Ahem," the Black Wing Commander began as he folded long, jet-black wings and frowned at us. "I—and every other Avii in the castle—can hear you quite clearly," he said. "While I find it entertaining, I really would prefer that King Justis not discover what polar opposites the Karathian guards for his Queen are."

"Sorry," I apologized.

"My apologies, Commander," Ilya gave a half-bow.

Showoff, I sent to Ilya.

He didn't raise his head for several seconds. It took me that long to realize he was struggling not to laugh.

"Unbelievable," I muttered and folded space to my suite.

〜

Quin

"I heard there was an argument on the lawn," Justis noted as a plate of food was set in front of him. "Your new guards, if I'm not mistaken."

"They've worked together one day," I said as a plate was set in front of me. "You can't expect perfection in a matter of hours."

"If Caylon hadn't passed on both of them," Justis cut into the chunk of meat on his plate, "I'd have sent them away myself."

"But I like them," I said.

"You like them?" Justis' fork was poised halfway to his mouth as he blinked in surprise.

"I do. Zaria wastes no time in telling males off. If I have her as a guard, I'm hoping to learn from her."

"That doesn't sound promising," Justis muttered before stuffing the chunk of steak in his mouth and chewing.

"If I am forced to have guards, then these are the ones I want," I declared.

"I'm not sure you need to learn anything from Zaria," Justis remarked after swallowing. "I think you have things well enough in hand already."

I didn't reply, I merely rustled my wings, letting him know what I thought of his assessment.

~

Le-Ath Veronis
   Sun City
   Terrett
Berel and I had been out all day, in Sun City. Sun City was the closest large city to Avii Castle, and Justis had asked us to shop for agricultural equipment and supplies for the Avii farmers.

Everything we'd selected would be delivered by boat the following day; neither of us had the ability to transport ourselves by folding space.

Therefore, we had to send mindspeech to Justis when we were done, thinking that Salidar, Caylon or someone else with folding talent would come for us.

We were quite surprised to see who did come.

"Zaria," she held out her hand. "One of Quin's new guards," she added. She studied me for several moments as we clasped fingers, before turning to Berel and offering her hand to him.

"You're Karathian?" Berel guessed.

"Yes, as is Ilya, the other guard. The Karathian King insisted on two guards for Quin and the Prince."

"I'm surprised you lasted a day," Berel grinned. "Quin doesn't like guards."

"But I'm so likable and nonjudgmental," Zaria grinned back.

I like her, I sent to Berel.

Me, too, he replied.

"Ready to go?" Zaria asked.

"Absolutely," Berel grinned.

Avii Castle

Quin

"Honey, I'm home," Zaria announced as she landed Berel and Terrett inside my sitting room. Bleek and Barc were there ahead of them; Barc wanted to show me the drawing he'd made in day class.

Ilya, who stood guard by the door, barely lifted an eyebrow, although I read in him that he wanted to laugh—for a second time that day.

"Look," Barc wagged his comp-vid drawing at Zaria.

"What is this?" Zaria took the comp-vid. "Why, it's a reptagator," she breathed. "And a very good one, I might add."

"She guessed it," Barc was overjoyed and clapped all four hands.

"You figured that out?" Bleek said, taking the comp-vid from Zaria. "I didn't get it."

"Here—see, this is his snout, with all the teeth," Zaria pointed at the drawing. "His legs, rubbery hide—it's a reptagator."

"Come here, you," Berel swung Barc into the air, making him squeal with delight.

"Dearest?" Kaldill appeared inside my sitting room, careful not to knock into anyone else. For a moment, he stared at Zaria while a fleeting expression of recognition moved across his features.

"Do we have new guards?" he turned to me then, while ignoring her.

Perhaps I was mistaken, but I could have sworn for just a moment that she was terrified.

Kaldill no longer cared that she was there, so I dismissed it as unimportant.

~

Ilya

Zaria excused herself, explaining that she'd spend the next two hours guarding the terrace outside Quin's suite so the two Avii guards stationed there could get a meal and rest.

"It's raining out," I said as she passed.

"I can form a shield," she muttered, brushing past me on her way through the door. I saw it, then.

The sadness. Perhaps it was because of her past—her mother's death and her forced exit from Karathia. I didn't know for certain and at that moment, I dismissed it. I hoped her skills as a witch wouldn't fail us when real trouble came. She had yet to learn what I'd asked about already—those who hunted Quin and Bel Erland.

They'd destroyed an entire planet in their attempts to kill Quin before. Things could get worse from here on out—the very throne of Karathia was their goal and they'd proven that they had no qualms about murdering anyone who stood in their way.

At least I was coming to see Zaria as something more useful than a pretty cook's assistant. She was already turning heads and deliberately ignoring all of it.

CHAPTER 2

Q uin

"We have new information," Caylon said when he and Salidar joined us at the breakfast table. "It appears the Arden twins are taking up Cayetes' old habits and pirating the shipping lanes. Three ships were taken two days ago. The information we have indicates that some of Cayetes' old crew boarded one of the ships before the recording devices were shut down."

"Where are the ships now?" Lafe asked.

"One is missing, the other two's crews were killed and the ships left to drift after everything of value was stripped out of them."

"The one that's missing—was it a freighter?"

"Passenger ship, with a few wealthy people on board," Caylon frowned.

"You think they're looking to ransom them?" Ilya asked. He and Zaria were at the table—with several people between them. I hadn't failed to notice the distance they placed between themselves.

"We don't know, and the pirates have Sirenali, so even the most powerful can't find the hostages—wherever they are."

Terrett hmmphed in his throat, pointing out his displeasure at their use of Sirenali, all of whom were little more than slaves. Like him, they'd had their tongues removed at an early age so they couldn't place obsession—and somehow, they'd been obsessed at the same time, so they'd never be able to fold space.

"So their ID chips have been deactivated? The hostages, I mean," Zaria asked.

"It looks that way. All mundane methods of tracking have been destroyed or neutralized," Caylon replied. "No surprise, really, when you consider that we're dealing with a Fifth-level warlock and a strong, Fourth-level witch."

"These are the ones King Rylend worries about?" Ilya asked.

"Yes." I couldn't help thinking of all the lives lost, because of them and Vardil Cayetes, the master who'd commanded them.

Why they'd taken Vardil with them remained a mystery. I hoped we'd solve before it morphed into something we couldn't deal with. As far as we knew, Vardil was little more than a babbling idiot, even with the dark spells they'd placed upon him.

"So they needed Cayetes for something; that's why they took him with them," Zaria spoke. She'd said aloud what I'd been wondering myself.

"He's little more than a rag doll, according to Karzac," Caylon pointed out.

"Until they need a fingerprint, DNA, an eyescan or something else that only he has," Zaria replied.

"That's disturbing," Lafe sighed. "And could likely prove true."

"It's also a way to keep Cayetes' underlings in line—if Deris and Daris can make them believe that Cayetes is still in charge. Perhaps that's why they've started their pirating business again," Zaria pointed out. "To keep those underlings occupied with their usual duties while the Arden twins work on getting what they want from Cayetes. Once that happens, then the rest of them should watch their steps or they'll be fried—or worse—by those two."

I noticed Ilya staring at her, then; he couldn't understand how she'd gotten so much information in so little time.

As I couldn't read her, still, I was unable to tell him what he wanted to know, although I was just as curious as he was about it.

"You think we should actively hunt them, then?" I pointed my question at Zaria. "The ASD is already hunting them, for the obvious reasons. They've merely had little luck in finding them."

"Oh, we should hunt them, all right," Zaria replied. "I want to see those suckers die."

"Suckers?" Berel asked. It was an unusual term and one most of us wouldn't have used.

"Better than saying fuckers in royal company," Zaria replied, nodding to Bel Erland and me. "Excuse me, please." She scooted her chair away from the library table where we'd met for breakfast.

We watched as she made her plate disappear; I imagined it plopped onto the table in the kitchen, where it would wait to be washed by the Yellow Wings there. Then, she disappeared from our sight.

I understood the need to be alone at times. I imagined she'd return if Bel Erland or I had need of her. That was her job, after all.

Bel Erland, who sat next to me, rubbed my back gently. *She'll be back*, he sent. *I think this is new for her—she expected to be working in a kitchen.*

I understand that, I replied. *I still like her—there's just some sadness and urgency in her. I can't put my finger on it.*

"Those words rhyme in the English language, while they don't in Alliance common," Salidar pointed out. "Sucker and fucker." He spoke in the designated language to prove his point.

"I guess you'd know," Caylon huffed before turning back to his eggs and bacon. I could tell that Sal knew something Caylon didn't, and that irked Caylon. The trouble was, that's all I could see in either of them. Whatever Sal knew, it was blocked from me for some reason, and I couldn't figure that out.

My talent appeared to be fine with everyone else, so I didn't quibble about it. I'd either learn it in time or I wouldn't. Still, it made me curious; I'd met few I couldn't read and somehow, Zaria was on that list.

"We're set to have a meeting with Justis this afternoon," Caylon said, breaking the tension at the table. "Queen Lissa is scheduled to come, too, to discuss continuing our involvement in the pirating trade. We're holding the meeting in her library."

∾

I wasn't surprised to see the ones who'd manned the BlackWing ships before. Amos and Flossie Thompson were having tea with Queen Lissa in her library when we arrived.

Yanzi, who'd been visiting his brothers, arrived with two of them —Farzi and Nenzi. Those two had captained BlackWing II, so of course they'd be there. Yanzi gave me a firm hug and kiss before taking my hand and sitting beside me. Bel Erland grinned and let Yanzi have his seat.

Jayna had also come; Caylon was happy with her progress as a trainee and with his permission, she'd volunteered to serve aboard a BlackWing ship. His stipulation was that she continue with her training, and I imagined that someone would be on the same ship to ensure that she received it.

I'm sure he'd say the same to me; I spent two hours each day training with Justis' troops—Caylon now taught hand-to-hand combat while Ardis only taught aerial combat. In fact, Ardis lined up with the others when Caylon held training sessions. Salidar, Drake and Drew assisted Caylon, because of the sheer number of troops they trained.

Once we were all together in Lissa's library, Ilya and Zaria took up positions by the door, to guard us. I didn't imagine that anyone or anything could successfully attack Lissa in her palace, but they were ready, in case that happened.

Zaria had found a better wardrobe for her new position—suitable pants and shirts that allowed for easy movement. I imagined they'd also provide some protection if she were attacked.

Ilya wore leathers like most Falchani warriors did and, like them, he was quite serious when on duty.

"While it appears that Cayetes' ships are back in business," Lissa announced, "Kooper says they've found evidence that drakus seed has been traded between criminal factions. I think the Arden twins have used this past six months to grow more of that shit and now they're selling it."

"No word on where they're growing it?" Lafe asked.

"Nothing yet. It may be that it's growing wherever they're hiding out. As a side note, there are six more planets infected with the poison."

"So we can be assured they're not on a poisoned planet, then," Kaldill appeared inside the library. "Sorry I'm late; I've been instructing Lendill on court protocol. He has little patience, and that is a must when hearing complaints."

He turned toward me then and offered a brilliant smile. I couldn't help it—I smiled back at him.

"I suppose that means we can weed out all those planets affected," Lissa hunched her shoulders. She knew, just as I did, that something needed to be done soon or the poison would destroy the worlds it infected.

I wanted to curse the rogue gods responsible for that, but didn't fully understand which ones to blame. Liron, after all, had provided protection from the poison for Siriaa—until his death. Then, due to the failure of a physician to do as Liron asked, followed by the rise of a grasping Prince and his evil advisor, Siriaa had been overcome by the spreading menace.

I would never forget, too, the part Vardil Cayetes played in spreading the poison throughout the universe by blasting a dying Siriaa to bits.

Those bits were now traveling, unhindered, to other worlds, where the poison was more than willing to grow and spread through fertile ground.

"They need plenty of water to grow drakus seed," Kaldill pointed out, bringing me back to the present. "On Vic'Law, the fields were near the ocean, where it was easy enough to supply desalinated water to the plants during dry periods."

Kaldill knew plants and trees—I think it was in his blood,

somehow. The Elf King could grow roses in solid rock if he wanted, and in seconds, too—I'd seen him do it.

He smiled at me again while a beautiful, red rose appeared in his hand. It floated toward me until I could pluck it from the air.

Thank you, I sent to him.

You are more lovely, he replied, *than any flower I have ever seen.*

"The Larentii have gone *Looking* for the Arden twins," Daragar announced after appearing behind my sofa. "There is obvious Sirenali involvement—we can find nothing relating to them or to the drakus seed."

"So they have Sirenali at the seed fields and Sirenali aboard the ships taking it offworld," Zaria spoke up. "Or someone would be able to find it."

"True," Daragar turned toward her. "Q'elindi," he bowed to her.

Ilya and Bel Erland drew in a breath.

Bel Erland

"Did you know?" I demanded.

"I suspected," Zaria shrugged. "I've never been tested again, so you see why it remained a suspicion."

We'd adjourned our meeting shortly after Daragar's arrival, which meant I could question Zaria about her hidden talents. I considered calling Dad, but he was in a meeting. I decided to contact him later.

"How have you survived with the visions this long?" I asked.

"I learned to block them," she said. "Some were just too painful."

"If you've learned to block them, then you're the first Q'elindi to do it," I sighed. "Why didn't you contact my father about this? He'd have welcomed you to court."

"I think he'd have been somewhat dubious," she replied. "How many do you get every year, claiming the same thing?"

"Several," I admitted. "Dad doesn't go easy on them after they lie to him and the court."

"I don't want to do that as my job," she hunched her shoulders. "I

21

just had a bad feeling about everything—that's why I wanted a job at the palace. Something is threatening the throne. I found out what it was when I saw you the first time."

"You read me?" I blinked at her.

"Yes. Sorry, but that was information I needed to know. It confirmed my suspicions. Now I know what's keeping me awake at night."

"Your only concern was to protect the throne?" I asked.

"When you have terrible nightmares of what may come if you don't," she said, "Then yes, my concern—and my self-appointed mission—is to protect the rightful King of Karathia and his son, the Prince."

"Jeez-Louise," I muttered one of Gran's favorite phrases while rubbing my forehead.

"Look, I can't see past a Sirenali's fog any better than anyone else," she said. "But that doesn't mean I'm not working on ways to get around it."

"Will you keep me updated?" I asked. "And I apologize for the paperweight incident. That was a stupid thing to do."

"You call what a Sirenali can do a fog?" Gran, who was also in this impromptu meeting with Ilya, Daragar and me, asked.

"It's what it looks like when I see their obsession in someone," Zaria replied. "Like their brain has been fogged and all they know from that point forward is whatever obsession has been planted there."

"We see it as much the same," Daragar admitted. "It is impossible to see through; there is information in the Archives concerning such."

"Where did you see someone who'd been obsessed?" Gran asked.

"On my way home from the market," she said. "On Tulgalan. Three men ran down the street toward me, while Targis' constables raced after them. I dropped my shield long enough to attempt to read them. That attempt was futile—I only saw the fog. Then, the one who'd obsessed them appeared from nothing. By that time, I'd transported myself to a safer place so I wouldn't be caught in the weapons crossfire. That didn't mean I couldn't read the Sirenali, however, who had murder and thievery on his mind. He disappeared with one of the culprits; the constables captured the other two, who suddenly dropped dead on the walkway and exploded. This incident is recorded in the constable's records; the three constables present would have died if I hadn't thrown a shield about them at the last moment."

"Dear God," Gran muttered. "Did the dreams start after that?"

"Shortly after, yes."

"Can you describe the Sirenali you saw?"

"Do you have paper?" she asked.

Gran *Pulled* in several sheets of paper. We watched as Zaria placed her hand on the top sheet. An image appeared beneath her fingers. It was an advanced spell that few warlocks or witches could do; it required perfect recall. Somehow, I wasn't surprised that the Q'elindi could do it.

"I'll hand this to Kooper," Gran said. "Although I worry that this Sirenali may have ordered someone to change his appearance by now."

"I will know him if I ever see him again," Zaria said. "If I understand things properly, Quin may also know."

"She will," I said, lowering my gaze. I did—and didn't—understand Zaria's reluctance to come to Dad before. It wasn't until Karathia was threatened that she'd made her way to the palace, and then, she'd applied to be a cook's assistant.

She probably found the prospect of serving the crown until the end of time somewhat smothering, Gran pointed out in mindspeech.

Try being royal—wait, you are, I teased back.

I hear that. She probably realized early on what going to see your father would entail. It's a shame in some ways and perfectly understandable in others. For now, I'd rather keep her where she is—guarding you and Quin. She seems happy enough to do that, Gran said. *If you keep her at your side, I can't imagine there'll be many unwelcome surprises coming in your direction.*

True and exactly what I was thinking, I responded.

"Zaria," I said aloud, "I'd like to keep you where you are—guarding Quin and me. I hope that's agreeable to you, too."

23

"It is, or I'd have said no in the beginning," she said.

"You need to keep this to yourselves," Daragar warned. "A Q'elindi would be considered a great prize to many, most of whom have less than legitimate reasons to want one."

"I can take care of myself," Zaria grumped.

"Honey," Gran turned to me, "Make sure the others can't say what Zaria is. Her kind are a myth and legend to most people."

"Karathian Witch, Third-level it is," I declared. "That's what she is—to all of us—from now on. I'll let Dad know, but he'll keep the secret, too."

"Come on, we have ships to stock and outfit," Gran said, rising from her chair. "Seven is the largest in the fleet, I think you should take that one," she added.

"Then we'll take seven," I agreed.

~

Ilya

I stole several glances at Zaria as we walked out of Queen Lissa's private study, but she ignored me. Again, the sadness flitted across her face and I guessed that Daragar had announced to all of us what she'd have preferred to keep secret.

I'd studied Karathian history extensively; I knew of the handful of Q'elindi who'd served the throne throughout the millennia. None had ever gone out to do battle, before. This one—she'd already said the King and Prince were in danger. If a Q'elindi predicted it, one should heed her words.

A new respect was growing for a certain witch, and I felt guilty for judging her on her beauty before I learned anything else about her.

~

Avii Castle

Quin

Kaldill and I were waiting until Bel Erland arrived before having

24

dinner; we wanted to hear what his decisions were on Zaria as much as anyone else. I wanted her to stay with me—for purely selfish reasons. I liked her, and there weren't many guards I'd willingly accept.

That she was Q'elindi surprised me greatly, and likely accounted for the fact that I couldn't read her. After all, only a few Q'elindi had ever been born. Zaria was the only one living, to my knowledge.

Bel Erland wore the biggest smile when he arrived with Ilya and Zaria. You'd think he'd been given the best gift ever. In seconds, his father, King Rylend, his grandfather, Erland Morphis, and two royal guards also arrived.

We'd have to add a few chairs to Justis' dining table, but that wouldn't be a problem.

~

Zaria

I had a private meeting with King Rylend and his father, Erland, after dinner. I was offered a glass of wine but declined; I didn't want wine clouding my thoughts when I spoke to the King.

Yes, I'd felt shaky most of the day, after Daragar spilled my secret. I'd done my best to hide my dismay—after all, if nobody is expecting what you can do, the greater the threat you can become to them.

I didn't want the enemy knowing what I was. For many reasons.

"We're not going to command you," Rylend began after we settled on comfortable chairs in Justis' sitting room. "But we'd like to hire you for certain events and court dates in the future. You'll be well-paid for your services," he added.

"I'll think on that," I replied, struggling to keep my voice even. "I'd like to eliminate this threat, first, before we make any agreements about the future."

"Understandable," Erland nodded. "We'll present this again," he promised. "At the proper time. Just keep my grandson safe."

"I intend to do just that—he and Quin," I agreed. "I will give my life to keep them safe."

"We can't ask more than that," Rylend said. "And I thank you for your dedication."

"There's something you should know," I said.

"What's that?" the King asked.

"It has to do with my past, and the trauma I experienced," I said. "I get shaky now and then—the doctor calls it trauma-induced-anxiety, but it doesn't affect me other than making me shake," I said. "I just want you to know that ahead of time—in the interest of full disclosure."

"I remember Didge and the attack by the Ra'Ak," Erland looked grim. "I'm not surprised you were affected by all that."

I wasn't about to tell him that Didge didn't cause my trauma. Other things caused it, but those were my secrets to keep.

∾

Ilya

"You're staying?" I asked as Zaria appeared outside Quin's sitting room.

"That's the plan," she said. "I think we're moving to BlackWing VII in the next day or so," she added. She sounded as if she were exhausted.

"I'll be fine," she waved off my unspoken concern. "I'll see if Quin needs anything before I go to bed."

She knocked on the door and went in when Quin answered. Only a few moments passed before she was out the door again and heading toward her bedroom. *Good-night,* I sent to her.

Thanks, she replied softly and disappeared inside her suite.

∾

Quin

"I have five suitable outfits," Zaria replied to my question at breakfast. "I probably should buy another pair of boots."

"Ilya?" I turned to him. "What about you?"

26

"I could use new boots."

"I take," Yanzi offered. "Terrett come, too."

"Yanzi, take them to Falchan," Lafe said. "I'll come with you. They ought to have boots with a knife sheath, I think."

"Good," Yanzi agreed. "We get things for Quin, too."

That's how I ended up with Lafe, Yanzi and Terrett on Falchan, where leather goods were sold. Lafe steered us away from the shops where tourists bought; we ended up on the edge of Cedar Falls, where the leather workers took orders and sold to the locals.

"Hmm, small," the shop owner studied Zaria and me. "I have something that will work," he added. Ilya already had three new sets of leathers—they'd waited on him, first.

"I can alter these in the waist and shorten them," the shop owner nodded as Zaria and I tried on leather pants meant for a tall, slender boy.

"There's no need, I can do it," Ilya offered. "It's a simple spell," he nodded to the man.

"You're Karathian?" the shop owner asked.

"He is, but he trained on Falchan," Lafe explained. "He has the tattoos to prove it."

"Have I heard of you?" the shop owner turned to Ilya.

"Ilya Ironsmith," Ilya extended his hand.

"I have heard of you," the shop owner nodded. "The warlock who refused to employ his spells in battle, unless the General commanded."

"It wasn't fair to do otherwise," Ilya remarked. "I was on loan from the Karathian King until recently," he added.

"Ah, yes. I've heard that tale. I will give a fourth of your money back if you will make the necessary alterations for these," he nodded toward Zaria and me.

"I'll accept that," Ilya agreed.

I watched as the alterations were performed on my clothing first—the hems fell where they should and the waist tightened. Then, Ilya turned to Zaria.

"Not too tight in the crotch," Zaria warned before Ilya performed the spell.

"I know better," he grinned before taking up her leathers so they fit properly. He did the same for three more outfits each, then we left the shop owner behind and went in search of boots.

"Comp-vid pouch on one side, knife sheath on the other," the bootmaker showed us what he had. The comp-vid pouch was designed for one of the smaller brands, which would fit easily if I wanted to carry one.

"Two pair, brown and black for this one," Ilya held a finger over Zaria's head. "And whatever Quin wants, of course."

Terrett, Yanzi and Lafe bought things, too, so everyone went home with something.

"We're scheduled to be on BlackWing VII before lunch tomorrow," Kaldill announced when we arrived at Avii Castle with our bundles. "Queen Lissa says to let her know what we need to get it outfitted and into the shipping lanes after that."

∽

Avii Castle

Ilya

I'd never served on a ship before; I'd only traveled on one twice in my lifetime. Folding space was much faster and a more elegant mode of transportation. I admitted to myself that this wasn't a crowded passenger ship, like I'd been on in the past. I hoped there'd be private quarters and room to walk freely throughout the vessel.

All my missions—if you could call them that, had been on Falchan's plains and in its mountains, as a scout or in small raiding parties, searching for marauders from the other side of the mountains. I hoped a closed-in space wouldn't adversely affect my capabilities, as I'd probably need my warlock's talents rather than a warrior's skills.

Therefore, I went in search of Caylon Black, to ask about the ship's schematics. He would have them, as he was placed in charge of the ship and any missions performed by the crew, with Salidar DeLuca acting as Second-in Command.

The pilots hadn't been named as yet, and I imagined they'd join our group aboard ship. I found Caylon and Salidar in the castle library, poring over the ship's schematics with Gurnil, the Blue Wing Master Scholar.

"It's big," Sal said, lifting his gaze from the three-dimensional image splayed across a table by his comp-vid. "Enough berths for everyone, including the pilots, although a few will bunk together—there's more than one bed in several berths."

"Not enough room for Quin to fly, but there is a small exercise room, a galley and dining area," Caylon pointed to those sections at the back of the ship. "Three decks," he pointed those out. "Engine and propulsion here," he indicated the back section of the lower deck. "Command Center on the upper deck," he tapped the smaller, appropriate space. "Room in the command center for two pilots and a captain, plus two or three others," he added. "It's a big ship, with berths, galley and dining on the second deck. I figure Kaldill or Daragar will shield the ship from normal sight. Terrett will keep it hidden from anyone powerful enough to scry for it."

I blinked at Caylon's remark, only then realizing that the mute Terrett was Sirenali. "He has mindspeech," Caylon said, as if reading my mind. "He speaks very well that way."

"Good to know," I mumbled. "Does Zaria have this information? Wait, that was a stupid question," I held up a hand before Caylon could point out the obvious. It probably wasn't necessary to inform the Q'elindi about anyone she'd already met.

Le-Ath Veronis
   Queen's Palace
   Lissa
"With information supplied by Caylon and Ilya, I think Zaria is at least a strong Fourth-level, and quite possibly a Fifth-level. She had Ilya walking in place inside a bubble shield that he couldn't find the exit in," Erland explained.

"I wish I'd seen that," I said. I wanted to laugh but didn't—Zaria had chosen the best way possible to contain someone without harming them.

"No other Q'elindi on record—with the exception of your sister, of course, has ever held that degree of power. Do you think she was born into this time because Karathia needs her?" Erland asked.

"That's happened before," I sighed. After all, my father had planned my birth, because, in his words, *I was the answer to so many things that troubled him.* It let me know early on that love wasn't the real reason I existed.

At least I had love now. I hoped Zaria would find love—there was a sadness in her that I couldn't define. Perhaps Bree would know, but she could be the only one.

"Lunch?" Winkler poked his head inside my study door, where Erland and I were talking.

"What do they have?" I asked, realizing suddenly that I was hungry.

"Chicken-fried steak," Winkler grinned.

No wonder he was ready to eat—chicken-fried steak was his favorite meal. "Let's go," I said. "We can talk while we eat."

~

Avii Castle

Quin

"My love," Justis kissed me again. He didn't want to let me go. He certainly didn't want me to leave Avii Castle. A part of me didn't want to leave, either. The other part of me was determined to destroy what was left of Vardil Cayetes and the Arden twins. I had Siriaa, Vic'Law and all the poisoned worlds to avenge, after all.

"My King," Dena spoke softly behind us, "Lunch is packed and ready to be transported to the ship."

"I must go," I pulled away from Justis. I found Jayna standing next to Dena when I turned; Dena looked sad that she wasn't coming with us. I knew as well as anyone that Ardis wanted her with him.

A part of me was glad she was staying at the castle; I feared for her safety where we were going.

I worried, too, that the Orb would appear and fling me and those connected to me to a dangerous place. Dena was ill-equipped to deal with that.

Jayna, on the other hand, had become adept in handling weapons and at hand-fighting. In fact, Sal said recently that if Jayna wanted a position with the ASD, all she had to do was approach Kooper Griff, the Director.

I could see plainly in her face, however, that she wanted revenge against Cayetes and the twins as much or more than I did. Her family died on Vic'Law, and she was determined to do something about it.

"We have information," Caylon appeared nearby. "Morid Belancour, who took a short trip away from Grey Planet with a Grey House wizard, has been kidnapped and the wizard with him was wounded severely. They need Quin immediately to heal the wizard so he can tell us what he knows."

CHAPTER 3

*G*rey Planet

Quin

The ship—and lunch—had to wait. I found myself transported quickly to Grey Planet, where the wizard lay mortally wounded in their tiny, family-run hospital.

Caylon, Sal, Ilya and Zaria stood nearby as I placed my hands on the blast wound in the wizard's chest, exerting all my healing talent to bring him back from certain death. After a while, I felt it when Zaria joined her talents with mine; she worked on the lower chest while I repaired the upper.

If she hadn't helped, I would have been drained completely after the healing, the wounds were so severe. Whoever had leveled the blast —and I suspected another wizard or warlock—had intended for this one to die.

"He needs to sleep so his body can adapt to the sudden changes," Zaria mumbled after she and I pulled away. Our combined work had been seamless, which astounded me. She was powerful as a healer; that much was evident.

"I need to ask questions," Caylon growled.

"I've seen everything he knows in his face," Zaria retorted. I blinked at her—she'd done already what I should have done. "Here," she held up a hand and formed a two-dimensional display of what the wizard had witnessed.

I wasn't surprised to learn that Daris had snatched Morid Belancour at a restaurant, while Deris leveled a blast at Morid's wizard companion, nearly destroying his heart. If another wizard hadn't arrived to place the wounded one in stasis, he'd have died before Zaria and I could heal him.

"Fuck," I heard Ilya mumble. "What the hell do they want with him? Morid wouldn't make Second-level as a warlock."

"Information," Zaria sighed. "Damn, I'm tired."

Caylon transported us back to Queen Lissa's palace to deliver the news we had; that Morid Belancour, Marid's eldest son, had been kidnapped on Tulgalan by the twins. Zaria and I—we'd seen the same thing in the wizard's face—that Daris and Deris had demanded information while exerting power on Morid. Morid claimed he didn't have the spell they asked about, so they'd taken him and tried to kill his companion.

"What spell?" Queen Lissa asked. I didn't know.

Zaria did.

"You need to hide that coffin in the dungeon at Avii Castle," she said. "It belongs to them and there's something hidden in the base they can't get to without the spoken words of a spell Marid of Belancour laid years ago. Likely at Vardil Cayetes' command," she added. "The coffin will destroy itself if the proper words aren't spoken to open it."

"To keep the twins in their place and in service to him, no doubt," Lissa huffed. I could tell she was angry. "Well, let's move that infernal thing to my dungeon. I'd like to see them get past me to get to it."

"Thank you," I breathed. I'd suddenly felt terrified for Justis and everyone else in Avii Castle. They had no way to combat a murderous witch and warlock, bent on taking what they saw as theirs.

"Do you know what's in it?" Lissa asked, turning back to Zaria and me.

"It's empty," Zaria shrugged. "Except for a ring and a book."

Lissa went perfectly still. "What ring?"

"It's important to them in their bid for the Karathian throne—that's all I saw in my vision of Daris and Deris."

"Oh, dear God," Lissa muttered.

Justis and I watched as the coffin was pulled out of the cell in the castle dungeon, before Lissa's Falchani mates transported it to a similar cell beneath her palace.

"Will they realize it's gone?" Justis asked. "I don't want an attack here if I can help it."

Queen Lissa, who'd come with her Falchani to remove the thing, shook her head. "I hope there's some sort of location device or spell on it," she replied. "So they'll know it isn't here any longer. It'll piss them off, but that's their problem."

I wanted to giggle at her choice of words, but held it back. Bleek was nearby; he wanted to see the thing gone, too, since it had held Barc captive inside it for so long. He wanted no reminders—for him or his son—about his enslavement while believing a promise Cayetes never intended to fulfill.

"Well, that's done," Justis remarked. "Love, stay for dinner, then go to your ship if you must," he kissed my forehead.

"I think you'll be fine," Lissa shrugged. "We've had enough excitement for today."

"Then I'll be pleased to have dinner with you," I smiled at Justis, who tipped my chin up and kissed me in front of Bleek and the Queen.

Le-Ath Veronis

Queen's Palace

Lissa

"Erland, I can mist inside it and bring out the ring, but I admit, it scares me. What if they did something to it, so it would go to one of them instead of the proper heir?"

He and I stood outside the last cell in my dungeon, staring at the jeweled coffin inside. "I suppose that's possible," he admitted. "Perhaps that's how Helsa died—subverting the ring so it would recognize one of her children instead of the one it should go to."

"So—she could have performed a black spell to exchange her life for that?" I guessed.

"It's possible. She always was a power-hungry bitch. She hated Wylend's mother, that's why they never stayed at the palace at the same time. She wanted both her sons to be first and second-in-line to the throne, since she provided the first heir, but Karathian law always said birth order determined that. She wanted the law changed."

"I just had a terrible thought," I said.

"What's that?"

"Those few days that Wellend was officially King?"

"Yes?"

"What if he changed the law during that time? After all, he'd probably listen to his mother, don't you think?"

"Fuck," Erland muttered. "Look, I need to talk with our son—and with Wylend. I'll let you know later what we find."

Avii Castle

Quin

"Everything comes back to the Arden twins," Sal said at dinner. "Cayetes, drakus seed, a ring they want badly," he shrugged. "They want the Karathian throne, that's easy enough to see, but what I don't understand is how they'll convince the people of Karathia to accept them, if they manage to take the crown."

"They will not take the crown," Ilya hissed. "Not while I live."

"I will stand between them and the real King," Zaria said, her words softer but no less resolute. "I know what they are. They are content to ignore those rather dubious facts."

"What are they—in your opinion?" Justis asked Zaria.

"Murderers. Thieves. Users of the outlawed drug, and I'm not talking about drakus seed. I'm talking about the Lyristolyi drug. The one everybody thinks has been eradicated. Drakus seed is bad enough —the other—that's worse."

"Gurnil, do we have information on this drug?" Justis turned to the Master Scholar.

"We do not," he replied, rustling his wings. "I will do research, my King, and present my findings to you soon."

"Zaria, how do you know about that drug?" Caylon asked. "It's not common knowledge anymore."

"I've done plenty of research," she said. "The information is still there, if you dig far enough."

"Perhaps you could suggest reading material?" Gurnil turned to her.

"I can," she agreed. "I'll send it to your comp-vid after dinner. In fact, the Queen's library holds books that provide information on the drug, as does the library at the University of Le-Ath Veronis. So many vampires were alive when the drug was still found and used on alien worlds, that you may be able to get firsthand accounts of it."

"I never thought of that," Gurnil breathed. I could tell he was excited about a new subject and the research it entailed. Gurnil was seldom bored; there was always something new to learn.

"I wish to help," Ordin offered. "I wish to study the records concerning the effects of this drug on its recipients."

"Prepare to be shocked," Zaria warned. "Records of its use may seem benign and even helpful at first, until it reveals its true self, which is terrifying. Worlds have died because of it. If you don't believe me, ask the Larentii."

"Ah, another resource to tap," Gurnil smiled.

"Whatever you do, though, don't approach the Lyristolyi about it," she added. "They'll do anything, up to and including murder, just to destroy a single grain of it. I hope the ASD handles this without bringing them into it."

~

Ilya

I made a mental note to research the Lyristolyi drug for myself. Drakus seed was dangerous enough. I couldn't imagine something worse. After all, drakus seed had come and gone, then come again during my lifetime.

I doubted there were many normal Alliance citizens, Reth or Campiaan, who knew anything about this one. That spelled centuries since this one had last been seen. The fact that the Arden twins apparently had both drugs troubled me greatly. What could—or would—they do with them?

"We'll cover the necessary information on-board the ship," Caylon announced. "Both drugs are in the possession of our enemy, and they've employed them for their own gain. I hope we can answer all the questions that will surely come after this discussion."

After dinner, the rest of us made our final preparations for boarding the ship while Quin had a glass of wine with Justis in private. Bel Erland found me in the Library, cleaning and polishing my blades—it was something to do to fill the time.

"I can't find Zaria by *Looking* or scrying—Dad says it's a talent belonging to the Q'elindi," he settled on a chair across from mine.

"You have a wondrous gift if you can *Look* for others," I said, holding up a blade and checking the edge.

"I get it from my grandmother," he shrugged. "But I still can't locate Zaria. I was hoping you'd know where she was."

"Outside, taking over for the guards at the terrace doors so they can get a bite to eat," I said. "I think she likes the solitude of it."

"I'm wondering how she knew so much about that drug," Bel said, looking down at his hands and sighing. "I asked Gran about it in mindspeech. She says it's just as terrible as Zaria claims it is. Gran's of an age and in a position to know that. Zaria," he lifted his eyes and shook his head at me.

"She is Q'elindi. I'm not sure any of us might predict what she knows."

"I'm surprised you're defending her. When I introduced her to you, I could almost hear you saying that I hired her for her looks. I wanted to tell you then that Quin is all I see. I'm telling you that, now."

"I've seen it for myself," I muttered, setting down one blade and lifting the other.

"I'm merely hoping—that you and Zaria come to some sort of truce where Quin and I are concerned. I hope you can work together without belittling her—well, you know what I mean."

"Zaria doesn't know much at all of a warrior's skills," I said.

"But," he began.

"My Prince, allow me to finish. Zaria hasn't been trained as a warrior. Her skills as a witch are formidable. Combine that with a Q'elindi's talent and ability, and you have a weapon in your hand that will do whatever it takes to defend you and your intended. The other —is merely training. I ask that you approach either Caylon or Sal, to give her basic instruction in hand-to-hand, as it could prove useful when a spell might be unwise."

"You don't want that duty?"

"I think she'd kill me," I stated flatly. "One of the others—she would take instruction better from them, I think."

"You don't think you'll get along, is that what you're saying?" the Prince asked.

"No, I think we can work together just fine. I know to rein in my— lack of humility, let's say—and things will likely work out. I wish I'd done it from the start, but I thought I'd be forced to work double duty to cover for someone whose only ability was her beauty."

"You should hear Corolan," the Prince snorted. "I thought he was going to write poetry after she stopped that paperweight in midair and dressed me down in front of my father."

I couldn't help the smile; I didn't want to offend the Prince, but I found the incident amusing. I wished I'd seen it for myself. If I'd known those things about Zaria before our introduction, I'd have known better than to think Bel Erland hired her for her looks.

She wouldn't mince words if she disagreed with him concerning his safety; of that much I was certain.

"So," he slapped a knee before standing to stretch. "I'll find Caylon and see what he says about training for Zaria."

"You should probably approach Zaria about it, too," I pointed out as he walked away.

"Good idea." He waved a hand and kept walking.

Quin

"I received this from Liron," Justis handed his comp-vid to me. The image was of Justis' smiling nephew, standing beside a huge, white wolf and a beautiful, pale-haired woman.

"He's growing so fast," I sighed.

"At least his mother isn't harping in my ear; word has it she actually likes it on Avendor."

"I feel bad that Liron had to be taken away from his uncle," I slipped my arm through Justis' as we studied the image together.

"He'll come back—when we determine it's safe enough," Justis said. "I'm still worried about that infernal coffin, though. I had no idea it could prove so dangerous."

"Queen Lissa has it, now. Let her worry about it," I brushed dark hair away from his forehead.

He smiled, grabbed my hand and kissed it. "Never forget that this is where you belong, too," he said. "At Avii Castle, as my Queen."

"I won't forget," I bumped my forehead against his. "I just have some things to do, first."

"Then be safe, beloved," he whispered and kissed me.

When Kaldill transported us aboard BlackWing VII, we found the crew waiting for us. Some I'd never met; one I had and I was so happy to see him I flung my arms around his neck.

Somehow, Edden Charkisul, Berel's father, had coaxed Queen Lissa into allowing him to ride along with us, in case a spokesman or ambassador was needed. The pilot and copilot I'd never seen before, but the cook and his assistant vouched for them.

The cook, as it turned out, was one of Yanzi's brothers—Bekzi. His assistant was another surprise—a mute Sirenali named Gerrett. I understood immediately that Gerrett was Terrett's younger brother, but I didn't want to release that information too soon, in case it upset them.

Our pilot and copilot, James and Nathan, were a couple. Yes, the names were strange ones, but I'd heard stranger in my short lifetime. James, Nathan, Bekzi and Gerrett knew one another and had worked together before on Avendor. James and Nathan received their pilot training from Nenzi, one of Yanzi's brothers, whom some said was the best pilot they'd ever seen.

Zaria, who followed Bel and me toward our suites, hesitated for a moment upon seeing the four crew members. They smiled politely at her; her shoulders sagged and she followed me when I moved away.

It made me think that she'd heard of them before, but as I couldn't read her, I couldn't say it for certain.

"May I have a private word with you?" Edden had followed us, with Berel and Terrett right behind.

"Of course. Will my suite be acceptable?" I asked.

"I think it will," he said. "We've had word that all banking accounts belonging to one of the wealthy captives aboard the missing ship have been emptied of funds. His family, understandably, is more than upset that they've been—in their words —raped in this way, with no word on the status of their missing patriarch."

"I thought the ASD would freeze accounts," Zaria said.

"They did. Somehow, that action was reversed in this case and the accounts emptied."

"Where were these accounts? On one world or several?" Ilya asked.

"On one world—Tulgalan," Edden said as he strode ahead of us toward my suite.

"Then I know what the thief looks like," Zaria muttered. "That's why he was there when I saw him. I'm sure he made an attempt at petty theft, just so he could get a feel for the employees and the targeted bank."

"A Sirenali that can speak," Bel Erland shook his head. "A very dangerous thing."

"Not all Sirenali are thieves and murderers," I pointed out. Bel nodded reluctantly.

"Many were corrupted by rogue gods," Zaria agreed with me. "Now, many are mute slaves. Both those things are wrong and a terrible injustice to the race itself."

Terrett stopped in his tracks and kissed me, then took Zaria's hand and kissed it, nodding his thanks.

You shine brightly together, Zaria sent to Terrett and me.

Will you help us capture these that threaten us? Terrett asked.

That's why I'm here, Zaria replied. *Come on, let's hear what Ambassador Edden has to say.*

"It's likely that employees at the bank were obsessed," Caylon agreed. Our meeting had spilled into the dining area, after it became too large for my suite. We now had an image on a comp-vid of the Sirenali Zaria had seen on Tulgalan. With information on the bank involved, it appeared that some of us needed to go to Tulgalan to interview employees.

We needed Kooper Griff's help to achieve that. Kaldill offered to transport those necessary for the questioning to Tulgalan, where we'd meet with Director Griff at the bank.

But that would wait for the morning—or at least after we'd slept. Zaria and Ilya had taken up their position at the entrance to the dining hall, as if there weren't a heavy shield placed by Kaldill about the ship already.

We were headed for the shipping lanes shared by the Reth and Campiaan Alliances where the missing ships had been taken. For now, it was the only lead we had as to the location of Cayetes' ships; every one of them had at least one Sirenali slave aboard, who kept the ship hidden from the powerful.

"Here's my thought," Zaria spoke up. "We can't find those ships by scrying or employing other, powerful methods, but they show up on mundane scans, like any other. Someone should probably track those things on the ship's systems, searching for the one or ones that show up there but not when they scry or *Look* for them."

"You mean they'll show up on the screen, but be a blank spot when we *Look*?" Salidar asked.

"Their blip will resonate when they pass through the lanes, like a werewolf who can scent those fuckers when they walk across your lawn," Zaria shrugged. "They can't hide their scent unless someone with power erases it for them. They probably don't bother in most cases."

"That makes sense," Caylon nodded. "It's reasonable to assume that they wouldn't have a wizard or warlock aboard every ship to hide them from other ships that look exactly the same. That would be too expensive."

"Why are they emptying bank accounts?" Berel asked. "I thought Cayetes had more money than he knew what to do with."

"They have to buy a planet full of warlocks and witches, or at least buy enough to fight for them and claim the throne," Zaria stated bluntly. "You have no idea how much that's going to take. Plus, if they buy what they can and obsess the rest," she shrugged.

"Warlocks can't be obsessed," Ilya began.

"Yes, they can," Zaria disagreed. "Frankly, that's something I never want to see again."

I'd remained silent through most of the meeting, but it was time for me to speak. "Unless you are a god or a Larentii, or belong to one of a few special races, you can be obsessed," I said. "Zaria is correct. A witch or warlock is susceptible."

"May the gods be merciful," Edden breathed. "I never knew we were in such trouble."

"Not all of them are ready to obsess anyone they see," I said. "The few who are will be most dangerous, however."

"I'll speak with Griff," Caylon said. "It's late and past time for sleep. We'll deal with Tulgalan and obsessions tomorrow, while the ship finds its way to the proper shipping lanes."

Kaldill waited for me by the door; I could tell by his smile that it was time.

Time for us to be together in bed. I admit, I felt nervous.

There is nothing to fear, dearest, he reassured me and took my hand.

That night, I learned what it was like to make love with an elf. I'm sure it was enhanced, too, because Kaldill was King of the Elves. There is a rush that infuses your blood; a heady, all-consuming desire to have more of the elf who is loving you.

It went on through the night; I'm sure I'd have been exhausted, except Daragar arrived and bent time so I might sleep.

Caylon took no pity on me during my lessons after I woke; I hadn't expected him to. The one I did pity, however, was Zaria.

Somehow, Caylon, Ilya and Sal had arrived at the decision to train her in hand-to-hand fighting, which she plainly didn't want. Sal did the training; Caylon glanced their way from time to time and Ilya made himself scarce after Zaria glared in his direction.

I wanted to laugh—the whole thing had been his idea and she knew it without anyone telling her.

He needed to become used to that—that she could see those things in him whenever she wanted.

I heard a loud thump; Caylon and I both turned to look.

Zaria lay on her back, gasping for breath. She'd been forbidden to use any power during her training and had to rely on her physical ability only. Sal had shown her how to drop someone by sweeping their feet and applying a swift punch to the face or shoulder.

He'd caught her on the chin when she'd flailed in an unsuccessful attempt to keep her balance. He hadn't intended to hit her; her flailing had thrown his fist into her face. In some ways, she was just as responsible for the contact as Sal was.

"That'll leave a bruise," Caylon muttered before attending to our lesson.

~

"I'll live with it," Zaria waved off my offer to heal the darkening bruise after training. She stalked past Ilya, who stood guard outside the door. I saw him wince as she passed; he'd seen the mess Sal made of her face.

~

Kooper Griff met us outside the bank in Targis, Tulgalan's capital city, as promised. Lendill Schaff, his co-Director and Kaldill's son, was with him.

"Who's watching Gaelar N'Seith?" I asked Kaldill.

"He's only here for this interview," Kaldill shrugged. "He'll go back afterward."

We walked into the bank behind Kooper and Lendill—Kaldill, Bel, Ilya, Zaria and I. I imagined that Zaria and I would glean more information by looking at employees than Kooper or Lendill would ever receive during questioning.

After all, those funds should have been safeguarded. Somehow, an employee had released them and they'd been siphoned away. Kooper explained that the funds had bounced from one banking institution to another after they were siphoned from this one, before disappearing altogether.

There was no word on where or how that had happened. It could involve more obsession at another bank, but that information could wait. We had employees to see here.

The bank president smiled nervously when Kooper identified himself. He turned, then, to lead us toward a meeting room, where employees would be summoned and questioned.

No need, I sent to Kooper. *He's the one.*

～

"He's fogged, just like the others I've seen," Zaria confirmed my discovery. "He probably doesn't even remember that he did it."

The bank president sat alone in the meeting room. He was terrified—as anyone in his situation would be.

That's how I'd known—by what Zaria called the fog on his brain. A blank spot of sorts enveloped his mind, indicating he'd been obsessed. Nobody would question him if he accessed certain files. His password overrode all others, including security.

"We have to arrest him," Kooper grimly shook his head.

"You'll never get the needed information," Zaria responded. "I suggest you place him somewhere so he can receive therapy. I think he's going to need it. This is something he'd never do, had he been in control of his faculties."

"I get that," Kooper agreed. "But I still have to arrest him."

"Somewhere, another employee at a different bank is likely in the same situation," I said. "Funds have disappeared and he has no recollection that he—or she—facilitated it."

"It'll take a while to attempt to track it," Lendill observed. "I can do that much from Gaelar N'Seith."

"Then you get on that; I'll see what I can do from another standpoint," Kooper said. "Thank you for your help," he nodded to Zaria and me. "It would have taken us many hours to get this the usual way."

"We're still no farther along than we were," Zaria admitted as we walked out of the building. "All we have is a terrified man with a family he can no longer support."

"I think temporary support can be arranged," Kaldill said. "We still have funds from Cayetes' shipments that we seized."

"Will you do that for us?" I asked.

"Dearest, I would do anything for you," Kaldill smiled at me.

BlackWing VII

Ilya

Zaria released the spell she'd held about herself while we'd been away from the ship; I watched her sigh as the purpling bruise reappeared on her chin. She should have let Quin heal it; it had to be painful.

"It's a reminder," she brushed past me.

"Of what?" I asked.

"Of how people see me as useless unless I can punch somebody in the face." She didn't turn around to look at me; she merely kept walking. I wanted to curse. At her and myself.

Somewhere, in her past, someone had bullied her. I found myself hoping that she'd fried them with her power.

"I'll talk to her," Salidar passed me in the hallway. "Sometimes a punch is better than a spell," he added. "I just have to make her see that."

Yes, I admit that I felt the smallest twinge of jealousy as he began to walk faster to catch up with Zaria.

Zaria

I wanted to be alone. Salidar came barging through my door anyway. "We need to talk," he said.

"About what?"

"About that bruise on your chin."

"Look, I was just as responsible as you. That ought to be the end of it."

He shut the door to my berth and placed a shield about the room. I turned my back on him. "It's soundproof, so I can speak frankly. Bree didn't know that jolting the coffin when it landed in Avii Castle would wake you for an early release and frankly, we can't put the genie back in the bottle at this point. I know who you are and right now, only three people are aware of that. Two, as you may have guessed, are in the Mighty category. I didn't mean to get anywhere near your chin with my fist. You have to work with me on this, all right? Bree says you'll have to make friends with those you knew in the past all over again—it can't be helped."

"Is that supposed to make me feel better? Or less lonely?" I turned to look at him, then. Dark eyes studied me for a moment before he answered.

"No. And I'm sorry about that. We need you—that's the simple truth of things."

"How much did she tell you?" I turned away again.

"Most of it. Some, I already knew because it's a legend with the Larentii, now. That their Vhanaraszh turned rebel to save billions of lives."

"Yet they'd separate my particles in a second if they found me again." My hand shook as I wiped tears away.

"No. Look, your sentence has been wiped from the Council records and the Larentii Archives. None of them would raise a hand against you, now."

"I don't belong anywhere," I quavered.

"I didn't mean to make you cry, either," he said. "I wish there was something I could do about it."

"Except I mean nothing to you and you mean nothing to me."

"Sort of. I was hoping we'd be friends—when I'm not swinging at you."

"I'll consider it. At least it's you swinging at me instead of Ilya. Before—he was the one who attempted to teach me Krav Maga. I think I'd just lie there and cry if he tried it, now."

"You still have PTSD," he stated flatly.

"I don't think it'll ever go away as long as I'm alive. Honestly, I

47

thought I'd taken care of that problem around four hundred Earth years ago."

"We need you, remember?" He repeated softly. "I can probably get Kevis Halivar here if you need to talk to somebody."

"I've talked to someone in the past," I said. "It didn't help much."

"I know you can't just go out there and tell everybody what you've been through—it will mess things up. You have to keep your chin up and hope for the best."

"The same chin that has a big bruise on it?"

"Want me to kiss it and make it better? Or, do you want me to ask Ilya to kiss it instead?"

He wore a crooked grin when I turned to face him again. "How about you run out that door while I throw pillows at you?"

"That'll work," his grin became wider.

Before dinner that night, the entire ship was gossiping about how I'd tossed Salidar de Luca out of my berth and then thrown pillows at his head.

CHAPTER 4

Quin

uin
　　I wasn't sure what Sal had talked about with Zaria, but she tried harder the following morning during training. He didn't hit her again, she was more in control of her limbs and they ended on a truce, bowing to one another while Zaria reluctantly thanked him for the lesson.

I didn't realize how tense I'd become over the situation until it drained out of me afterward. Jayna, who was training with Caylon while I watched Sal and Zaria, bowed to him and thanked him for her lesson, too.

"Anything else?" Caylon lifted an eyebrow in my direction.

"No, sursee," I said.

"Good. Breakfast is waiting."

When I arrived in the dining area, I found Kaldill, Bel Erland, Berel, Yanzi, Lafe and Terrett waiting for me.

"Why didn't you get your plates already?" I asked.

"We want eat with you," Yanzi declared. "You poke along."

"I want to eat with you, too," Barc declared, hugging me with all four arms. Bleek, standing behind Barc, gave a lopsided grin.

"Then let's eat together," I said and held one of Barc's hands as we walked toward the serving line. Somehow, Zaria had cleaned up and gotten to the galley before I did; she stood behind the line, helping the cooks serve breakfast.

"I suppose that makes sense; she did apply as a cook's assistant at Dad's palace," Bel Erland muttered.

"Hey, Barc," Zaria offered him a smile as he went ahead of us. "Want bacon? Ham? Turkey fritters?"

"What's a turkey fritter?" He laughed at the sound of it.

"No idea and we don't have any anyway," she grinned back.

"I want bacon," he declared. She gave him what he asked for, then offered to float his plate to an empty table large enough to hold all of us. Barc laughed when his tray took off on its own, floating gently through the small dining room until it landed on the table. Not even a drop of milk was spilled.

"Thank you," Barc clapped his hands at the simple trick.

"I'll never be able to serve his breakfast again," Bleek pretended to frown at Zaria.

"You want me to float yours, too?" she asked.

"Want to arm wrestle?" Bleek laughed.

"I guess that's a no," Zaria grinned at Bleek's overabundance of arms and piled food on his plate.

"Is it scary that she knew what I wanted?" Berel asked when he took his seat at our table.

"I doubt she means any harm—she probably wants you to be happy at breakfast. I believe she turns it off otherwise around those she knows—the legends abound of how the Q'elindis in the past wearied of what they constantly saw in others. They wore a veil most of the time, to obscure any images that might come." Bel grinned. "Come on, eat and stop worrying about it."

"I wasn't really worried about it," Berel pointed a fork at Bel

Erland. "I've just never had that kind of service, before. Can you imagine if every waitress knew what you wanted when they came to your table?"

"Sounds like a time-saver," Bleek grabbed a basket of bread in one hand while helping himself to the butter and sipping tea at the same time.

"I don't think Zaria should hire herself out as a waitress," Lafe observed. "Kings, Queens and rulers in both Alliances would pay almost anything for her services."

"She's working with us," Bel pointed out. "Don't give her any ideas. We need her."

"I don't think she intends to go anywhere," Kaldill said. "This is her mission, I believe."

∽

Ilya

I waited until everyone else was served and Zaria took her plate of food to a now-empty table. She barely looked up when I set my plate on the table across from hers and sat down to eat.

"I hear you had an argument with Sal," I began.

"I threw pillows at him." She dipped into her bowl of oatmeal.

"Heard that, too. I doubt he received any bruising."

"Hmmph." Her bruise had lightened some, making it appear deep brown instead of purple, with yellowing around the edges.

"I can get cream for it, if you won't accept the healing," I said.

"I'm fine. Really."

"Then eat your food instead of pushing it around. How do you expect to throw a proper punch if you don't take care of yourself?"

"Is that all you're concerned about?"

I'd upset her, when that wasn't my intention.

"No. Fuck, no." I lifted my plate and turned to walk away.

"Please, sit."

For a moment, I caught the bitter loneliness in her voice. It squeezed my heart in a way I didn't expect. Setting my plate gently on the table, I pulled the chair back as silently as I could and sat.

"I cannot guess at the troubles of your life," I began. "I wish I could take the sadness from your face. You will have to make that decision, someday, I think. Whether you choose to allow it or not."

"What nickname would you use?" She lifted her eyes to me and I saw they glittered with unshed tears. "For me?" she added.

"It would have to be special, as you are special," I replied. "Something out of the ordinary, that only I might use for you. I will think on this."

"All right."

"Eat," I gestured with my fork. "I will reheat it if necessary, with power."

"It's fine." She scooped a spoonful of oatmeal and lifted it to her lips. I hoped she'd made it sweet—to feed her energy.

Quin

Just before lunch, we received information concerning a distress call. Caylon had the information from Director Griff, with the last-known location of a beleaguered ship. This was a freighter, filled to capacity with food, vehicles and pharmaceuticals.

"Kooper believes that they may want the pharmaceutical packaging, in order to pass the drakus seed off to buyers without appearing illegal," Caylon informed us. "I've already instructed James and Nathan to set our course for the location of the distress call."

"I'll get us there faster," Kaldill offered. He intended to fold space with the BlackWing VII and everyone on-board. Caylon barked the coordinates; there was a moment of disorientation, which righted itself almost immediately.

"They're still unloading the ship," James called out from the helm. An image of the crippled freighter came into view, with another ship lined up beside it and connected through a makeshift walkway.

They'd punched a hole in the freighter's hull to remove the cargo, then intended to pull the walkway back to their ship, leaving the gaping hole in the other unprotected. If anyone remained alive on the freighter, they'd die.

"Who's going?" Caylon barked.

"Really? You have to ask?" Zaria spat before disappearing. Ilya cursed as he followed her.

"Ready?" Caylon lifted an eyebrow at Sal.

"Thought you'd never ask," Sal quipped and disappeared when Caylon did.

Ilya

I already thought Zaria was made of myth and legend. Q'elindis were so rare they almost didn't exist.

What I saw upon landing on the main freight deck of the captured ship was a child's tale come true.

While wrapped in a golden shield, Zaria, from a distance, destroyed any pirate who fired a weapon at her.

Yes, I'd read of the talent in an old book of tales. It was called mind-kill. I was forced to shield myself quickly, but found that Zaria turned her attention to anyone who fired at me, too.

One by one, they fell. I had no idea why they didn't give up and attempt to flee, but they didn't.

It wouldn't have mattered after a while; once all the vermin had crowded onto the freighter, I fired off a spell to seal the hull breach while Zaria took care of the rest. Caylon and Salidar stood nearby, also shielded but holding their weapons at rest while they watched Zaria work.

How had she escaped notice for so long?

How?

I heard that Quin had done something similar, but I wasn't sure whether to believe it. Quin—she had to be near the ones she killed— or so Caylon had said.

In the tale I'd read, the hero with Zaria's skill could do so from long distances; he only had to focus on the target.

So long as the target wasn't blocked.

Yes, I recalled in the tale that there were certain individuals who could block the targets.

I realized they meant Sirenali. After all, if one part of the tale were true, it made sense that the rest of it could also be. Without lifting a finger, I watched the last pirate die.

"Is anyone on-board this ship still living?" Caylon released his shield and strode toward Zaria. She was surrounded by the bodies of those she'd killed.

"In the small cargo hold," Sal supplied. Zaria didn't answer; she gazed instead at the bodies of the fallen.

They'd tried to kill her. If they'd given up, I think she'd have taken them prisoner, but they'd still be alive.

I probably should have been afraid of her. I was afraid *for* her, instead. How many would hunt her if they knew what she could do? Either to use her, or kill her outright?

Q'elindis were always protected by the crown of Karathia, and they'd never been so talented.

"Zaria?" I called out when she didn't move. She didn't acknowledge my voice. Something had happened.

Zaria? I sent instead. Still she didn't respond.

Cabbage?

I don't know why I called her that. It just came to me. Her eyes locked on mine. *Ilya?* She sent. *My Ilya?*

"Come," I said, beckoning to her. "If you cannot bring yourself away, I will do so."

She couldn't move; I discovered that quickly. Therefore, I employed power to pull her away from the mountain of bodies and set her on a bare spot next to me.

"Do you need help?" I asked, taking her elbow.

I barely had time to catch her as she lost consciousness and fell.

~

Quin

"Zaria's exhausted. We have four from the cargo hold who need healing," Caylon said.

I'd watched as Ilya carried an unconscious Zaria past me, once he'd folded space to get back to our ship. Caylon and Sal had transported the others, several of whom needed my immediate attention. I went to work, although a part of my mind wondered what happened and why only Zaria had exhausted herself.

~

Bel Erland

"My Prince," Ilya spoke softly from behind. I'd been watching Quin healing what remained of the freighter's crew. Most were dead, according to Caylon. All the pirates were dead. He and Sal had gone aboard the pirate ship to rescue the young Sirenali, but he required Quin's attention, too.

"Ilya?" I turned to him, then. He'd carried Zaria back; she was unconscious when he did so.

"Zaria is sleeping. I must speak with you," he said. I heard the urgency in his voice, although he attempted to mask it.

"Where?" I asked.

"I'd prefer to speak with you in Zaria's quarters," he replied. "It concerns her, after all."

"I'll transport us," I offered. At his nod, I did so, landing us inside Zaria's small berth where she lay asleep on her bed, just as Ilya said.

"Do you recall the old tale of Kepple?" Ilya asked.

"Kepple the Brave?" I asked. It was a favorite story of young Karathians for millennia.

"Yes. That's the one," Ilya nodded. "I think it may not be a tale after all."

"What are you talking about?" I asked.

"The part about mind-killing?" he said. I studied his face—deep, solemn brown eyes stared into mine. There was no lie or subterfuge there.

"What about it?" I shrugged.

"I just saw Zaria do it," he replied. "More than a hundred pirates are dead because of it."

CHAPTER 5

*L*e-Ath Veronis
Queen's Palace
Bel Erland

My conversation with Dad and Granddad took place roughly an hour later, in Gran's Palace library.

"You're sure about this?" Dad asked.

"Caylon and Salidar saw it, Dad. It wasn't just Ilya."

"Holy crap," Gran muttered.

"I don't think she's dangerous," I began.

"Honey, that's not my worry," Gran said. "I don't think she'll be dangerous to anybody who doesn't deserve it. What I'm worried about is who may end up with this information—how many criminals would love to have that kind of firepower under their thumb?"

"Gran, Quin can do it, too, remember? None of us will talk, but what if word gets out about both of them? Caylon says Zaria's talent likely is farther-reaching than Quin's, but they both have it in some measure."

"Then we have to maintain silence, or discredit any information that may be leaked," Gran shrugged. "Is anybody aboard ship afraid of Zaria, now?"

"No," I shook my head in absolute denial. "I think most of them are glad to have someone with that talent watching their backs. Zaria was the first to land on the freighter. We have a few of the freighter's crew who owe their lives to her swift action."

"I think we should do our best not to make her uncomfortable about this," Granddad sighed. "I don't want her feeling ostracized for the talents she possesses. Damn, I wish she'd come to us before now."

"Erland, honey, I think she had her reasons," Gran smiled at Granddad. "I might have done the same thing in her place."

"So we should treat this like business as usual?" I asked.

"I'd like to speak with her," Granddad said. "To reassure her that we support her in this."

"What happened to the Sirenali on the pirate ship?" Gran asked.

"All were dead except one," I replied. "There were three, but the last of the pirates killed two before boarding the freighter to attack us. They left the youngest for dead, too, but Quin managed to save him."

"This is something new," Gran muttered. "Killing their Sirenali."

"Mom, do you think they're attempting to keep the Sirenali and their talents away from us?" Dad asked.

"It could be, but since most of them died, we can't really ask them, can we?"

"Perhaps Zaria saw that in the pirates—the last ones she killed," Dad suggested.

"I'll ask about that," Granddad said. "Come, my Prince. Let's see what Zaria has to say."

BlackWing VII

Zaria

Something had happened, there at the end. I'd said the wrong thing, out of hope. Or desperation. Probably both.

I hadn't seen Ilya since I'd fainted.

That was a dumb thing to do and I ridiculed myself for it—both the weakness and the fainting afterward.

He'd run and I'd never get close to him again.

The story of my life.

Lives.

All of them I could remember, anyway.

"Zaria?" Bel Erland knocked on my door.

"Come in," I blew out a sigh and stood to receive the Prince. He and his grandfather, Erland, walked inside my berth.

"You want to know about the remote-killing, don't you?" I said after catching a glimpse of their expressions. No, it wasn't horror—it was curiosity more than anything. Erland—his curiosity was combined with admiration.

"First off, I don't like to do it," I said. "In this case, there wasn't any other way, unless I wanted those obsessed murderers who wanted to kill all of us to live."

"I have no argument about your reasons," Erland gestured for me to sit on the side of my bed while he and Bel Erland took the two chairs in my small living space. "I merely desire that you not punish yourself, or keep yourself away from the others—they still feel the same about you."

"Hmmph." I didn't add that Ilya was noticeably absent. It only added to the growing burden of friends long dead or those who didn't remember me because in their minds, they'd never met me before.

Yes, depression is a terrible, terrible thing, and one I'd been fighting since I'd wakened in blackness, only to find myself locked inside a hideous, shallow coffin. If Leo Shaw were still around, I'm sure he'd have some label to slap on the growing list of phobias I had.

The only person I could blame for all of this, of course, was me. I'd taken matters into my own hands in an attempt to save lives, and I'd screwed myself to do it.

"Zaria, stop it," Erland said, jerking me away from my unhappy thoughts. He must have caught the sadness that overwhelmed me, causing my hands to shake.

"This is what we wanted to prevent," Erland reminded me. "Self-harm is often the worst kind."

"I know," I whispered and looked away.

Quin

Zaria isn't feeling well, Bel Erland sent.

Do you need my help? I returned.

She says she doesn't want help, but I'm concerned, he said. *Granddad is trying to talk her around. I think we should ask Kevis Halivar to join us—at least for a while,* he added.

Kevis Halivar?

He's sort of related, Bel explained. *He's a physician who treats this sort of thing. Zaria is upset because of all the people she killed. Granddad and Sal think it's a good idea to bring him in.*

I hope she feels better, I said. *Barc really likes her, and so does everybody else.*

I know. She's the only one who doesn't like her, I think.

She blames herself, and that shouldn't be.

I agree.

∼

Zaria

"Kevis," he introduced himself and held out a hand. Yes, he could be as serious as any medical professional, but underneath that stern exterior was a streak of humor that he hid most of the time.

"Doctor Halivar, I presume? Sorry, I didn't put up a jungle illusion for your arrival." I shook his hand.

"Not many would get that reference," he grinned.

"They haven't told you? About the Q'elindi thing?"

"They did. I see that part works just fine."

"I warn you, you're not the first to want a tour of my head," I told him.

"I ah, had a discussion with Salidar earlier," he said.

"Great. Lovely. Additional descriptive terms that I will surely recall later," I grumped.

Sal and I are connected to Bree, he sent mindspeech. *You can talk about anything with me, including your former lives. Our sessions will be private, I assure you.*

I didn't answer, I merely rubbed my forehead with a hand. How did I tell him that talking about some things would reduce me to a useless pile of jelly?

You're afraid. I understand that.

Do you remember previous lives? I snapped. *How and why you died in them? Say yes and I'll believe you. How many suicide patients have you talked to, after they successfully committed suicide?*

I didn't mean that, I only meant I understood you were fearful.

"Oh. Fine." I blew out a breath. "You're my designated shrink. Welcome to the circus."

"We'll have our first session tomorrow, after breakfast," he said. "Want me to clear up the last of that bruise on your chin?"

"It doesn't hurt anymore," I said.

"You should learn to accept help when it's offered," he chided.

"Accepting makes me cry," I said and folded space to get away from him.

~

Quin

"We had a hard time finding her," Bel Erland settled beside me in my sitting room.

"Where was she?"

"In the hold of the ship, with the cargo," Bel said. "She was lodged between crates and looked like she'd been crying. Kevis didn't say anything; he just helped her to her feet and folded her away. He took her to her berth and placed her in a healing sleep."

"I want to know what happened to her," I sighed.

"Dad says Didge was pretty messed up by the Ra'Ak; that's where the former heir to the throne died—killed by one of those hideous creatures. It's a miracle Zaria survived the attack."

"This was before your father was named heir?" I asked.

"Yes. Dad was next in line, because Gran and her father refused it."

"Your grandmother already had a kingdom to run. What made her father refuse the throne?"

"Because of what he is, although he's retired. Besides, some of his decisions haven't been the best or most prudent, where family is concerned."

"At least he helped us out," I said.

"And we're grateful. Get Gran to tell you his history, sometime; it's not pretty. It was his son who died in Didge," Bel added.

"Sounds like a tangled mess," I agreed, smoothing a dark lock of hair away from his forehead. He leaned in to kiss me. We forgot the world for a while, in the comfort of our love.

⁓

Ilya

"I can't discuss it, as you know," Kevis Halivar shut off his comp-vid and blinked at me from across a small table in the dining room. A cup of hot tea sat at his elbow; he'd taken a break to complete his notes—probably on his latest patient, Zaria.

I should have known better than to blurt out the question that occupied my mind—what was wrong with her?

"But what can I—we—do to help her?" I demanded.

"I won't know the answer to that until she tells me what's upsetting her," he replied. "Even you should realize that could take a while."

"I want to get to know her." I was back to divulging my difficulties.

"Then do so. Just because something troubles her from her past doesn't mean she can't forge a new friendship or relationship," he scolded. "Just be patient with her, all right?"

"I can do that," I dropped my eyes and stared at my hands. "Thank you." Pushing my chair back, I rose to leave.

"Be consistent," Dr. Halivar called out as I walked away. "She needs a source of solid, constant support in her life."

"I can do that," I whispered.

~

Quin

"The body is at an ASD facility," Caylon informed Bel and me at breakfast. Sometime during the night while we slept, the body of the wealthy kidnap victim—the one whose fortune had disappeared from his bank account, had been dumped on a moon orbiting Tulgalan.

"They have his money—he was no longer useful," Bel said. His brow furrowed as he frowned—we understood that electronic surveillance and recognition bots now had the images of those who'd forced a bank president to unlock those funds.

If any of those people walked into another Alliance bank, they'd be recognized. What Bel and I also understood, however, was that with a warlock or witch's help, people could be made to look like someone else.

Someone completely innocent.

So far, no more accounts had been drained; Kooper kept Caylon and Salidar updated on that information.

Now—one victim was dead and we were still no closer to discovering the others.

"ASD drones and manned ships were sent out to scan all of Tulgalan's moons, but they're too smart to dump a body where they're hiding," Caylon continued.

Even the stupid ones know not to do that, Bel informed me.

"This probably happened the moment they had the credits in their possession," I said.

"That's what Kooper thinks," Caylon agreed.

"Here's my question," Zaria appeared unannounced at our table. "Why did it take so long for them to kill and dispose of him, and why aren't we seeing more of the same with the other kidnap victims?"

"I agree," Ilya set his tray of food on the table and pulled out a chair to join us. "It should be simple to convince these victims to hand over information—we're dealing with a powerful witch and warlock who can extract information from nearly anyone, should they so desire."

"Yes, but," Zaria took a chair at the table and pointed a finger at Ilya, "They wanted information from Vardil Cayetes, too, and weren't able to pry that away from him."

"Perhaps they wanted to use Cayetes as long as they could, to further their own agenda. The information needed could wait—until Cayetes was reduced to a drooling fool. Good luck on getting information after that," Ilya said. He bit into a slice of bacon to punctuate his statement.

"True, but we're back to getting information from kidnap victims," Zaria said.

"Well, what's your theory, then?" Ilya finished his bacon and went after the eggs.

"I think they used this poor sap as an example," Zaria sighed. "For the others. After all, they're wealthy and have assets other than their wealth. What if Deris and Daris want those assets, too? If you show them what can happen if they don't cooperate, well, you could have a shipload of victims willing to do whatever you ask. Right?"

"I hadn't considered that," Caylon muttered.

"If they're neck-deep in drakus seed production and sales, you don't want to grow all your drakus seed in one place. You'll diversify, so if one place is discovered, you still have several others to meet the demands."

"So we should look for lands, warehouses and other things in the possession of those victims," Caylon rose immediately and nodded to Zaria. "Anything suitable for the production, storage or shipping of that filth." He disappeared, and I imagined that he'd be in contact with Kooper Griff the moment he reached his cabin.

"Have you had breakfast?" Ilya asked Zaria.

"No. I'll go get something," she said and moved to push her chair back.

"I'll take care of it," Ilya offered. "I just sent mindspeech to Bekzi, asking for an omelet for you. He says it'll be out shortly, with coffee and juice," he added after a moment.

"Thank you. Coffee sounds wonderful."

I wanted to smile—Ilya was doing his best to take care of Zaria without upsetting her. Too bad Sal and Lafe sat between her and Ilya.

"May I join you?" Edden Charkisul carried his tray to our table. "I heard we may have other investigations in the works," he added when I gave him a smile and gestured toward Caylon's empty chair.

"I think we're getting lessons on how a criminal's mind works," Sal grinned when Edden set his tray on the table and took the offered chair.

Bekzi arrived at that moment with Zaria's tray. He offered her a wide grin as he set it in front of her. "Tell if you not like—we make again," he said.

"Honey, it'll be fine," she said. "You're an amazing cook."

"I thank," his grin widened. "Sit here—have coffee—with you?"

"If that's what you want." Zaria was surprised that he'd asked. Gerrett appeared seconds later, two cups of coffee in his hands. He took a second chair on Zaria's other side, while Bekzi occupied the first.

Ilya frowned deeply and concentrated on finishing his meal.

Don't be upset, I sent to him. *If you could see Zaria's eyes following you every moment you aren't looking, you'd know she cares for you.*

He went still for a moment before nodding imperceptibly and lifting his cup of tea to drink. *Dr. Halivar says not to take things for granted*, he replied. I was surprised to hear mindspeech from him—he was reluctant to speak most of the time.

"Zaria," I turned to her. She lifted her eyes from her plate to blink at me. She understood I wanted to ask for something.

She tilted her head as she considered my unspoken request. "I can form a wind-tunnel of sorts, so you can fly in place," she said. "I can adjust the wind speeds, too, to give you the workout you want to keep your wings strong."

"That brilliant," Bekzi said. "Not room on ship to fly."

"Want help?" Ilya offered.

"If you want to," Zaria smiled at him. You'd have thought the sun had become visible after days of gloom when Ilya's eyes brightened.

"When?" Zaria turned back to me.

"Every afternoon, when we don't have something else to do? At three bells—for half an hour?"

"That's fine," Zaria said. "I'd love to watch you fly. It sounds amazing."

"Want to start this afternoon?" Ilya asked.

"I'd love to stretch my wings," I said. "Yes."

I flew in a windy, oval tunnel. At first, Zaria consulted me as I flapped my wings to keep myself aloft. She adjusted the speed of the circulating wind to give me the exercise I desired.

At least Caylon waited with his news until I'd finished my exercise. We met with him in the captain's study behind the bridge. "Zaria was correct," Caylon appeared grim. "We have found unusual activity surrounding property and facilities owned by kidnap victims. We have ASD agents researching this, although Director Griff doesn't want to move in too quickly. That could shut everything down, leaving us with no clues as to the safety or whereabouts of these victims."

"So we wait and watch until we can move in with certainty?" Lafe asked.

"Yes. Kooper wants leads on the Ardens and Cayetes, unless things get so bad there's no choice but to go in before then."

"What about Morid? Do you think he's still being held captive?" Bel asked.

"I think as long as the coffin is in your grandmother's dungeon, they'll have Morid," Zaria spoke. "I worry that he's not in comfortable circumstances, however."

"I think so, too," I nodded at Zaria. "While I believe him weak for not opposing his father, he didn't agree with many of his father's decisions. If we rescue the others, we should also rescue Morid."

"We have to find them, first," Caylon growled. "Do that for me and I'll authorize anybody's rescue."

Zaria's and my eyes met. Without words, we were committed. There would be no waiting for authorization from Caylon. The moment we could effect a rescue, we were determined to do it.

It's the right thing to do, Zaria sent.

Agreed, I returned.

Zaria

"I feel terrible about Valegar." I sat in Kevis Halivar's makeshift study after dinner, to talk, as he put it. His first question?

Tell me something that troubles you.

"Why?" he asked.

"Because he thinks I'm dead, and that I left him without a good-bye."

"So you feel guilty about that."

"Feel is too mild a word. Struggling with crushing guilt is a better phrase."

"Do you love him, still?"

"Yes."

"And you worry that he may not love you, now, since you mistreated him."

"Yes."

"There is one way to figure this out," Kevis shifted in his chair.

"What's that?"

"Speak to him."

"Out of the blue? What do you think that will do to him?"

"Would you rather he found out another way? Larentii can and will keep secrets until the end of time. Probably beyond that, if necessary."

"My worry is that Kalenegar will attempt to pull me away from this," I swept out a hand.

"I doubt that very much, since Breanne wants you right where you are."

"I just," I covered my face with both hands. "I can't handle his anger," I mumbled, feeling close to tears. "Not now. I'm only one word away from a total meltdown most of the time."

"Breanne admits that she should have kept the Larentii from passing sentence against you," Kevis sighed. "I know that felt like a betrayal to you. That your race abandoned you, there at the end, when you were trying to set things right. You feel as if they failed to understand your motives, and the resulting pain you suffered as a result."

"Yeah."

"Are you angry with Valegar?"

"No," I huffed. "He could find me to stop me. He and his father, both. He did the only thing he could and stayed away."

"You don't blame him?"

"Absolutely not. What is there to blame? He was nothing but good to me and loved me no matter what, even when I was turning most of my attention on Ilya. I feel bad that I didn't give him his due."

"Do you blame the drug for this? The confusion you feel?"

"I blame that fucking drug for almost everything. On Karathia, I was supposed to be with Ilya only during our lifetime, only that was fucked up when I got the drug a second time and Valegar came along. It's like having three people in your head all the time."

"Because you remember three lives."

"Yes. With distinct clarity."

"What would you say to Valegar if he were here, now?"

"I'd say I'm sorry. It's all I have." I wiped tears away while ducking my head—I didn't want a relative stranger to see me cry.

Ilya

I'd just finished a sparring session with Caylon, and was walking toward my cabin when the Larentii arrived. His unexpected presence almost made me jump, but as Larentii don't have violent tendencies, I understood that I was safe.

"Who?" I glanced up at him as he matched his stride to mine.

"I am Valegar," he smiled. "You knew me in another lifetime."

~

Quin

"We have an addition to the crew," Sal said. He'd found me having herbal tea with Lafe and Berel, before we retired for the evening.

"Who?" I asked.

"A Larentii."

"Do I know him?"

"Nefrigar's second son, Valegar."

"I haven't met him, but he's welcome here. Will he come and go, like Daragar?"

"It's possible, I suppose. You can ask him yourself, if you want. He's officially here to record our actions for the Archives."

"Then we could see much of him," I said.

"Very true." Sal grinned. Something else was afoot, here; I merely couldn't read it in him. "Word of the Q'elindi spread rapidly, once Daragar discovered her," Sal explained. "Of course the Larentii want to record that. They are also very interested in you, as you know, but they rely on Daragar to provide that information for Nefrigar. They have no desire to intrude on your privacy."

"Then I am grateful for the concession," I mumbled while considering the talk I intended to have with Daragar when I saw him next.

"Dearest, you wish to speak with me?" Daragar appeared—his smile broad and glowing.

"Is there something you haven't told me?" I asked. I couldn't help smiling back at him—that's how infectious his grin was.

"Dearest, of course you are in the Archives, as your history is tied to that of Siriaa and the events following its destruction. I hope this does not offend you." His smile disappeared.

"You mean this is in a historical context?"

"Yes. Berel is also listed in this history, as is his father and many others."

"Oh. All right, then. I just didn't want," I sighed.

"We know this," the smile was back. "Do not fear, all is historically well in the Archives. Now, may I interest you in my company this night?"

Hot damn, Berel sent. *We get energy sex.*

He'd used one of Queen Lissa's archaic idioms. I didn't care; I wasn't about to turn Daragar down.

Ilya

If the information had come from anyone else, I wouldn't believe it. Still, it was difficult to process.

"You remember this?" I stared at Valegar.

"Yes. As difficult as it is for you, I have been in mourning for many years as a result of this—both for her and for you."

"How much did she love me? How much did I love her?"

"She grieves for you. Is terrified that you will never love her, and are lost to her forever. What she did in the past—you were the catalyst. Her actions kept you from terrible harm."

"But you won't tell me what that was."

"No. I can only tell you that in your previous life, she loved you more than anything."

"Why are you telling me this, then?"

"To give you a choice. If you do not wish to be connected to her, then I can arrange to have the connection broken."

"What?" I went still, while my entire being was suffused with fear. "No," I whispered. "Please, never say that to me again."

"She saved you before. You must help save her this time."

"How do I do that?"

"How much do you wish to touch her? To tell her how you feel?"

"You should know," I grumbled, lowering my eyes. "Larentii know everything, or so I hear."

"Don't wait, then. Tell her how you feel. Show her. I hope you know to back away if she becomes uncomfortable."

"Of course. I received my instructions in proper sexual conduct, just as any other warlock and witch in training."

"Very good. There is one more thing."

"What's that?"

"Your jealousy. It is now removed."

CHAPTER 6

*Q*uin

The pleasures of the night were quickly forgotten when we were roused from our beds after only a few hours' sleep. Another freighter had been attacked, only this one didn't get the chance to send out a distress signal before it was overtaken two days earlier.

We were pulling alongside the drifting hulk, now, where a gaping hole remained in the cargo hold, with no apparent signs of life to give us hope.

"What was the cargo?" Caylon snapped as we prepared to board the abandoned ship.

"More medical supplies, in addition to food packs destined for the ASD," Sal responded.

"They took everything? Why do they want ASD food packs?" Bel asked.

"Tell the ASD to quarantine every food pack in their possession," Zaria shook her head. "Tell them to take care when testing some of them."

"What the fuck?" Sal turned in her direction.

"If you can't beat them, kill them," Zaria said. "Too much drakus seed will kill anybody. That stuff has to be carefully measured if you want the benefit without the very considerable side effect of waking up dead."

"You can't be serious?" Caylon growled.

"Tell them to test that crap. Then tell me how serious it can be."

Caylon sent mindspeech—I watched his eyes lose focus for several seconds. When he blinked, he turned back to Zaria. "It will be done," he said. "They'll run a sampling. Kooper will keep us informed."

"You may want to issue a recall for all food packs distributed or sold to anyone else," I said. Zaria nodded at my request.

"How," Caylon began before shaking his head. "Never mind," he held up a hand.

"I worry that somebody won't get the message, or will disregard it," I said. Zaria nodded again.

Are you two thinking with the same brain? Bel Erland sent to Zaria and me. I could tell there was a smile in his mental sending.

You think we'd tell you that? Zaria snipped. I stifled a snicker.

How do you wake up dead? he teased.

Believe me, it's less complicated than you think, Zaria replied.

You're not getting out of training, just because you got out of bed early, Sal interrupted.

You moonlight as a wet blanket, don't you? Zaria returned.

Sal laughed, causing Caylon to frown. It took a moment for me to understand the meaning of Zaria's words. When I did, I laughed as well.

"What's so funny?" Caylon demanded.

"Zaria told Sal that he moonlights as a wet blanket," I said.

James and Nathan, our pilots, fell into each other's arms, they laughed so hard.

"Thank you. I'll be here all week," Zaria stood and bowed, which brought on fresh laughter.

Caylon tossed up a hand and walked out of the meeting.

Zaria

"I'll train her today," Caylon nodded to Sal before our session began. My breath caught. I was about to be taught a lesson for disrupting Caylon's meeting. Who knew Caylon Black had a sense of humor that ran into negative territory?

"Then I'll see to Quin and Jayna," Sal said and stepped away.

"Now, then," Caylon said. "One of the things that advanced students learn is the art of mockery. The talent can often distract the enemy, depending upon the effectiveness of the derision involved."

"Yes, but," I said.

"But what?"

"Doesn't it normally entail that the one doing the mockery is at least skilled enough to hold his or her own with his or her opponent?" I asked.

"Under normal circumstances."

"You know I can see anything in just about anybody, including their weaknesses?"

"I understand that."

"If I insult someone, it will make them all the more determined to kill me," I said.

"What would you do if you faced an enemy at this moment?" Caylon asked.

"It depends."

"On what?"

"How much of an enemy he was."

"Who is the worst enemy you can think of?"

"Alive or dead?"

"Alive."

"Deris and Daris," I said.

"What would you do if they stood in front of you?"

"Kill them."

"No words beforehand?"

"Honey," I let my shoulders sag, "those two have given up any right to keep their lives. They would die as quickly as I can make them dead."

"You have no questions for them?"

"Did you forget who I am? I can see everything in their faces. There's no need to waste time asking for information."

"Then apply that talent to what I wish to teach you."

"What?"

"Go ahead. Turn off your filter and see everything in me that I want you to know about hand-to-hand combat. Then I'll test your knowledge."

"Knowing and doing are two different things," I pointed out.

"Then how do you know you can kill Deris and Daris before they can kill you?"

"You want to test me? Or is this your version of the verbal mockery mentioned earlier?"

"You're far too quick for me," Caylon snarled.

"Oh, look, your misogyny is showing," I snapped back. "Better tuck that back in before your mate sees it."

"Keep my mate out of this."

"Seriously?" I *Pulled* in four wooden practice blades, thumping two of them against his chest. "Come on; flatten me like you want to."

"Aren't you afraid I might bruise that fragile skin?"

"Ooh, now the claws come out," I said. "Big, bad Caylon wants a piece of me. Come on, panther-man, get your licks in before your daughter's born." I shook a wooden sword at him.

"What?" Both wooden blades dropped from his hands as he gaped at me.

"She's pregnant. Your mate," I snapped. "This is why she couldn't perform the healing for the Grey House wizard, so Quin and I had to do it. The baby is yours—a daughter. Better hide that misogyny good, dude."

"That secret was not yours to give," Valegar suddenly stood beside me. "His mate was waiting to tell him."

I blinked up at Valegar for two seconds, tops, before I dropped bonelessly to the floor.

∾

75

Quin

"I asked for it," Caylon waved a hand. It was now six hours later; he'd spent most of that time with his mate, Cleo, who was pregnant, just as Zaria said. "I wanted to goad Zaria; instead, it blew up in my face."

"I suppose it isn't the best idea to bait the Q'elindi," Sal handed Caylon a cup of Falchani black tea.

"No. Cleo wasn't as upset as I thought she'd be, but still it rankles to hear it from a near-stranger."

"Was what she said true—about the misogyny?" I asked.

"I do have misgivings, as often as not," Caylon mumbled. "When a female refuses to explore her full potential," he hesitated.

"And I suppose you don't feel the same about the males not living up to their potential?"

"I know how lopsided this sounds," Caylon admitted. "I was born in a time when all able-bodied males served in the Warlord's army. Females had the right to choose whether they fought."

"Yet many of those males washed out, did they not?" I was beginning to see what Zaria had known all along. Caylon had a weakness.

"Yes."

"Yet you still considered the women as less than they?"

"Because they didn't try, or weren't forced to try," Caylon insisted.

"If Zaria were here, I believe she would point out the additional hardship any woman faces who chooses to fight alongside the men. Not least of that is the general contempt and sexual references tossed about by the males."

"I'm aware—more so now than before."

"Zaria handed your ass to you, I believe Queen Lissa would say. I would also tell you this—that women serve in their own ways. I suggest you adjust your attitude and beliefs to accommodate that truth."

"I'll take that under advisement." Caylon disappeared.

"He's old school," Sal said, sitting across from me and sipping his own cup of Falchani black. "He needed a bit of updating. He just got it in a way he never saw coming."

~

Zaria

"My love, please stop pacing and tell me what's wrong," Valegar begged.

"How long?" I whirled to face him.

"Father and I guessed the moment Daragar brought news of a Q'elindi. When he revealed your image, we were sure."

"Right."

"Lara'Kayan, I didn't intend to upset you."

"Well, I didn't intend to upset you, either. So there." I hugged myself and went back to pacing.

"I know." His voice had gone soft. Gentle.

"I made you suffer," I admitted. "I can't tell you how sorry I am about that."

"Have you not suffered, too?"

"It doesn't matter if I suffer. I deserve it."

"Dearest, you saved so many. Never tell me you deserve to suffer again. Come here, now; I will massage your neck and sing to you."

I hesitated. "Come," he said and held his arms open. I was in them in seconds while he trilled the Larentii love song reserved for his mate.

~

Bel Erland

I stood beside Lafe as we watched the ASD remove bodies from the freighter. Some—only minutia remained. They'd been nearest the door, and were blown apart by the raiding party.

I imagined shipping prices going up across the universe, because shipments weren't arriving as scheduled, creating shortages. Freight companies would be forced to hire additional security, feed and

77

house them on-board the ship while displacing cargo to do it and that would either cut into profits or raise prices on the cargo in question.

"We've had word," Caylon appeared beside me. "An entire ASD training unit is dead on one of Gribak's moons. They consumed food packs containing drakus seed. Kooper wants Zaria and Quin to come —in case they can see anything in the dead."

"How many?" I turned toward Caylon. His face was set in a grim mask.

"More than three hundred. A training exercise meant to teach them how to survive under minimal conditions and no atmosphere."

"Fifty died here," I nodded at frozen blood spattered across the inside of the cargo hold. "Quin wanted to come with me. I really dislike the idea of her seeing this—it will upset her."

"Nobody needs to see this." Caylon shook his head. "This was a slaughter, not a real fight."

"Yeah."

"I have no words." Zaria appeared with Valegar right behind her. Both studied the grisly evidence of the attack—on floors, walls and equipment.

"Kooper wants you and Quin to go to Gribak's third moon to see the dead there," Caylon said.

"Then we'll go," Zaria said. "At least those won't be bloody, like these poor souls."

Valegar's hands were on Zaria's shoulders—he'd shortened his height to better suit hers. I understood he was feeding her energy; she didn't like this mess any more than the rest of us did.

"I will take you," Valegar offered. "When you are ready."

"Zaria?" Ilya now appeared next to Valegar.

"Ilya, this is awful," she sighed. "So many, hoping someone would come."

"Do you know what that feels like?" Caylon asked.

Zaria turned to him. "Better than you think," she said. "I know you understand it, too."

Caylon almost took a step backward. Few knew his history, and that he'd officially perished after watching all his men die around him from an overwhelming attack by Falchan's enemies.

Zaria had seen that in him. If he hadn't attacked her as he had, she'd probably show even more sympathy.

What just happened? Ilya sent.

I'll explain later, I said.

Zaria

Caylon remained silent, but behind his enigmatic, dark gaze, he was thinking. Much of his mortal life, he'd measured those he knew by their fighting skills. During that time, he'd never taken a mate. He'd had sex with those who took his money and nothing else.

He'd reluctantly accepted Cleo as his mate after his placement with the Saa Thalarr. Caylon Black was coming to realize that fighting skills were only a small part of the whole picture, where others were concerned.

For now, he disliked me for pointing out his weakness. Something in me didn't want his daughter to see it in him if she chose a path other than that of the warrior. Perhaps he would call a truce between us.

Eventually.

Kooper Griff strode onto the ship, then. Caylon nodded to the Director of the ASD. "When will Quin and Zaria be ready?" he asked.

"You can ask me directly," I said. "I'm ready, now. I'm sure Quin can be, too."

Kooper turned toward me, then. His brows furrowed as he considered my statement.

I didn't sign up with the ASD or Caylon Black, I pointed out in mindspeech. *My job is to protect Quin and Bel Erland. I'm happy to assist both of you, but I can answer for myself, thanks.*

My apologies, Q'elindi, he returned. *Caylon and I—we're used to giving orders.*

Understood. I'm used to making my own decisions.

I see that. Will you ask Quin if she's ready?

Already on it. Terrett, Lafe and Berel wish to come as well. They're ready, I replied.

~

Quin

Ilya and Zaria stayed close as we surveyed the temporary facility erected by the trainees on Gribak's moon. They'd built it before consuming food packs laced with drakus seed, in quantities sufficient to kill them.

Bodies lay in groups around tables—it hadn't taken long for the seed to do its destruction. Remnants of the food packs had already been removed—for testing as well as safety purposes. Only the bodies, portable equipment and other supplies remained.

"Can you see anything?" Caylon asked. He addressed Zaria and me.

"The food packs were replaced without their knowledge," I turned to Caylon. "None of these," I swept out a hand, "had anything to do with this."

"Are you sorting through ASD employees?" Zaria asked. "In case one or more have been compromised?"

"Like the bank employees?" Kooper interrupted.

"Yes," I said. "Which ones would have access to the information on training missions and such?"

"We have a department for that," Kooper nodded. "I can take you when we're finished here."

"I'd very much like to meet them," Zaria hissed.

~

Valegar had to hold Zaria back. I think she was angry enough to destroy the two culprits we found. These hadn't been obsessed by any Sirenali—they'd accepted money to sell information to an intermediary. More than three hundred ASD trainees died as a result of their greed.

"Pargun is a well-known information broker," Kooper raked fingers through his hair as he described the intermediary in question. Zaria sat in a corner of Kooper's study, arms crossed tightly and refusing to look at Kooper. "He hasn't been high on our radar —until now."

"Now we know where some of the money the Arden twins have stolen is going," I said. Pargun had paid the two employees Kooper had in custody half a million Alliance credits for what they'd handed over.

Neither Zaria nor I knew whether Pargun was obsessed—we'd have to see him to determine it. Kooper had all available agents tracking leads on Pargun's whereabouts, but my guess was that he was cozy enough with the Arden twins and protected by Sirenali by now. Bel Erland had already scryed and *Looked;* Pargun couldn't be found anywhere.

~

Vardil Cayetes' Compound
Dorgus

The Lyristolyi drug worked for Master Cayetes—up to a point. His mind wandered much of the time and very little intelligible conversation could be had.

Deris and Daris promised they wouldn't harm him, as long as I played Vardil's part with his vast empire.

Yes, they'd performed a spell to make me look like Master Vardil's latest incarnation. I sounded like him, too. And, as I knew Vardil so well, I could mimic him in every way.

Every day, I searched diligently for a way to get away from them— a means in which I could save Vardil and myself from their machinations. Nobody knew I was standing in Vardil's shoes and making his decisions—except those two infernal Karathians, who made constant threats.

Had Vardil known they had their own agenda, he'd never have

employed them. Others had offered their services; only these two had named a lower price, provided they be employed together.

I cursed the day they became Vardil's servants. Now, they were the masters.

"Dorgus! Stop daydreaming and send the messages," Deris hissed. Taking a breath and lifting the comp-vid from Vardil's desk with shaking fingers, I began to tap the messages he'd dictated.

~

New Fyris
   Morrett
My dreams invaded the waking world when Nefrigar, Chief Archivist of the Larentii Archives, appeared in Prince Amlis' library.

He must have understood my joy, as his eyes brightened and he smiled. *Greetings,* he sent to me. *I understand that you retain memories of Corinnelar, when others have failed to do so.*

Is that true? That none recall her? She saved me and gave me this, I gestured toward the shelves of books lining the Prince's library.

"That is what I wish to speak with you about—how she saved you," Nefrigar smiled again. "To record for our archives."

Shall we sit? I offered. *It is a good story.*

~

Le-Ath Veronis
   ASD Headquarters
   Zaria
"Zaria?"

I'd taken a seat in an interviewing room at Kooper's ASD headquarters on Le-Ath Veronis. Ilya took the chair beside mine. Falchani-trained, he made no sound as he settled there.

"Ilya?" I turned to him. There were so many things I wanted to say to him. Some of those things began with, "Remember when?"

Those were the things I could never say. Those things meant

nothing to him. I had no idea why he'd been given the same name this time, either. Perhaps it was a cruel joke or atonement for past sins.

"Have you ever been to Niff's?" he asked.

Of all the questions he might have asked, that one was the least expected.

"No." I turned toward him, then, and studied his handsome face. Like before, he had dark hair and dark eyes. The similarity ended there—his features were different. Still, I would recognize him anywhere and anytime.

"I hear they have gishi fruit ice cream," he said. "Have you tried that?"

"No. I've heard it's really good," I shrugged.

"I'd like to take you. If you want to go."

"When?"

"Now?"

"What about?"

"Daragar is guarding the Prince and Quin."

"Then ice cream sounds wonderful."

"Zaria?"

"What?"

"This." He leaned in to kiss me.

I wanted to weep with joy and melt into him at the same time.

"Where are we?" I asked as I looked about me. We hadn't stayed at Niff's, once we had our ice cream.

"This is my home—on Falchan."

"You don't have something on Karathia?" His home was sparsely furnished and decorated—in true Falchani style.

"I do. My parents gave me a parcel of land when I reached adulthood, but I haven't built anything there; I'm afraid I left home to join the Falchani army," he offered a wry smile.

"I'm not surprised," I said, touching the varnished woodwork of an intricate room divider. "I suppose your parents gave you land in an effort to keep you on your home planet?"

"That's right. I compromise with them by visiting at least once a month."

"Ah."

"My mother will be overjoyed to meet you," he began.

I froze. He wanted me to meet his parents. It pleased and terrified me at the same moment.

I'd never considered the concept of in-laws of any kind, before realizing I was getting ahead of myself.

Ilya and I had married in another life. Not this one.

He didn't recall the daughter and son-in-law he'd had, while I remembered them clearly.

Both gone, now.

For centuries.

"You're shaking." Ilya's words brought me back to the present.

"It will pass." I turned away from him.

"Shhh, Ilya's here," his arms dropped around me.

Le-Ath Veronis

Queen's Palace

Quin

Queen Lissa's arboretum was where Daragar had taken us after we left ASD headquarters. Justis waited there, where a table had been set with food for dinner. His arms and wings were folded about me quickly, and I was kissed many times in the privacy his feathers created.

Lissa and her werewolf mate, Winkler, joined us for dinner; we took our seats and wine was poured.

Quin, what's wrong? Lissa sent.

I have an uneasy feeling, I confessed. *I don't know why—it's as if someone caused a ripple on the far edge of a pond, and now I am hearing the wash of it on my side of the shore.*

I feel something isn't right, too, but I've felt it for a while, she replied. *We'll eat and study this after dinner.*

Thank you.

Terrett

I was happy to be off the ship for an evening. Yanzi and I were getting cabin fever, as Queen Lissa suggested when we had dinner with her in the palace arboretum. I had no idea how those who worked on-board the ship day after day continued in their jobs—I found it wearying to fly through constant darkness.

Terrett, are you well? Quin asked when we settled in Queen Lissa's library for drinks and talk after dinner.

I am. I am also grateful to be off the ship for the evening.

Me, too, she admitted. *I know it's a big ship, but it's so—claustrophobic at times.*

Yes. After seeing those ships attacked, where the crew had nowhere else to go to get away, I admitted. I preferred enough space for fight or flight, as most anyone would. Freighter ships were often filled with cargo, leaving little space for anything else, including room for combat.

Ilya had shown me the images of Zaria, surrounded by crates with the enemy approaching from all sides, as she desperately killed those who came too close, intending to take her life.

She'd done it with skill but eventually, all of them died when they should have realized quickly that there was no hope of getting to her.

Prince Bel was correct to tell everyone to keep that information safe; any criminal who learned what Zaria could do would be desperate to obtain her services, in whatever way they could.

Ways that included blackmail and hostages.

Like Quin, she needed our silence and protection, as best we could give it.

Terrett? Gerrett spoke to me from across the room. He'd settled for a place on the floor, next to a bookshelf.

Gerrett? I replied, the question in my mental voice. We'd nodded at one another on the ship, but had little direct contact.

Do you recall your mother's name? he asked.

Of course I do. She was an evil bitch, I replied.

As was mine, brother. As was mine.

~

How long have you known? I asked. Gerrett had joined me in the palace kitchen, where we were served a light cordial and allowed to sit at a small table to share mindspeech.

Zaria told me while serving breakfast one morning, he replied. *I was stunned, of course. I never imagined*, he didn't finish.

I should have known, I responded. *She sold us for a high price, I imagine, and told those who bought us how to control our gifts after they removed our tongues.*

Yes. I shudder when I think of all the evil committed while others had control of those gifts, Gerrett said.

I care for her—Zaria, he admitted. *I doubt she will look my way, however.*

I would not doubt it, I said. *She looks at you and Bekzi with longing, at times. At least be her friend, if nothing else.*

I want that with you—to at least be your friend. I do not know whether our father is the same, but we were birthed by the same evil. We have much in common, brother.

We do. I am happy to know you live, brother. I worry that there may be more, though, with less than honorable leanings.

As do I.

~

Quin

"Lissa, we have news." Adam Chessman and Merrill Leopard walked into the Queen's library while we talked.

I understood immediately that the news they had was important. "All here can stay, it affects them," Merrill said.

"What is it?" Lissa asked.

"Our management at the casino on Campiaa found this in a guest's room." He held out a comp-vid. "The guest has disappeared, although we have a good idea where he is."

"There's a message you need to see. I'm extremely happy that Joey was there at the casino, going through records when this was brought to the office. Otherwise, it would have ended up in the lost and found pile and eventually tossed out." Adam shook his head. I could see that he was quite upset, although his face wore no expression.

"Joey got past the necessary passcodes, didn't he?" Lissa said.

"Yes. He disabled them. You'll see the message once you turn the thing on." Merrill made a gesture with his hands, urging the Queen to do so.

"All right." Lissa turned on the comp-vid and read.

"Holy shit," she cursed. "Holy, fucking shit."

CHAPTER 7

 alchan
Zaria

Ilya and I—we were talking. Kissing now and then, too, when urgent mindspeech reached us. At least we had our clothes on when we folded space to Queen Lissa's library.

"This message was sent to Ruther Kend," Lissa explained as she handed a comp-vid to me.

"The manufacturer of high-tech weapons? The one who supplies the ASD?" Ilya asked.

"That's the one. His vacation on Campiaa was interrupted by this message. I think he may have left his comp-vid behind, hoping someone would break the code and find the message," Lissa explained.

"Wait, these are schematics for," I said, lifting my eyes and gazing at Lissa.

"Yeah. Only these won't have any safeguards built in," Lissa replied. "Deris and Daris want Kend to build these for them, in exchange for his wife and children."

"They have them?" Ilya asked.

"We checked discreetly—sources say the family is visiting other family. We checked out that story—it's a lie. The last of that message reads that they'll die unless Kend keeps this to himself and cooperates."

"Here's my worry," I said, handing the comp-vid to Ilya so he could read the message. "Have they sent similar messages to others, demanding who knows what to fight their war against the crown of Karathia?"

"It's possible." Merrill nodded before turning to Lissa. "I doubt anyone else would have the presence of mind to leave a comp-vid behind for us to read."

"These machines were outlawed everywhere before the creation of the Alliance," Adam pointed out. "For a very good reason. They were made for a single purpose, and that purpose destroyed worlds."

"Only this time, I'm sure they'll be the new, improved version, with advanced technology," I said.

"What were they called—before?" Quin asked.

"*N'il mo'erti*—death machines," Adam responded.

"Where did they get the schematics, then?" Lissa demanded. "I thought all that crap was destroyed."

"No idea," Merrill replied. "Yet here they are; therefore, they exist."

"Has Kend gone back home—to his manufacturing business?" Quin asked.

"Word has it that he's at his mountain retreat on Jaledis, where he keeps a facility for research and experimentation on new technology. Getting into that place is like breaching a fortress, because admission is only granted to those who work there," Adam said. "I've coordinated with Kooper and Lendill already; we'll have to approach cautiously. It's likely that either Deris or Daris will be there with Sirenali, to ensure that their demands are met without investigation or interference."

"That's not fucked up or anything," Lissa muttered. "And it doesn't include any others who may have received messages."

"I need photographs," I sighed. "Of anyone you think may have something to offer to the Arden twins. The more recent, the better."

"You can tell from photographs?" Merrill turned to me.

"If they're recent enough. Get me something taken after the messages were sent."

"We're assuming messages were sent," Caylon said.

"How well do you know the Arden twins?" Bel Erland spoke up. "By now, you should have determined that they don't put all their eggs in one basket."

"I understand that," Caylon agreed. "But have they sent out seven messages or seventy? We don't know."

"Then let's start with Jaledis," Lissa said. "If Deris or Daris is there, then we need Zaria or Quin to see them—to tell us what their plans are."

"That will require infiltration of the facility," Kooper appeared at the library door. "We are working out a plan, now. This is classified information and hasn't been distributed to any ASD employees."

"What do they wear on Jaledis?" I asked. Bel Erland snickered.

~

Jaledis

Quin

I hadn't gone shopping with Terrett in months. He, Daragar (in disguise) and I walked into the grocer's in the small city of Turbak, at the foot of the mountains that housed Kend's research facility.

Jaledis belonged to the Reth Alliance and had all the amenities any Alliance world possessed, including fresh food. Terrett would select meats while I bought vegetables for our table.

Some of our crew were still on BlackWing VII; Zaria, Bel Erland, Caylon, Sal, Ilya, Bekzi, Kevis, Terrett and I had been taken to Jaledis. Daragar and Valegar would stay as much as they could with us; Kaldill and Lafe were in charge of the ship in our absence.

Bekzi and Zaria gave me a list, Terrett grinned at me. I put my arm around his waist and hugged him. He leaned in to place a swift kiss on my cheek and strode toward the meat counter.

~

Zaria

Will you share a suite with me? Ilya asked. He and I were sorting luggage into suites at the large villa Kooper arranged for us.

Ilya's question caught me by surprise. In another life, sharing a suite would be automatic. What if we didn't get along this time?

We can try it, I answered, my mindspeech on the hesitant side.

I don't want you to be afraid, he said.

I don't want to upset you, I said.

You won't upset me unless you say no. Then I'll be disappointed.

That's not what I meant. I don't want to disappoint you in—you know.

You won't.

But.

"Don't mind me," Kevis Halivar interrupted a really nice kiss between Ilya and me.

"What is it?" Ilya didn't hide the growl in his voice. I let my forehead drop to Ilya's shoulder to hide my embarrassment.

"I merely wanted to see if Zaria had time for her appointment this afternoon."

"So I can run but I can't hide?" I pulled away from Ilya to face Kevis.

"I believe you can do both. I'd prefer you didn't."

"What's in it for me?" I asked. Kevis had a glint in his eye—he enjoyed verbal sparring.

"A comfortable spot on the sofa?"

"Come on, doctor boy, you can do better than that."

"Chocolate and a comfortable spot on the sofa?"

"Now you're talking my language," I said. "What kind of chocolate?"

"Strawberries covered in chocolate?"

"Hmmmm." Ilya cleared his throat.

"Strictly professional chocolate-covered strawberries," Kevis held up a hand. "I promise."

~

Quin

"I can barely see it," I said. Our compound had been supplied with a spy-screen in an upper-deck room facing Kend's mountain facility. Even with the far-sighted camera, the facility was so well-hidden by trees and outcroppings that I could only get a glimpse of the roof.

The roof, of course, was covered in sunlight-gathering squares filled with a special crystal.

"Those crystal beds on the roof are so effective, they power the entire facility that way," Sal explained as I squinted at the screen to get a better look. "Kend's great-great-great-grandfather developed those things and the family still holds the rights to their manufacture. That massive wealth funded this one's forays into research and development, and now they supply all weapons for the ASD."

"Are the crystals natural?" I turned away from the screen to look at Sal.

"They were in the beginning," he shrugged and offered a crooked grin. "They found a way to manufacture them and make them even more efficient, without flaws in the crystals. It brought down the price, too, so almost anyone can afford it. Most of the weapons requiring energy are powered by strips of those crystals."

"It's convenient," Bel Erland said. "The crystals hold a charge of sunlight for days, if it isn't expended."

"It takes many firings to deplete the charge, too," Sal explained. "That's why the ASD buys its weapons from Kend Industries."

"What sort of weapons will Kend have guarding his facility?" I asked, turning back to the screen.

"He could have anything that's available to the ASD, and possibly a few things the ASD doesn't know about. That's why we haven't sent drones or spy-bots—they'll likely be fried at the perimeter. Industrial espionage and design theft is a reality where Kend Industries is concerned," Sal said. "They've only ventured into weapon design when Ruther took over about twenty-five years ago. When he was fourteen."

"Does Ruther have any wizards or warlocks working for him?" I asked.

"We don't have that information yet and even if he did, it could be that they're being paid under the table, so to speak, and there may not be an official record of it. I've heard that many wealthy industrialists do this, to protect themselves and their company."

"I've attempted to scry, but with probable Sirenali involvement, there's really no way for me to get the information. If he's hired a witch or warlock, Dad doesn't have those records." Bel Erland frowned as he studied the screen beside me.

"So it could be a wizard, too." I shivered at the thought.

"We'll figure this out," Bel's arms went around me, holding me carefully.

～

Morid

They wanted me to suffer. Therefore, no obsession was laid. I imagine cost was involved, too, because the Sirenali who performs obsessions for Deris and Daris Arden charges per obsession.

The Arden twins do not argue about the cost because they are just as susceptible to obsession as any other. They tread carefully around V'ili, the Sirenali Prince.

I see it as an unholy alliance, as each one wants what they want, and aside from that desire, all else is expendable.

I do not have what they want to achieve their desire; therefore, they are happy to watch me squirm in my cage. The old enmity between wizard and warlock is strong within them.

I should have stayed on Grey Planet, as instructed.

The only brightness in my captivity was this; I was moved to Ruther Kend's private research facility on Jaledis, in the mountains above the small city of Turbak. Two housekeeping employees were assigned to bring me food and fresh water. They do more than that, when the Arden twins aren't looking.

Since I was placed in their care, I have clean clothing and the opportunity to bathe myself every other day. Before that, I was forced to wear what I'd worn when I left Grey Planet behind. At least I still have my ability to disguise what I wear—so far the twins haven't seen through that.

I wished I were powerful enough to escape the cage they'd placed me in, but I am not. Father always told clients we were more powerful than we were, in order to command greater amounts for our spells.

I learned humility on Grey Planet, after watching their Master Wizards perform spells I could never attempt.

If it weren't for the two who care for me here, I would wish myself dead. Norn and Gale give me hope, in addition to food and smuggled comforts.

~

Ilya

"This is the list of employees we think are at the mountain facility," Caylon handed a comp-vid to me. "This includes cooks and housekeeping staff. They get food and supply deliveries once per eight-day. Everything is inspected before it enters the gate."

He and Sal had found me inside my suite, where I'd unpacked nearly all of Zaria's things. It would be more difficult for her not to stay with me if her clothing and shoes were already here.

"Then what about this?" I asked. "Let Zaria and me take over for the delivery crew. She can see in the employees doing inspections whether it is safe to approach them or not."

"That's a decent idea," Sal said. "It beats whatever we had, which included folding into the facility. It's likely that the moment we become corporeal, an alarm would sound."

"That was my thought as well," I agreed. "Plus, if Deris has placed a disturbance spell, it could explode in our faces—quite literally."

"Disturbance spell?" Sal asked.

"It's a complicated spell, which detects anyone who doesn't belong in the designated area," I explained. "Only a Fourth or Fifth-level is capable of casting it."

"You can do it?"

"Yes. I believe Zaria is also capable."

"Let me coordinate with Kooper, and we'll work on getting you and Zaria on the delivery crew." Caylon strode out of my suite. Sal grinned and shrugged before following Caylon out the door.

I laid the comp-vid on my dresser and went back to settling Zaria's boots in my closet.

~

Zaria

"How is it going with Valegar?" Kevis asked.

"It'll take a while for the guilt to go away," I said. "I still feel bad about how I treated him."

"What about Kalenegar?" he asked.

"I haven't brought him up yet," I pointed out. "Where did your information come from?"

"From Kalenegar."

"Of course it did. That's sarcasm, in case you didn't know."

"I recognize all forms of sarcasm. I'm related to several deft practitioners."

I slapped a hand over my mouth to stop my snicker from becoming a full-blown laugh. Kevis didn't try to conceal his grin. "So, what about Kalenegar," he continued.

"Him." My shoulders drooped. "He was ready to wipe my atoms from existence. I think that statement says it all."

"You don't see a reconciliation?"

"I can't answer that."

"Because you don't want to or because you don't know?"

"Right now, it's both. My worry is this—if he were willing to kill me once for making a misstep, what's to keep him from doing it again? How can I trust that?"

"Nobody's asking you to."

"Then why did you bring it up? Were you trying to upset me?"

"No," he held up a hand. "You were reluctant to tell me about your marriage to Ilya centuries ago, therefore, I asked about Kal."

"I made it so Ilya died a horrible, painful death in prison, rather than being consumed by a terrible obsession and killing his friends." I wiped tears away at the thought of Ilya, suffering and dying of cancer in a Russian prison.

"What do you think his choice would have been?"

"I don't know," I flung out a hand. "I didn't give him a choice. It was my choice. All of it."

"And this is something for which you can never make amends, because he is a different person and has no recollection of it."

"Yes."

"Why do you not let it go, then?"

"Because I can't forgive myself. I believe that has to happen first, doesn't it?"

"It's generally a good idea."

"So you see my conundrum?"

"Yes, but it will only take your acceptance that things are different now and you have a fresh start."

"Except I have all these memories, and for me, they're still fresh. For you, centuries have passed and you weren't alive at the time, anyway."

"True. I'm merely a listener, not a firsthand witness," he reminded me.

"You're not sympathetic? You've just shattered my hopes and dreams," I quipped.

"I am sympathetic. In a detached way," he grinned. "Imagine what a basket case I'd be if I became emotionally involved in all my patients' troubles."

"You have a valid point, sir. Shrink on," I nodded while echoing his grin.

"Shrink on, shrink off," he laughed while waving each hand in a circular motion.

~

Karathia
  King Rylend Morphis

"I never considered Wellend's book," Dad pinched the bridge of his nose. "Wylend and I—we always assumed that he'd held the kingship for such a short time that there'd never been one, or that it was empty and disappeared when he died. Warlend's was destroyed with him—it was never found either."

"So the only person who may have known where Wellend's was—aside from him, could have been his mother, and Helsa's dead, too."

"Son, I think we both know where it is—we've looked everywhere else," Dad sighed and took a seat on the sofa inside my study. "We merely don't know what it contains, although our guesses may be eerily accurate."

"But I have a book," I began.

"Yes, that can be presented as an argument for our side," he agreed. "It could effectively split the planet, however, and that cannot be allowed to happen. What if our fears are true and Deris also has a book?"

"He's the eldest, so it would make sense that if either twin had a book, it would be him," I said, taking a seat next to my father. He placed an arm around my shoulders and pulled me into a hug.

"What are we going to do, Dad?" I whispered.

"Hope," he replied. "Hope that Zaria, Quin and Ilya can bring them down while keeping us out of it. You know what will happen if we challenge and there are two valid claims to the throne."

"Yeah. I do. The first and eldest claim wins."

"Exactly."

Jaledis

Quin

"Ildevar Wyyld thinks it better to have me here, in case an ambassador is needed in a delicate situation," Edden Charkisul smiled and pulled me into a hug. I wasn't surprised that Berel had arrived with him; either could act as a liaison with the Jaledi government.

I received a hug and kiss from Berel, who lingered on both.

"Bekzi, Zaria and Ilya are cooking tonight," I pulled Berel toward the combined kitchen and dining area. "If we beg, we may get a drink while we're waiting."

Ilya

My experience in cooking anything consisted mostly of grilling a catch or a kill over an outdoor flame. It fascinated me to watch Zaria make dumplings to drop into the chicken and broth Bekzi prepared.

"This good—you like," Bekzi grinned at me.

I didn't care what it tasted like—it was a pleasure to watch Zaria's graceful fingers work the dough before rolling it carefully with a pin and cutting it into evenly shaped, bite-sized squares.

She enjoyed cooking—that was easy enough to see.

"Chicken and dumplings, one of my favorites," Kevis Halivar said as he walked into the kitchen followed by Quin, Ambassador Charkisul and Berel.

"Ilya, will you get drinks for them?" Zaria asked.

If you'll give me a kiss, I replied. She leaned her head back; I took her lips. It should have been a chaste kiss. It was anything but. Forcing myself away after several seconds, I set about putting drinks for the new arrivals together, my mind on Zaria the entire time.

Zaria

That was more than a casual kiss, Kevis teased when I went back to making dumplings, my cheeks heating at the promise in Ilya's kiss.

I guess you'd know, Mr. Casual Observer, I huffed mentally.

Oh, I like sex just as much as anybody, he said. *More than some, maybe*, he added.

Tell me again why I'm making dumplings for you?

Now, that's something I hadn't considered, he responded.

You sound like my brother, I snapped.

You had a brother?

No. I was abandoned and adopted when I was a baby.

Ah. Why didn't you tell me that earlier?

It didn't come up, Doctor Boy.

I'll remind you in our next session.

Joy.

Zaria?

What, bro?

Let Ilya pamper you.

I closed my eyes as tears threatened.

"There. Done," Valegar appeared and made dumplings disappear into the pot in less than a blink. "Come, my love, we will go."

Quin

I couldn't say what happened, but Kevis Halivar wore a frown after Valegar disappeared with Zaria and Ilya. Our drinks plunked onto the table in front of us, almost as an afterthought, just as they disappeared.

"What happened?" Berel asked.

"I'll explain later," Kevis said. "A word of advice, however—never inform a Larentii that his mate is about to cry."

Larentii Homeworld

   Ilya

If it had happened any other way, with anyone else, I'd have been uncomfortable. Instead, I welcomed Valegar's strong, blue arms around both of us as Zaria huddled against me and wept.

When the Larentii song began, it soothed all of us. Eventually, Zaria slept. That's when another Larentii came. One with red hair curling about his shoulders. He settled himself beside us on the grass in a high meadow. I realized I was on the Larentii homeworld,

99

then, and that our visitor was Kalenegar, Head of the Larentii Council.

"If she were mortal, she'd worry herself into an early grave," Kalenegar whispered. Reaching out, he stroked a long blue finger against her cheek.

"She has two Larentii?" I asked softly.

"Yes, although she may never forgive me," Kalenegar replied.

"Why?" I couldn't help but ask.

"Because she was sentenced to death by the Larentii Council," Valegar supplied. "It is a long tale and one she should permit, before we tell anyone else."

"She's not sentenced now?" I barely kept the terror from my voice. I had no idea Larentii would sentence anyone to death.

"Her sentence was rescinded," Kalenegar reassured me. Valegar's arms tightened about Zaria and me, letting me know that all was well. "We eventually recognized her actions for what they were—heroic. She saved many, many lives as a result."

Will she tell me? I ventured to ask Valegar in mindspeech.

I know not. I think she has to become comfortable with what she is, first.

"She is the first of her kind," Kalenegar spoke, letting me know he'd heard our conversation. "She walks a lonely path, and with her past lodged firmly in her mind, she no longer knows whom to trust."

"You mean there has never been a Q'elindi like her?" I asked. I already knew the answer; I merely wanted to hear him say it.

"Zaria is many things, and none of those things have ever been, before."

"I worry that I don't deserve her," I sighed.

"You are as important to her as the breaths she takes," Kalenegar locked eyes with mine. They were a deep, cobalt-blue, filled with the experience of who knew how many eons. I understood then that he could see through anyone, much like Zaria could.

Jaledis

Quin

She is fine, Ilya replied to my hesitant mental query. *She cried herself to sleep, I think, so Valegar is taking care of both of us.*

"Daragar?" I looked up at him. He'd appeared shortly after Valegar took Zaria and Ilya away. Dinner was long past and he sat cross-legged on my bed while I snuggled in his embrace.

"What is it, dearest?" He smiled at me.

"Is Zaria strong enough to deal with this?" I swept out a hand.

"Ah. I understand your worry, my love, but Zaria is exactly where she should be. You and she are vital to this effort, and her will and determination are formidable. It is her past and not her present that troubles her."

Larentii Homeworld

Zaria

"What time is it?" The question came out garbled—I was only half-awake when I asked it.

"Time matters not," Valegar murmured.

"He says he can get us back anytime," Ilya soothed. "Go back to sleep if you want."

"No, I should get up," I said, lifting a hand to rub my eyes. "I'm hungry," I added.

"Quin said they saved our dinner for us," Ilya said.

"I'll take you," Valegar said. Moments later, we were in the kitchen at the compound in Turbak. Someone had placed our bowls of food in stasis—it waited, hot and fresh, for us to consume.

Ilya and I had almost finished our portions when the explosion rocked the far side of city.

Jaledis

Kend Enterprises Mountain Retreat

Morid

Ruther Kend sat next to my cage, his head in his hands. The prototype of the machine the Arden twins wanted had just been fired at the city below, with devastating results.

Deris ordered the killing machine to fire, and pinpointed the target. Unfortunately, it had performed flawlessly. Kend blamed himself for the ensuing deaths.

"They'll kill us all before it's over," I whispered.

"They have his family," Norn hissed from the other side. "What else can he do?"

"You see my circumstances," I muttered, gesturing toward the bars that held me. "There is nothing any of us can do."

"Ah, there you are," Deris strode into the room. "A good first effort, but I want the machine to be stronger, to cause a larger area of destruction. Come, Kend. You have work to do."

With slow deliberation, Ruther Kend pulled himself off the floor and followed Deris. Norn made himself smaller on the other side of my cage, grateful, no doubt, that Deris had chosen to ignore him.

∾

Quin

Ilya and Zaria trailed behind Bel and me as we walked the perimeter of the destruction. Three city blocks had been leveled; homes and businesses lay in rubble. Gorvis' rescue teams were frantically searching through debris, hoping to find living souls.

Only bodies remained, most of them broken and scattered amid the rubble. The chink of bricks tossed out of the way reached us. A man, not belonging to the rescue teams, wept as he tossed pieces and bits of his home away, calling the names of his wife and children as he did so.

"Dear heaven," Zaria muttered and strode toward him. Ilya reached for her, but failed to capture her hand.

"Wait," Bel held me back. On that evening, with light provided by a setting sun and emergency lamps supplied by the city, we watched as one by one, Zaria lifted the man's family from the wreckage, whole and alive.

His wife and four children were filthy, weeping and bearing cuts and bruises, but they lived.

"Quin, my darling, let the local medical crews help them," Bel held me back when I attempted to go to them and provide healing. "See, Zaria is doing the same thing. Do not call attention to us, my love."

The living victims, along with the now happy father, were taken to the nearest medical facility for treatment. It gave the other rescuers hope, but all through that long, weary night, no others were found alive.

Zaria stood beside us after the initial rescue, her face drawn.

We find the twins, they die, I whispered mentally to her.

Oh, yes, she replied. *Most definitely.*

CHAPTER 8

Q *uin*

"This is where the authorities say the blast originated," Caylon pointed to a location twenty clicks from the eastern edge of Turbak. It lay opposite the mountain where Ruther Kend's facility lay.

"Misdirection?" Sal asked.

"I believe so. Also, because Ruther gives generously and almost single-handedly keeps Turbak thriving, the authorities wouldn't be willing to entertain the thought that he could be responsible. While it is a temporary injustice to those who died, it also assists us in our efforts to infiltrate the facility."

"While allowing time for more people to die," Zaria said. None of us had slept; this was a morning meeting over breakfast. Zaria and I— we'd only picked at our food.

"This is a war," Caylon reminded her. "It is callous to say it, but there will be casualties."

"Are you always this cheerful in the mornings?" Zaria shot back.

Caylon stood still for a moment, at his place at the head of the table. Then he ducked his head and chuckled.

I don't recall that he's actually laughed in months, Sal sent to me. *I think—no, I'll get back to you,* he added.

He'd speculated on what I was beginning to realize—for perhaps the first time ever, Caylon Black actually respected a woman.

She'll stand toe-to-toe with him on any day, I said, verifying Sal's thoughts. *Maybe not with blades, but with wit and courage.*

I think he's only beginning to recognize the actual value in those things, Sal agreed. *In the past, he always won the battle of wits while sparring. The time with Zaria, well, he was overmatched and he knows it.*

"All of us need sleep," Caylon regained his composure. "I'll be in contact with Kooper, who's on his way now. When you wake, we'll have more information."

Any remaining energy I had deserted me then, and my shoulders sagged.

Come, Terrett sent. *I will make you comfortable.*

He led me away; I caught sight of Ilya doing the same with Zaria. I hoped she'd sleep—we both needed it. I understood that sixty-three deaths in Gorvis weighed heavily upon her; it was the same for me.

Le-Ath Veronis
Queen's Palace
Lissa

"It's not difficult—the original machines could do it," Rigo sat next to me with a sigh. "All of them capable of hitting a target from any direction, while they remain stationary and hidden."

"How do you know this?" I turned to my Hraedan mate.

"In Hraede's royal archives, once, we held information on these machines," he said. "The N'il Mo'erti—engines of death. Those books were removed from the archives and are carefully stored and protected by the Rith Naeri. I have already checked; those records are untouched. These plans came from elsewhere. I've studied them, and they were most certainly drawn by a different hand."

"I don't understand this," I rubbed my forehead.

"Tiessa, these were the machines that eventually destroyed Tiralia. Not only were they capable of terrible destruction at the command of a few, but were also capable of manufacturing poisonous gases."

"You make them sound as if they were almost sentient." I lifted my eyes and stared at Rigo.

"I believe that is how they were designed," he agreed. "Perhaps it is most fortunate that Tiralia waged a civil war against itself, rather than turning these terrible machines loose against the Alliance. Unless I err, Ildevar Wyyld likely knows something of them as well."

"He probably does; he's older than a lot of Larentii, even. I suppose he and I should talk."

"I would like to be included in that meeting," Rigo said. "This could signal an ending for those planets untouched by the poison."

"We don't need to let this get any farther than it has already," I snapped and stood. "I realize Ruther Kend's family is in danger, but maybe it's time to weigh a few deaths against the deaths of planets."

"My love, it may already be too late," Rigo advised, his expression grim. "Yes, this may be the first foray that Ruther Kend has made with these abominations. What if others are already manufacturing an army of them for the Arden twins, who are merely waiting for potential improvements made by the best military manufacturer currently alive?"

"You just scared the bejeezus out of me," I said.

Jaledis

Zaria

"Photographs." Caylon dumped a comp-vid on top of me, after barging into Ilya's and my shared bedroom.

Yes, we were still in bed. No, we hadn't done anything other than sleep—we'd been too exhausted.

"Let me," I held Ilya back. He was ready to leap from our bed and challenge Caylon Black to a duel.

"What are you going to do?" Caylon taunted.

"Nothing much," I said, handing the comp-vid to Ilya.

The element of surprise should be saved for an appropriate moment—I'd learned that from reading Caylon.

Now was such a moment.

In a blink, I'd folded myself out of bed and punched Caylon square in the face. I won't say I didn't put power behind that punch, because I did.

Caylon landed on his ass four feet away.

"Get out of my bedroom," I snapped, pointing toward the door. "Come in again without knocking and you'll be more sorry than you are right now."

"You will go," Valegar appeared, a deep frown marring his features. "I do not wish to see this behavior again."

"A Larentii is threatening me?" Caylon pulled himself off the floor.

"I'm threatening you, now."

Someone new had arrived. He was and wasn't High Demon. I say that because clouds of smoke poured from his nostrils, but he wore power like a second skin.

"Of course, Lord Rath," Caylon bowed.

"Why did you do this?" Li'Neruh Rath demanded. "You know it to be wrong, as well as rude."

"Because she won't look at me."

"What?" Ilya and I echoed one another.

"Because Zaria won't look at him the way he wants her to," Valegar's eyes brightened with understanding.

"Dear heavens," I muttered. "Look, I'll heal that bruise on your chin. Later. Much later." I glared at Caylon. "Then we'll talk. With Ilya and Valegar there with me."

"I, too," Bekzi peered through the open door. "With Gerrett."

"Very well. I must also approach my mate," Caylon ducked his head.

"Perfect. Great. Please leave. I need a shower and some alone time with a comp-vid."

"I must speak with you," Li'Neruh Rath dismissed the others with a nod. "You and Master Ironsmith. Valegar may also stay."

When Caylon walked out the door, Li'Neruh slammed it shut with power.

"What may we do for you, Mighty One?" Ilya inclined his head.

"We must make a plan," he said. "It may involve traversing the timeline."

~

Quin

"What is happening?" I asked, as packed bags appeared from nothing in the kitchen.

"A request from the Mighty," Sal said, taking a seat at the table. "You'll have to deal with new guards, I'm afraid; Zaria, Ilya and a few others are being sent on a separate mission."

"I don't want them to go," I whispered. Somehow, those two had become family to me, and it frightened me that they were leaving.

"Me either, but when the Mighty say you're needed elsewhere, then you're needed elsewhere. Queen Lissa is sending someone to help, and Corolan is coming at the Karathian King's request."

"Who else is going with them?" I quavered. I felt like crying; never had I found someone who supported me as thoroughly as Zaria did.

"Bekzi and Gerrett," Sal sighed. "Don't let this upset you—it's important."

"Will they come back?"

I sounded small.

Lost.

"I don't know," Sal lowered his eyes. "They didn't tell me that."

~

Ilya

As much as we'd been told about where we were going, there were things that hadn't been said. I saw concern in Zaria's eyes as she dressed for our destination. She knew things I didn't, of that I was certain.

"Going as servants. Not like," Bekzi shook his head. "They treat us bad, I think."

I dislike this, Gerrett's mental words echoed Bekzi's spoken ones.

Honey, I wish you weren't involved in this, Zaria strode toward Gerrett and took his face in her hands.

I go to protect you, he replied, fierce determination in his sending. *I will do what my talent allows, to hide you if necessary.*

"Thank you," Zaria put her arms around his waist and hugged him.

I watched as an expression of happiness transformed his face as his arms folded about her.

Somehow, I would have to share her with others, whose thoughts, like mine, were to protect her life with ours.

Quin

"Our objective remains the same," Kooper announced at our meeting. It upset me that I wouldn't get to tell Zaria good-bye before she left. I wasn't told whose decision it was, only that it was for the best.

It made me angry.

I sat in the compound's library where the meeting was held with the rest of us, my arms crossed tightly over my chest. If I were ever told who made the decision, I'd likely be tempted to treat them to the same punch Zaria delivered to Caylon's face.

He still wore the darkening bruise—he'd refused to ask for healing from Kevis Halivar.

Perhaps he knew better than to ask me; I might have refused.

Why were you not sent with Zaria? I sent to Kevis, who'd taken a chair near the door.

I may be transported back and forth, if it becomes necessary, he offered a mental shrug. *I will be invisible to all except those from our team*, he added. *It helps to have powerful friends—and mates.*

Yes it does, I agreed. I was more than grateful that Kaldill and Daragar protected BlackWing VII and all aboard.

Wait, I sent. *Since Gerrett is going with Zaria*, I didn't finish.

Valegar's father has suggested a substitute Sirenali, and he is already on board the ship, Kevis ducked his head to hide a smile.

Who?

His name is Morrett, Kevis replied.

Do you think? I began.

Yes, and I believe Nefrigar has already informed him that he has brothers.

Where did Nefrigar find him?

Working as Chief Librarian for Prince Amlis in New Fyris. Kevis didn't hide the smile this time—it had become a full-blown grin. *Well*, Kevis continued, *Morrett is an avid reader as well as a scholar. Nefrigar has supplied him with a comp-vid containing many volumes that can only be found in the Larentii Archives. Morrett is perhaps the happiest of librarians at the moment.*

I hope Terrett and I get to meet him soon.

It can be arranged.

"Therefore, we will send two of ours in disguise tomorrow, with the weekly delivery bound for the research facility," Kooper said. I turned back to his announcement; more news of Terrett's brother would have to wait.

Karathia—Past

Zaria

A Karathian month before the attack that killed Warlend, Wylend Arden's father, was the time in which when we arrived.

No, we weren't allowed to interfere with the coup; Li'Neruh Rath was very specific about that.

What I hadn't expected was where we'd end up—in the Queen's Palace, which was occupied by Helsa Blackmantle-Arden.

We were to be her servants, waiting on her, her children and grandchildren. She'd recently cleaned house, firing most of her servants and hiring new ones. She'd only kept a handful of those who'd previously served her. I suppose if you were one of King Warlend's Queens, you could do whatever you wanted.

Someone had cleared the way for our employment—Ilya, Bekzi, Gerrett and me. No, we weren't expected to perform any sort of sorcery in the execution of our duties. Gerrett was the one I'd worry for if that were the case. Bekzi held his own power and could do anything required of him.

Regardless, Gerrett was listed on his paperwork as a mute First-level, whose work would keep him cleaning, dusting and other various duties involving near-invisibility.

Bekzi and I—we'd been hired for the kitchen.

Ilya was hired as the stablemaster, since Helsa's family enjoyed riding. As Ilya was Falchani-trained to care for horses and such, I had no worries about him.

At least we didn't have to deal with Helsa right away; the hiring had already taken place and we only had to report to our superiors to learn what was necessary to serve the family.

I wondered when we'd meet Helsa's grandchildren, who were in their late teens and destined to cause more trouble than most people I'd ever met. That included a rogue god and others who practiced evil.

You see this? Bekzi sent as we were led through the enormous castle toward the kitchen at the back.

I see it. I did. If it weren't made of, or covered by, expensive fabric, it was gilded and decorated with precious stones or made of a precious metal or the rarest of woods. This home compared to the royal palace of Karathia, nearly one hundred miles away.

One hundred miles is nothing to those who can fold space. This home, unlike the palace, was nearly surrounded by a scenic lake bordered by a forest. To me, it looked like something from a fairy tale.

You think Warlend loves her this much, or rebuilt it for her to keep her away from the palace? I sent. It was more than evident that all the furnishings and embellishments were new or recently updated.

She complain. He give, Bekzi replied.

Yeah. I get the same idea. I stared up at a highly decorated plaster ceiling, washed over in gold.

"Be careful of the carpets," the servant who led us through the house cautioned. "They're from Serendaan and cost much."

They still cost, Bekzi informed me.

He and I wore the plain, black uniforms of the household. I'd already transformed my long, black skirt to a split skirt, because I hated it the other way. Nobody would know—it was still full and swished about my ankles as I walked behind Bekzi.

We expected to cook right away, Bekzi's mental sigh echoed his drooping shoulders.

Yeah, I saw it in the chamberlain's face when we walked in, I confirmed. *Welcome to the world of being on duty all the damn time*, I told myself.

∾

Jaledis

Quin

I understood that I'd have to go with the delivery; I merely hadn't considered who else might go with me. My duty was to read whoever came to inspect the goods destined for Ruther Kend's research facility. The one assigned to go with me would protect me as well as he or she could.

Queen Lissa was the one to volunteer.

"I don't go into the field as often as I once did," she reassured me when my jaw dropped at her appearance. "In this case, it's for the best."

"Thanks, Gran," Bel Erland stepped forward to embrace her. I received a hug from her after Bel Erland stepped aside. *Never forget how much we love you*, the Queen whispered in mindspeech before letting me go.

"We have information on how to present yourself and the protocol of the delivery job," Kooper said. "We'll meet after dinner to make sure everything is in place."

"It'll be fine," Lissa smiled at me.

How could I tell her that something churned in my belly, and I hadn't a clue about what it meant.

~

Karathia—Past

Gerrett

Queen Helsa had already dismissed three of her new servants. Two she sent out the door with burned flesh from the spells she'd thrown at them as they cowered.

I'd been pressed into serving her tea in her massive sitting room, which held a window overlooking the most scenic portion of the lake about her home.

"This had better be right," she snapped as I poured tea carefully into her cup and added two small spoons of sugar, just as Zaria had directed. I didn't question Zaria's knowledge; I did question Helsa's sanity and unpredictable anger.

She wore her long, blonde hair braided and pinned atop her head, like a makeshift crown. No doubt she'd had it lightened with a spell. Her features were even and would be considered beautiful by those just as shallow as she.

"This is the mute servant, Mother," a man strode into the room to take a chair near the Queen's.

"Good. He can't talk back like that other filth. I've been forced to get rid of three already," she waved a hand that a servant had worked on to carefully shape the nails and stain them red.

That's Wellend, Zaria reported. She'd asked to look through my eyes and I'd gratefully allowed it. *He takes his tea with no sugar, and usually has two cups. Wait for him to get nearly to the bottom of the first before refilling his cup. Serve his tea, then place two of the tiny cakes on a saucer for Helsa, and lay the fork carefully by her right hand so she can reach it easily.*

I did as Zaria said, moving carefully but not so slow as to draw Helsa's ire. Wellend nodded distractedly when I served his tea; Helsa watched like a bird of prey as I set two tiny cakes on a saucer in front of her before placing her fork exactly as Zaria said.

"Hmmph," Helsa rumbled and lifted the fork to examine it for stains or spots. Temporarily satisfied, she cut into the first cake and lifted a bite to her mouth. I waited, worried that she'd find something wrong with Zaria and Bekzi's baking. I knew they were exceptional at it, but taste is always subjective.

Helsa rolled the taste of it on her tongue before swallowing and nodding. Turning toward Wellend to hide the relief in my eyes, I saw that he'd almost reached the bottom of his cup.

Lifting the teapot, I silently offered to refill it. With a nod, Wellend set the cup down so I could pour.

"Where's Wallend?" he asked.

"Oh, he and Valia went to visit her mother. The twins wanted a holiday. They'll be back in three days."

"Ah."

Wellend's thinking that Valia merely wanted to get away from Helsa, Zaria sent. *He's wishing he could have gone with his brother.*

Wasn't he invited? I asked.

He's just gotten back from court with his father, Zaria explained. *Helsa has no love for Warlend—or Warlend's other wife, Terez. Mostly, Helsa loves Helsa.*

I can see that for myself, I returned. *Is that the ring—the heir's ring—on his finger?*

Wellend wore a ring on his right hand. It held one large, clear, faceted jewel, surrounded by black diamonds in a pale gold setting.

Tiralian crystal, Zaria confirmed my guess. *It holds the heir's spell.*

Was it made by a warlock or a witch? I asked.

Neither, Zaria answered. *This bears consideration,* she added.

Zaria

The ring I'd seen in the casket had been perverted. Not only did it bear a red stone instead of Tiralian crystal, the gold around it was plain instead of the paler, more expensive version. No black diamonds surrounded the stone, either.

Something was very, very wrong, here—there was no other way to explain it. The ring Wellend wore had been crafted by a Grey House wizard, more than fifty thousand years before it came to him. Warlend had worn it before he took the throne, but it was Warlend's father, Worlend, who'd had the ring made to designate the heir.

I couldn't say as yet who'd perverted the ring in the casket, or what it had been designed to do in the beginning; it wasn't a face I could easily read. And, as it hadn't been perverted yet where I currently was, I only had a houseful of suspects at this point.

Poor Gerrett had been pressed into serving tea to Queen Helsa, who truly was a privileged bitch, used to getting whatever she wanted. She didn't care whom or what she hurt in order to get it, either.

"More servants come tomorrow," Bekzi sighed beside me, tossing the kitchen towel he held over a shoulder and shaking his head at the ingredients covering the prep table for the feast we'd planned for dinner.

We'd put a beef and chicken dish on the menu for the evening meal; Helsa favored both, so we hoped to appease her by giving her and the rest of her household a choice.

Any of her family in residence was expected to join her for dinner and dress appropriately. I could think of nothing worse than dressing in uncomfortable clothing just to have a meal with the sow. Except Bekzi and I had to prepare the meal and hope to please her unpredictable whims.

～

Jaledis

Quin

"What's wrong?" Berel asked. He'd wakened after midnight to find me sitting up in bed beside him.

"I don't know," I said, wrapping arms about myself to stop the shivering. "Something's wrong, I just can't understand what it is."

"Something about tomorrow?" He pulled himself into a sitting position beside me.

"I don't know," I mumbled. "I feel like something terrible will happen, but I have no idea when or what."

"To you or someone else?" He pulled me onto his lap and wrapped me in the blanket from the foot of our bed.

"I don't know that either." I settled my forehead against his neck and shoulder while he ran a soothing hand down my back and feathers.

"Queen Lissa will be with you tomorrow, sweetheart," he whispered before planting a kiss on my hair. "She is quite powerful, although not everyone knows it."

"I know it." I settled into a more comfortable position in his arms.

"Father likes Zaria. Very much," he whispered against my hair. "If you wish to discuss her absence, he will be more than willing to listen."

"Because we both miss her?" I guessed.

"I think so."

"I wish she were here to go with us tomorrow," I said. "She'd know what to do."

I couldn't say why I'd said what I did; I merely felt it, somehow.

"She is elsewhere and needed there," Berel rumbled softly. His heartbeat soothed me and soon I fell asleep.

Karathia—Past

Zaria

"Dinner was exceptional. Mother will never say it, but she ate with good appetite." Wellend appeared in the kitchen, scaring Bekzi and me half to death by his unexpected arrival.

"Thank you, Prince Wellend." Bekzi and I bowed our heads to the current Crown Prince of Karathia.

"If Mother ever dismisses you for any reason, take this to my Father, the King," he handed Bekzi a small, gold token. "He will hire you for the palace kitchen with no question."

With that, Wellend disappeared, folding space to who knew where. Bekzi turned to me, then. *This—your father. Should have been. You look like. Dark hair, blue eyes. Should have been.*

My eyes widened in surprise. Had Bekzi recalled my past?

"I know some things always," he hmmphed and turned to inspect the cleaning job the kitchen assistants had performed earlier.

I love you, I whispered into his mind.

I love you, he replied and turned to me. *Gerrett—he not remember. He know he love you anyway.*

That's more than some people. My shoulders sagged.

Not let that upset you. All will come. Time for bed.

Yeah. We have an early morning and no days off in sight, I agreed. Waving an arm, I turned off the spelled lights in the kitchen.

∽

Ilya

Zaria?

Ilya? Her reply sounded sleepy.

Never mind. Sleep, my love. Tomorrow is another day.

∽

Jaledis

Quin

I hadn't ridden in ground transportation in moon-turns. The hovervan lurched along the narrow, winding path toward the research facility, while the occasional tree reached out to slap the windshield of our vehicle as it passed.

At times, the limbs would scrape and screech down the sides of the van, causing me to jump.

It's just the trees, nothing to worry about, Lissa turned to me with a smile.

We sat directly behind our driver—Caylon Black in disguise. Behind us were boxes piled almost to the roof of the van, all filled with food and other necessities ordered by Ruther Kend and his staff.

That staff probably included either Deris or Daris Arden and an unknown Sirenali.

"Two more clicks," Caylon announced as another tree limb whacked the windscreen in front of his face. Ruther Kend had made it more than difficult for anyone to go in or out of the property located on the steep side of a mountain.

"You can see it now," Lissa pointed through the windshield.

The facility, painted white and green, rose above the trees on a higher stretch of the mountain. To me, it looked almost like a castle, complete with turrets. Perhaps Kend fancied himself some sort of king. If he had in the past, it no longer mattered. He was a hostage to evil, now.

We passed our first visible security camera, which followed our passage along the road. Somebody watched us from the facility; had probably watched us all along, but now we knew it for sure.

Two minutes, Caylon informed us in mindspeech. Apparently, he'd detected voice receptors as well as camera-operated weaponry. We had to look and sound just like a delivery crew or we'd be targeted. If the Arden twins had become involved with the weaponry, they'd kill anything they found suspicious.

We're fine, Lissa reassured me. The uneasiness in my belly increased.

∽

Karathia—Past
Zaria

Two new servants walked into the kitchen for the Queen's breakfast tray early the following morning. Two young men; Norn and Gale. Gale was handsome and tall, with blond hair. Norn was shorter, not as handsome and had close-cropped dark hair. A shiver went through me as I studied them.

No, they weren't bad. They were good.

They were also employed by the Karathian King—as spies.

Warlend was spying on his wife and her household, including one of his sons, who stayed there most of the time.

I wasn't about to report them; they had a job to do. And, if I'd been Warlend, I'd have spied on Helsa, too.

I wondered if Helsa would ever know that it was due to the fact that Wellend had reported Helsa's treatment of her servants to his father, because he certainly had.

"Set the currant jam at her right hand, about three-quarters up the side of her plate," I instructed as Bekzi piled items on the tray to be taken to the Queen's suite. "Place the small spoon next to the jar and remove the lid. Make sure her toast is crisp when it arrives; if it isn't, send mindspeech and I'll have more brought."

"Of course," Norn bobbed his head.

I placed a heating spell on the eggs, small sausages and strips of bacon on the covered plate before Norn and Gale left the room. I sincerely hoped they knew how to serve royalty. I didn't want to see them mistreated and tossed out like garbage after only one meal.

Those are the King's spies, I informed Bekzi as they rushed out the door with the tray. *He's looking into Helsa's mistreatment of his subjects—at Wellend's request.*

Plot thickens, Bekzi wiped off the prep table behind the stove.

It sure does, I agreed.

❧

Jaledis

Quin

One minute, Caylon informed us. I felt so ill by that time, I thought I might be sick. Caylon pulled to a stop in front of two employees, who wore what looked to be servant's uniforms for Kend Industries.

Caylon stepped out of the van to greet the two servants.

The Orb blinded Lissa and me when it appeared inside the van. I remember shrieking as it seared the wings from my back and flung me away from Jaledis.

CHAPTER 9

*J*aledis
Lissa

Caylon understood what I'd done to keep everything from blowing up around us. I'd been forced to hold back; The Orb would have killed Quin if I hadn't. Instead, the foul thing had sent its threats against Quin if I failed to cooperate. Then, I was commanded by the Orb to step back while it muted her screams and seared the wings from her back.

I wept when I sent her black wings back to the compound before Kend's employees signaled others to come forward and unload the van.

We'd needed Quin's talent to identify those who'd come from Kend's facility, in order to transfer information as to what was going on inside it. The Orb had appeared and crippled her while I watched in helpless horror.

Yes, I was angry and intended to become mist and go through the facility myself, but that idea was short-lived. For whatever reason, those inside the facility got spooked. Kend Industry employees disappeared around us and the mountain facility behind them imploded with an ear-deafening roar.

I turned to mist, then, just to get Caylon and myself away from the destruction. The machine Kend built for the Arden twins had likely been ordered to destroy the facility. Whether it was planned or set in motion by our appearance, I didn't know.

A horrifying and terribly sad spectacle met us when Caylon and I arrived at the compound. Bel Erland couldn't move. Berel wept. Terrett wore the grimmest of expressions as he cradled Quin's severed wings in his arms.

Somehow, their link to Quin had been broken by the Orb. Whatever the Orb was, it had acted in a sentient manner to solve what it saw as a problem. It recognized me as a threat, so it threatened Quin in return. Because of her continued link to the Orb, I'd understood the threat was real.

As for removing Quin's wings, I only had one guess as to why it was done. Wherever the Orb had sent her, she had to appear humanoid. Therefore, her wings were gone.

I was more than furious, and I'd already sent mindspeech to Bree, along with mental images of what had happened.

"What in the most holy of bloody fucking hells and purgatories has happened?" Kaldill appeared, his anger barely held in check.

"The Orb," I said flatly. "It took our girl and cut her wings."

Quin

My back was still on fire as I was dumped outside a door. Wherever I was, wealth was involved. The rug I'd landed on was hand-woven and thick.

"Who's there?" Someone opened the door and found me attempting to lift myself off the rug. I blinked up at him.

His name was Dorgus, and he was Vardil Cayetes' trusted servant. He was also acting in Cayetes' stead at the Arden twins' orders. They'd disguised him to look like Vardil's current incarnation, but I could see easily through their spells.

You will serve him and his current masters until I say otherwise, the Orb whispered in my mind. I knew better than to argue; the Orb had stripped the wings from my back without mercy and threatened to kill me so Lissa wouldn't attempt to intervene. Therefore, I was here so I could serve its calculated whims once more.

"I suppose I can't complain; at least they sent someone," Dorgus muttered above me. "Get in here. I need help with Master Vardil."

I didn't recognize my face in Vardil Cayetes' mirror. My dark hair had been close-cropped—at least it wasn't painful, like the removal of my wings. My features were irregular at best; it was the only way I could describe them.

I'd decided to be mute again; perhaps it was for the best that I never speak to anyone here. I'd learned in my past that they'd consider me incapable of carrying tales.

Vardil Cayetes' eyes barely focused on me as Dorgus and I removed him from his bath. Even with a healthy body, it looked as if his mind were wasting away.

Yes, I could probably heal him.

I wasn't going to, unless there were no other choice.

"Dinner will be brought," Dorgus waved a hand as he dressed Cayetes. "Then we'll put him to bed and you can amuse yourself in your room until the morning. His breakfast is at six bells; be up and ready by that time to help."

I could see in Dorgus what most people had likely never guessed—he was in love with Cayetes the criminal and would be loyal to him until the end.

Sadly, Vardil had only ever been partial to women, even in his current state. And, if he ever had a flash of true consciousness in my presence, I would know it. I had my own plans if that happened, and I was willing to accept the consequences when I acted.

Zaria

Milar, the Queen's chamberlain, appeared in the kitchen, clearing his throat while Bekzi and I prepared breakfast on our second morning. "Prince Wallend and Princess Valia are returning tomorrow. In two days, Princesses Palia and Titia will return from the King's Palace. In four days, the King and his second son, Wylend, will visit to celebrate the King's birthday. The Queen wishes to have special dishes prepared in honor of the King's visit."

Milar let out a breath, as if he'd saved it for the end of his announcement. I noticed that he'd made no mention of Wylend's mother, Queen Terez. Obviously, she wouldn't be visiting Helsa.

I didn't blame her.

"We will make sure the birthday meal is fit enough for a monarch," I dipped my head. "You may taste beforehand, if you wish."

"I do," he said. "And I will be quite judgmental if it is not to my liking."

"You like," Bekzi frowned. "We make best. You see."

"Is he slow?" Milar turned to me.

"Bekzi is swifter than you can ever imagine, Lord Chamberlain," I said. "He understands perfectly, and merely thinks many of the words the rest of us use are superfluous."

"Strange," Milar turned away from us. "One who uses less than plain speech, one who could speak at court, and both in the Queen's kitchen." He folded away.

"Get used to it," I muttered to the space Milar had occupied.

"Agree," Bekzi growled.

We see King before he die, Bekzi sent.

Yeah, my shoulders drooped. Warlend would have been my grandfather. What if he were someone I could love? Li'Neruh Rath had already said I couldn't interfere with the coup.

How could I deal with that? Knowing that someone I cared for would—*wait.*

I'd already dealt with it before.

This time, I had to use better sense.

Vardil's Compound

  Quin

"They're returning," Dorgus whispered as he and I settled a limp Vardil on an exercise machine and strapped him in. The machine would work his limbs while his body remained seated in a chair designed to fit his height and weight.

"I asked for a robotic walker, so he could carry himself about, but they wouldn't allow it," Dorgus grumbled. "Yet there they are, with the man who could enable my master to walk and use his hands, and they won't do anything."

I blinked, knowing he'd spoken of Ruther Kend. I wanted to point out that Ruther was busy making death machines for the Arden twins so his family might survive their kidnapping. I merely shook my head in feigned sympathy at Dorgus' words.

"How long have you been mute?" Dorgus asked.

I held up a hand and touched my fingers twenty times.

"Twenty turns? I'd wager that's how old you are," he said.

I nodded—no need to tell him otherwise.

He also didn't know what had precipitated the twins' return; I'd seen in Dorgus that this elaborate home on a hillside outside the capital city on Hraede belonged to one of their wealthier kidnap victims. Whether that victim was still alive, neither of us knew.

Yes, I'd already attempted mindspeech to let Kaldill know where I was, but it had echoed inside my mind and never went farther than that.

The Orb had its own plans and hadn't advised me of them. I also hoped this was one of the places Kooper and Caylon had on their watch list. Perhaps they'd find me. After a moment's reflection, I recalled that I no longer looked like myself.

Even if they had experienced eyes on this place, none would recognize me. Without my wings and facial features, it was a hopeless cause.

"Master Vardil, they're here," a servant poked his head inside the door. Dorgus shared his suite with the real Vardil, but like him, the twins had altered Vardil's features with a spell. To most, he'd be Dorgus, whom Vardil had chosen to care for after years of faithful service.

Dorgus was now Vardil Cayetes to all of Vardil's employees.

"Time to bow our heads and play the fool," Dorgus hissed. With a nod, he motioned for me to care for Vardil while he went to welcome the Arden twins and whomever they'd brought with them.

Morid

Gale and Norn flanked my cage as I was transported into the massive, hillside home. "We're on Hraede," Norn whispered softly. "They'll keep you in the main house and we'll help as much as we can, but I can't guarantee there will be no mistreatment."

"I know," I replied with my head bowed so I wouldn't draw attention. Ahead, Deris and Daris were greeted by someone they apparently knew. With my limited knowledge of Hraede, I understood this man wasn't from this world; he was someone the Arden twins had positioned there to further their cause.

Why had they chosen Hraede? It made little sense. Of all the worlds available, it would be the least hospitable if their machinations were discovered. Hraede was peace-loving, but there was a core of iron in the monarchy. If you broke the laws or threatened the peace, you would pay dearly for your actions. For that reason—and many others—the population adored Rigovarnus the Seventh, the current Hraedan King.

My late father hated Hraede, because they'd refused to allow him to do business on the planet long ago—before the Alliance stepped in to regulate spelled items and such. When Grey Planet was allowed membership in the Reth Alliance, he was angry enough to kill over it.

In reality he had killed many, not just because of those he'd worked for, but with what he'd taken from Siriaa.

He'd been responsible for Siriaa's destruction.

He and Vardil Cayetes.

He'd also left me with his legacy—a spell I hadn't been privy to, which led to my capture and current imprisonment. Without Gale and Norn, I'd likely have lost my mind already.

"Ah, Pargun, my friend," Deris greeted the one responsible for my capture. My fists clenched automatically as Pargun embraced Deris Arden like an old friend.

~

Quin

The massive house and surrounding grounds belonged to Yerbys Rovell, a wealthy businessman who used it for vacations with his family. I'd learned that by opening a drawer in a small study just outside Dorgus and Vardil's suite.

I'd carefully placed the information back in the drawer after reading it quickly; I'd found extra paper invitations from Yerbys' wife for three parties held the last time the family was in residence.

I wished for a comp-vid to read information on Yerbys' disappearance—if it had been reported. I hadn't known to look for such in Kooper the last time I'd seen him. Now that I was in possession of specific information, there was nobody to read who might tell me what I wanted to know.

Things such as how his family was doing and where they were, or whether they'd been kidnapped like Ruther Kend's family.

The other things I learned was that Pargun was in a large suite on a lower level of the house, and that Deris and Daris had brought a prisoner with them when they arrived with Ruther Kend and his employees.

That prisoner was Morid Belancour.

The last (and most puzzling) thing I discovered while sneaking clothing and wash packs to Morid, was that two of Ruther Kend's servants had taken it upon themselves to help Morid as best they could.

They'd introduced themselves as Gale and Norn, and I couldn't read either of them.

～

The kitchen floor was covered by flagstones; it brought back memories of working silently in the palace kitchen in Lironis. Instead of Wolter, shuffling from table to stove on long, storklike legs while shouting and herding kitchen boys about, however, there was a surly woman who frowned at everyone if they failed to do her bidding.

"I don't know why Master Vardil bothers to keep that freeloader alive," she muttered while dumping breakfast mush in a bowl and dropping it on a tray. Two slices of burned bacon followed on a small plate; I poured a glass of milk and set it carefully beside the rest before lifting the tray.

"At least you can't carry tales," she snapped as I carried the tray out of the kitchen. "Got lucky when they found you."

I pondered who might have gotten lucky, as I intended to expose all of them the moment I could, while they believed what they saw and failed to understand—that the least among them might bring about their downfall.

"I shall deal that witch a blow myself, when it becomes possible," Dorgus muttered as I settled the tray of less-than-appetizing food on a small table near Vardil's chair. Whether I'd been there to carry the tray or not, the food would have been the same.

Much better fare would be served to the Arden twins and their collaborators. Dorgus had already eaten; he'd been forced to have breakfast with the twins and Pargun, in addition to a few of Vardil's highly placed employees.

Dorgus had given orders to them, acting as Vardil while the twins supervised and watched for anything out of the ordinary from Vardil's erstwhile assistant.

A part of me wanted to feel sorry for Dorgus, but he'd been complicit in Vardil's doings for too long. Perhaps in different circumstances, he might have been a better person.

I held no hope that he'd change if Vardil suddenly regained his faculties and carried on as before. Whatever sympathy I had for him was because he was faithful in his love for a man who would never love him in return.

"That's right," Dorgus crooned as Vardil's hand lifted the spoon. Dorgus helped dip mush, holding Vardil's shaking hand in his own so the witless criminal could eat.

~

Karathia—Present

Bel Erland

I can't count the number of times I attempted mindspeech to reach Quin. Gran was sure Quin was alive; she explained that there was no need to remove Quin's wings if the Orb only intended her death.

"She's in a place where wings would only mark her as a spy or worse," Gran told me.

I'm sure she was right, but it didn't quell my worries. At times, the explanation only made things more horrible in my mind.

The Orb, after all, didn't have a stellar track record of placing Quin in comfortable situations. My guess was that she was somewhere near the Arden twins, serving the Orb's current whims.

Her life in those circumstances would hang by a thread, and it didn't guarantee that she wouldn't take harm from those who considered themselves her masters.

Berel and Edden, both just as devastated as I, offered to take the news to Justis. I couldn't do that; it was hard enough thinking about it. Telling someone else and then offering comfort would kill me.

I'd placed the stasis spell on Quin's severed wings myself, in order to send them to the Avii King. That's where they belonged, although I did allow a single feather for each of the rest of us.

Kaldill—I'd never seen him so stricken. He'd taken his feather and returned to Gaelar N'Seith to mourn.

I hoped he merely mourned Quin's absence and not her death; the Elf King often knew more than any of us, and that included Gran.

Lafe had asked to be taken to Le-Ath Veronis; I imagined that he'd meet there with Dragon, Crane, Drake and Drew. They'd know how to keep him occupied while he grieved. Terrett went back to BlackWing VII, to look after Bleek and Barc.

Barc was terrified for Quin and clung to his father's right hands as I appeared on board with Terrett. Bleek—I'd never seen such a look of desolation on his face. I was beginning to realize it wasn't just for Quin, but for Zaria, too.

Dad and Granddad were grim and tight-lipped about all of it. They worried that Quin would be harmed or worse—either killed or bent to the will of the Arden twins in their twisted grasping for the Karathian throne.

I stood in my suite at the palace on Karathia now, studying my image in the dressing room mirror before going to meet them. Dad ordered a meal to be served in his study so we could discuss the situation privately.

The news of Quin's disappearance hadn't been released to anyone outside the royal family on Karathia. For some reason, Dad worried it could be dangerous to do so.

To me, that meant he suspected that some citizens had already aligned with the Arden twins. I wished Ilya were still with us; I trusted him and he'd willingly assist me in any endeavor to ferret out those with treasonous leanings. Straightening the collar on my shirt, I sighed and folded into Dad's study.

Hraede
   Quin

I didn't learn until the fifth day that Ruther Kend and his staff were working in the basement of the massive Yerbys mansion. I'd followed Dorgus to the servant's lift past the kitchen; he'd motioned me inside and I rode down with him.

When the lift doors swept aside to allow our exit, I found a hive of activity going on inside the cavernous basement.

Whatever the family had stored there—it was now gone, replaced by machines, comp-vids and worktables. A large, box-like device took up a corner near the lift; it would manufacture metal parts and such for the machines and motors Ruther and his assistants were building.

"The problem," Ruther Kend tossed a piece of fabricated metal onto his table with a curse as the metal rang its loud complaint, "is that whoever made those drawings had no idea what they were drawing."

"Perhaps it's merely because you fail to understand them," Deris snarled as he appeared nearby. I cringed at his arrival; he was angry that this was taking so long. I read that anger easily in his eyes and the downward curve of his lips.

I understood that many who'd vexed him less in the past had died due to his anger. He only kept Ruther Kend alive because he was his only hope for getting the machines right.

Ruther was right, too; I read in him that the one who'd drawn the plans for these terrible machines had been neither scientist nor artist. Something was fundamentally wrong with the drawings as a result. While the machine loosed upon Jaledis was effective, it wasn't the elite killing machine it could become.

Somewhere in Deris' past, he'd experimented with this flawed version of the machine. Ruther Kend was his only hope of rectifying the flaws; therefore, Kend was still alive.

I shuddered to think what could be done with an unflawed, fully functional version of this killing contraption.

"Where did the drawings come from?" Ruther set his safety goggles carefully on the table and studied Deris.

"My grandmother paid for these copies," Deris snapped. "The originals were in the King's vaults here on Hraede. Before you ask," he held up a hand, "they're no longer there. They've been destroyed, I think—my sister and I have already checked. You, my friend, will solve this problem or a member of your family will die in two days. Get back to work and show me something better before then." Deris disappeared.

Was this why they'd chosen Hraede—to search the King's vaults for something that no longer existed? Then, once they were here, they'd elected to stay, since nobody had noticed their presence?

The nearest inhabited property was more than a click away, as Hraedans measured distance, and a narrow forest of trees filled the space in between. Small vehicles could come and go without any the wiser, unless someone were watching closely.

Wait.

That was one of the things Zaria brought up—that Deris and Daris could be interested in property as well as other holdings, to further their dangerous plotting.

I silently sent up a prayer that someone was watching this property as closely as needed. Even if none would recognize me now, I hoped someone would stop the Arden twins before Ruther Kend perfected their machines.

Catacombs—Rith Naeri Headquarters

Hraede

Halimel I

"There's definite activity." I shoved the comp-vid toward Brin. "The problem, of course, is that we don't know for sure who is there or what will happen if we infiltrate. Kooper Griff says the lives of kidnap victims are at stake. One wrong move and everybody dies. It doesn't help that Yerbys isn't a permanent citizen of Hraede; he merely vacations here one or two moon-turns per year."

"We don't have a tunnel near the property, either," Brin thumbed through the images delivered by one of our vampire spies. "I'll send this information to Rigo; he can decide what to share with Griff."

"I say we call the others in for a meeting. Ask Rigo if he's free to come. I want more eyes on this property, although it doesn't fit the bill as far as drakus seed production goes. The land isn't suitable and it's covered in trees."

CONNIE SUTTLE

"I'm hoping Rigo has better intelligence to share," Brin shrugged. "Perhaps its headquarters to important lieutenants or such. If we take one or two of those," he didn't finish.

We could place compulsion, as long as there'd been no obsession placed beforehand. That was a delicate situation and could end up exposing all of us. It angered me that these rogue Karathians had bred Sirenali—enough to cover their tracks from the powerful—in their bid for domination and the takeover of the Karathian throne.

Brin rubbed the Night Flower tattoo on the side of his neck. He did that whenever he worried—it was unconscious on his part. We'd taken an oath when the tattoo was applied—to protect Hraede and its citizens with our lives, our strength and our wits.

Once, we'd been kings of Hraede, and all of us had the advantage of being advised in secret by the wisest of vampires while we sat the throne. As for our turning, they only offered it to the best among Hraede's monarchs. Sadly, no queens had survived the attempt at turning, although Rigo said that Queen Lissa might consider offering her blood when the next suitable Hraedan Queen came along.

Rigo was the first King made vampire, but his sire hadn't been seen in years; he was so ancient, even when he made Rigo vampire, we feared he'd greeted the sun and quietly left this existence behind.

I think we felt Kellik's absence most acutely now, as we might be dealing with rogues from Karathia who held a power we couldn't combat properly.

"Done," Brin said, tossing the comp-vid onto the table. "Rigo is set to come to the meeting tomorrow night."

"I wish Kell were here," I said, lifting the comp-vid and studying the first image of the Rovell vacation home high on a hill outside our city. "Maybe he'd have some ideas."

∾

BlackWing VII
  Terrett

I joined James and Nathan on the bridge of BlackWing VII. It was near midnight, ship-time, and I should have been in bed. Since Quin's disappearance, my ability to sleep had vanished with her.

"It's a weak distress signal," James turned toward me. I'd learned he could hear my mindspeech, so we communicated easily.

From where? I asked.

"Not far—we just picked it up," he replied. "Will you ask Caylon to join us? This worries me."

I sent mindspeech to Caylon and Salidar, then informed James that they were on the way. "Don't venture too close," Nathan cautioned. "It could be a trap."

"I'm waiting for Caylon's orders," James confirmed. "Full stop, please," he ordered the ship.

"Full stop as requested," BlackWing VII's soft, mechanical voice replied. "All systems functional."

"What's going on?" Caylon shrugged into a shirt as he appeared on the bridge. Sal, fully dressed, arrived right behind him.

"Distress signal, Commander," James said. "A weak one. We're afraid it's a trap. There's been no word from the ASD that they've received it, yet, and we passed a sat-sensor not long ago."

"Daragar?" Caylon spoke to empty air. In no time, the tall Larentii, accompanied by Valegar, arrived on the ship's bridge.

"Can you help shield the ship?" Caylon asked. "I want to check this out."

"We must go quickly," Daragar turned bright-blue eyes on Caylon. "This is not what you think."

"Full speed," Caylon snapped. The ship, recognizing his command, jerked into motion immediately.

"Follow the signal," James ordered. The ship responded with a lurch. We were traveling as swiftly as we could and leaving the shipping lanes far behind.

Another Larentii I didn't recognize joined us.

"We won't be in time," he said, "and with the interference, I cannot get a proper location."

"Then allow me."

Someone else came. I gaped. He was tall, with light-brown hair and blue eyes. I'd never seen such power radiating off anyone before. "I just need to send out echolocation," he said.

"Yes, I have you now," he hissed. BlackWing VII and all on-board were flung forward in a blinding rush.

CHAPTER 10

errett

I had no idea where all the healers came from, but I was more than happy to see them. The floating space city we'd found had almost run out of power to supply oxygen to its inhabitants.

Oxygen had arrived with the healers, who rushed this way and that to save lives of hundreds. BlackWing VII was currently tied to a dock in something that shouldn't exist in a crushzone—multitudes of floating asteroids, small planets and debris dumps would have destroyed it, had it been towed here by traditional means.

It wasn't difficult to sort out; I recognized several hostages from the comp-vid images distributed by Director Griff.

We'd found where the Arden twins had placed most of their kidnap victims.

What they hadn't taken into consideration, however, was the genius and fierce determination of a fourteen-year-old girl—the eldest daughter of Ruther Kend.

She'd diverted energy from the floating city after consulting its other inhabitants, in order to send out the distress signal.

She'd almost killed them in the attempt, but I realized they were willing to accept that fate rather than fall into the hands of the Arden twins again.

We also found six mute Sirenali, all young and emaciated.

Sadly, Quin wasn't here to help them, and one died before a healer could get to him. The others had no mindspeech. Somehow, Deris and Daris had taken away their only hope of communication. Even their hearing was damaged, so they couldn't hear the soothing words of those who struggled to help them.

They needed Quin's help to regain any sort of life, or perhaps Zaria's healing. Either would give these a better chance.

We had neither of those things at the moment.

The tall stranger had disappeared. I was determined to ask Caylon who he was, once things had settled down.

Brother? Morrett placed a hand on my shoulder as I gazed at the beds containing young Sirenali patients.

I went still for a moment before turning toward him.

Brother? I repeated his greeting.

Corinne will help them, he said.

Corinne?

You do not know her?

I don't recognize that name.

She saved my life, Morrett said, beckoning me to come away. *If she can do that, I think she can help these, too.*

Le-Ath Veronis

Lissa

"Were all of them there?" I asked.

"Yerbys Rovell is missing, and only Kend's children were there," Merrill said. "Kend's wife—I have no idea where she is. His son and daughter didn't know either—they were separated when the children were transported to the space city."

"So Yerbys may be dead already and Barra Kend is scheduled to die next, if Kend doesn't do as directed," I slapped a hand on my desk and stood.

"That's my thought as well."

"There's activity on at least six worlds, on property owned by six of those kidnap victims," I said. "That we know of. Rigo says there's something going on outside Choridi, Hraede's capital city, but there's no evidence yet that it's anything other than a lieutenant or two who wanted to live in a fancy house. The property isn't suited for any other criminal activity that I know of."

"Are they keeping watch?" Merrill asked.

"Like hawks," I said. "Rigo has a meeting with the Order tonight. Maybe he'll get something new after he talks to the others."

"BlackWing VII is scheduled back here tomorrow morning," Merrill observed. "Karzac says he'll transport the victims to a hidden facility on the light side, with nobody the wiser."

"Kooper Griff is here," Renée, my assistant, announced.

"Lissa," Kooper walked in and nodded deferentially. "We've placed ASD agents on-board the space city, after repairing the systems. That child is a genius in what she did to divert energy to a makeshift distress signal. So far, there's no evidence that they've been there, or to any of the other places where we've seen activity. That means we still watch and wait."

"Here's my question," I gestured for Kooper to have a seat. "Will Deris and Daris go back to the space city themselves? If so, how are your agents going to fend off a powerful witch and warlock?"

Zaria

What the hell just happened? I asked.

Gale and Norn, without a backward glance, were rushed out of the house while Wellend kept watch.

The reason appeared moments later; Helsa, screeching that one of the two had stepped on her skirt while serving lunch, was ready to blast both into oblivion. I imagined that they'd folded space to get away from Helsa, or Wellend had returned them to his father's palace himself, in order to keep Helsa from murdering them.

What made me angriest was that she held more than enough power to remove any dust or shoeprint from the skirt herself.

She crazy, Bekzi sent and went back inside the kitchen.

Deciding that being out of sight meant out of Helsa's less than logical mind, I followed him.

We were treated to Helsa's shouting at Wellend, then, because he, in her words, failed to stop those two bastards so she could deal with them appropriately.

"Do we have everything to make the cake?" I attempted to shut out Helsa's shouted verbal meltdown.

Yes. We also have edible gold flakes. All in place. You see. Bekzi cringed as Helsa launched something at the servant's door near the kitchen. It shattered (whatever it was) while glassy shards tinkled and scattered across the stone floor.

With barely a thought, I exerted power to clean the floor, making the glass disappear while Helsa continued her tirade outside the kitchen.

Where glass go? Bekzi asked.

I put the vase back together. It's in the attic, now, I said. We went back to our meal planning, deliberately ignoring Helsa's shouting. At least Gale and Norn were safe from bodily harm, and likely making their report to the Karathian King while Helsa vented her irrational rage.

Ilya

Cabbage?

I'm here. She sounded tired.

What's going on?

Helsa just tried to kill two servants. Wellend sent them out the door before she could hit them with a spell, then flung an expensive vase at the back door after they folded away. It's just as well—Warlend sent them to spy on Helsa because Wellend asked him to. She's as irrational as they come, and half the time I can't see through the madness that's eating at her mind. What's going on with you?

I was informed that Helsa's father is on his way, and told to make room for his horse, because he's riding in for the King's birthday.

Oh, no, she said.

What's wrong?

I get the idea that Hegatt Blackmantle is adept at puppetry, just not the traditional kind.

You mean manipulation?

Yes. Exactly. It's what I've seen of him in Wellend so far.

This is his grandfather, love.

I get that. If your own grandfather is considered an unwelcome guest, how might others see him? Was Warlend manipulated into marrying Helsa for some reason? I think I'm seeing history with new eyes, she replied.

It's certainly different from the history I read, I agreed. *Of course, that could have been deftly manipulated. What else have you seen in Wellend?*

That this place was a crumbling mess when Helsa married Warlend. You see what it is, now, and on top of that, the other Blackmantle estate, where Hegatt lives, has also been significantly enhanced and upgraded.

In present day, I said, *both places still stand and are occupied by distant relatives of the Blackmantle family.*

Has anybody checked in with them? Zaria asked. *That sounds like an easy path for the Arden twins, if they can get someone to sponsor their takeover—quietly, of course.*

Yes. I'm beginning to be concerned about that, I said. *There's nothing we can do right now; all we're allowed to do is accurately assess this past and then work against it when we're returned to our own time.*

I know. She sounded depressed.

My love, I will come to you tonight, I said. *All will be well, I promise.*

Thank you.

Zaria

My hands shook as I kneaded bread dough; the bread would be set to rise and then baked to serve with dinner.

You not worry, Bekzi soothed. *We deal with Blackmantle, same as we deal with crazy daughter.*

We haven't met the crazy great-grandchildren yet, I pointed out while punching the mound of dough with a fist. *They're in their teens, and that makes it worse. Who knew the family would be a tree-full of nutjobs?*

That funny, Bekzi grinned. *Come, I finish.* He stepped behind me, his arms reached around my shoulders as he placed his hands atop mine. I certainly wasn't going to complain when the kisses trailed down the side of my neck, or that he guided me through the rest of the kneading before letting the dough rest.

Not worry, he said when he pulled away. *I hear from Ilya. We spend time together later.*

Yeah. I let my shoulders droop.

Yes, I knew he was mated to someone else, who didn't care that he and I were also intended to be together. Perhaps someday, when my anxiety wouldn't drive me away, I wanted to meet her.

He, like a gentleman, waited for Ilya to come to me first, as Ilya had no other mates. Turning away, I checked the soup base simmering at the back of the stove. Later, when the time was right, we'd add shrimp and seafood before serving.

It smells heavenly, I complimented Bekzi, who'd put it together.

Reah create, he smiled. *I learn all from her.*

Then she's a magnificent cook, I replied.

Best, he nodded.

Hraede

Kellik of Abenott

Even Rigo thought me dead; I'd kept away from him so long. Yes, once I'd been a noble in the King's court, a thousand years before Rigovarnus I ascended the throne of Hraede. I'd chosen to make Rigo vampire, and he, in turn had chosen those to make after him.

They'd kept Hraede safe from harm, ruling from the shadows, as I'd taught them. Many times since then, I'd considered ending my long life.

My vampire sire was certainly dead—I'd watched until the last moment as he walked steadily into the sunrise.

A wise and honorable man was my grandfather, who'd become a wise and honorable vampire. I still missed his calm demeanor and steady hand.

Something always held me back from a walk in the sun; perhaps it was because a part of me knew that someday, I might become useful again.

From the dark confines of the nearby forest, I studied the large vacation home belonging to an off-worlder. I had my methods of spying, as I'd taught Rigo everything he knew of it.

Something was going on in the Rovell home, and I doubted it was closely acquainted with anything considered legal.

Yes, I knew Yerbys Rovell had been kidnapped while on a business retreat with several others in the same income bracket. They'd thought themselves safe, with the best ship their money could purchase, which was guarded by the best security their money could buy.

Where they miscalculated, however, was hiring only mortals to provide security. Those mortals in turn relied solely on weapons to protect their employers. They hadn't taken into consideration that a powerful wizard or warlock might augment what they already had.

Therefore, when two powerful criminals, who happened to come from Karathia attacked the ship, the wealthy were kidnapped and their security guards were murdered.

I understood Kooper Griff, Director of the ASD, was using every asset he had to combat the two responsible, but so far, he was trailing far behind them.

Yes, I understood they'd taken over Vardil Cayetes' empire, with their sights set on bigger things. I could only assume that somewhere in their future, the throne of Karathia could come under attack.

I considered contacting Rigo, in order to gain an audience with the

King of Karathia. As I'd been gone so long, Rigo could be less than cooperative with my request. I held that idea in reserve while I watched the Rovell house carefully.

Yes, I imagined that it was spelled against intruders, so I hadn't approached it, yet. For now, I would be content to watch and carry any findings to Rigo, who had the ear of the ASD when needed.

Hraede

Quin

Barra Kend would be delivered to the mansion after nightfall; I read that in Dorgus after he returned from a meeting with Pargun.

I was beginning to despise Pargun almost as much as I despised Deris and Daris. In my mind, I pictured him as a Brakka slug, a creature that consumed almost anything organic and left a trail of poison behind to kill potential predators and anything else that happened across it.

Pargun wouldn't care that Barra Kend would die; he merely wanted payment for keeping her in an undisclosed location until called for.

When Pargun himself appeared in the kitchen while I gathered food for Vardil at midday, I also saw something he knew but Dorgus and the others didn't; Barra Kend was pregnant.

Deris and Daris would kill her and the child without a second thought, if they failed to get what they wanted from Barra's husband.

A plan was forming in my mind; I'd been ordered to serve Dorgus and the twins, but Pargun, as far as I knew, hadn't been included in the Orb's command. If I couldn't prevent Barra Kend's death, then I would have another in exchange.

Setting a bowl of soup that hadn't been burned on the tray, I was out the kitchen door before the cook could call me back.

Karathia—Past

Zaria

It was late before the kitchen was clean and Helsa sent off to her bedroom. While she hadn't said the food was bad, she'd made a fuss about it anyway, only taking two or three bites of what was set in front of her before flinging dishes at the servers.

Gerrett allowed me to see all of it in his eyes; Helsa railed against the guests arriving the following day while Wellend sat at the other end of the long table, eating his food without comment.

Afterward, I'd gone to clear away the mess with a spell so the others wouldn't have to; I'd waited for Helsa to retire to her sitting room with a brandy before arriving in the dining hall and eliminating the remaining mess before Gerrett and the others got down on hands and knees to clean up broken glass and smeared food on expensive rugs.

The glass and crockery returned to the kitchen whole, where it was washed by two kitchen helpers while Bekzi supervised.

This is a horrible mess, Gerrett informed me as I studied the clean dining hall. I understood he didn't mean the dining hall itself; I'd just set it to rights.

Helsa is horrible, I agreed. *I sure hope her father and the others aren't worse.*

I'm not sure they can be worse, only more of the same, Gerrett observed.

My hands were on my hips as I studied the rug beneath my feet— yes it was clean—cleaner than it had been before I'd cast the spell to remove the food and broken dishes.

"I feel I know you from somewhere," Wellend appeared and startled a half-scream from my lips before I could slap a hand over my mouth.

"We've never met, my Prince," I said when I caught my breath enough to bow my head respectfully and speak.

"I understand that, but the feeling persists. As if we knew one another in a different age."

Here was the father I'd never known, and I could never tell him

143

that, or call him Daddy. My soul wept for that terrible twist of fate, and once again I blamed the Lyristolyi and their drug for tearing apart the fabric of my life.

"My Prince, we have never met until now," I whispered.

He hesitated for a moment. "Dinner was excellent," he said and disappeared.

~

Hraede

Kellik

A hovercar the color of smoke traveled quietly through the trees on the way to the Rovell home. My eyes, as sharp as they ever were, saw three inside the vehicle.

One—the only woman, was bound.

A hostage.

Slipping silently off the high limb that bore my weight, I dropped quietly onto the track and followed. With darkness as my only shield, I gripped the crash-guard on the back of the vehicle and swung it around, smashing the front of the hovercar into a thick tree.

While two men fought to free themselves from the wreckage, I leapt on top of the vehicle, drew a line in the metal with a single claw and pulled one side away, as if I were ripping the lid off a pressboard box.

Without a thought, I removed the head of the man pointing his weapon at me.

The other pissed himself and shrank into the vehicle.

Careful not to harm her, I cut the bonds holding the woman and lifted her away.

"You will tell no one you saw me," I hissed compulsion at the man. "You wrecked the vehicle due to your own carelessness."

With a leap I was in the trees again, hauling the terrified woman with me.

~

Rigo

Hal's comp-vid rattled the warning tone—something had happened. He and the others never received messages from their team of vampire spies unless communication was necessary.

"A hovercar was wrecked outside the Rovell house," the vampire on the other end sputtered.

"What happened?" Hal demanded.

"Unsure at this time. We held back at a safe distance as directed, when the vehicle crashed. We heard it and moved in, but I can't explain what we found," he said.

"I can explain it."

I knew that voice.

Kell.

My sire.

"What?" I turned swiftly in his direction before the next words died on my lips. Kell, as mighty as he ever was, held an unconscious woman in his arms.

"Lissa," I shouted verbally and mentally. From my place at the meeting table, I could scent the woman's pregnancy. If something weren't done soon, she could lose the child.

Lissa

"She'll be fine," Karzac sighed as he turned away from the bed. Barra Kend slept peacefully, her pregnancy still intact. Karzac had healed the damage done by the wreck, then placed her in a healing sleep.

All she'd babbled the whole time I'd asked questions was her fear for her children and her husband.

I couldn't blame her. What concerned me was this; shortly after I'd gone to Hraede to help, the Rovell house went dark and any who'd inhabited it were now gone.

I suspected that included Ruther Kend. Rigo and the Rith Naeri had gone to the Rovell home to investigate—I asked him to search specifically for Kend's scent.

It's there, Rigo sent as I walked along a palace hall with Karzac. *Pargun's body is here*, he added. *Quite dead from no apparent injury. There's another scent you may be interested in, too.*

Who?

Quin was here.

I cursed.

~

Karathia—Present

Quin

In the twins' desperation to get away after the crash and abduction of Barra Kend, they failed to notice that Pargun never met with the others inside the basement for the move.

He was dead inside his suite; I'd made sure of it. In all the chaos, it was easy. Whatever Pargun knew, I also knew. The hostages he'd taken, I could find.

I felt no pity for him; he died swiftly and with less pain than he deserved.

I hoped someone would come to investigate, to find the body. Queen Lissa would understand that I'd been there, if nobody else would.

"We're on Karathia," Dorgus whispered as he and I settled Vardil on a bed in an unfamiliar suite. "This means we could die in an instant if the King and his spies learn we're here."

Karathia.

Bel Erland and King Rylend's home planet.

How could I get them to notice us?

Perhaps this was why the Orb had changed me. I no longer had my wings or a familiar face. If these died about me, I'd likely die with them.

"This is the ancestral home of the Arden twins," Dorgus continued. "Through their maternal great-grandfather, Hegatt Blackmantle and their grandmother, Queen Helsa Blackmantle-Arden. I can't say I'd miss them if the twins were killed, but I have to save him," he jerked his head toward Vardil.

I pitied Dorgus at that moment, because he refused to see anything but the criminal he still loved with all his heart.

Moreover, because I'd chosen silence, I couldn't tell him how I felt, and that was perhaps the wisest choice I'd inadvertently made. If I told him how many lives Vardil had taken, or the planets he was set to destroy beginning with Siriaa, Dorgus would only attempt to kill me himself.

He saw no wrong in Vardil Cayetes.

I realized then that I'd set aside the problem of poisoned planets; the Orb had me chasing other demons instead. Why it wanted me to serve Deris and Daris, however, I still didn't understand.

Why wouldn't it desire their deaths, like it desired Vardil Cayetes' death? Had it turned aside from Vardil, now that he was nothing more than a pathetic simpleton?

Did Deris and Daris play a role in the Orb's ultimate goal? Was that why I was with them now, and under their thumbs? Too many questions tumbled through my mind as Dorgus fed Vardil with the gentle hand of a parent feeding a baby.

When the meal was done and Dorgus began cleaning Vardil's face and hands, I slipped away.

Somewhere in the massive castle surrounded by a lake, Ruther Kend struggled to build a better death machine, unaware that his wife had been rescued by the unknown and was now likely out of reach of his captors.

The castle was grand and richly appointed, with gilt covering elaborate plasterwork and furniture carved by talented craftsmen scattered throughout. Rich, Serendaan rugs ran through rooms and hallways, lit with spell-lights in hand-blown glass.

Outside, elegant water birds graced the small lake, while squirrels, fox and other creatures chased and hunted through the forest. I understood then why Deris and Daris chose the home on Hraede—it had come closest to their ancestral domain.

Almost invisible as I slipped from one hallway to the next, I overheard snippets of conversation. One of those conversations involved Pargun and his absence. Stopping for a moment outside the half-closed door, I listened while Deris fumed that Pargun hadn't responded to his comp-vid messages.

Deris thought the information broker to be alive and merely ignoring his communications. Drawing in a breath, I slipped away as silent as a fox in the forest, heading for the rooms set aside for Ruther Kend and his assistants.

~

Karathia—Past

Ilya

My love, stop fretting, I brushed dark hair away from Zaria's forehead. Something troubled her and I couldn't get her to tell me what it was.

Maybe we should try this another time? Bright-blue eyes pleaded with me to understand.

"Shhh, cabbage," I soothed. "Come, let me love you and take your mind away from these things."

"But," she began.

"Hush." I held her face in my hands and kissed her—gently at first, then with more urgency. I and my body ached for her. "Yes," I murmured against her mouth as I lowered her onto the sheets. Her skin so soft against my mouth and fingers; her eyes closing with pleasure as I nipped her collarbone before traveling farther down.

It is a simple thing to remove clothing with a spell. I did it slowly, one piece at a time. "Ilya," she whimpered when my fingers found the sweetest spot.

"I won't be rough, my love," I promised, before lowering my head to where my fingers had been. The taste of her was exhilarating, like that of a perfectly cast spell, sweet on the tongue as it envelopes the caster with pleasure. I was more than pleased to bring her to climax that way, then I moved over her body and gave her another before taking my own.

~

Zaria

Ilya woke early, as did I; I had work to do in the kitchen while he went to tend the horses in the stable. I didn't want to let him go; his presence in my bed made me feel safe enough to sleep soundly.

After we'd made love.

No, I didn't want to delude myself. This Ilya I was still getting to know. Some things were the same, others vastly different.

He loved me—that was the most important part.

"Don't let the new arrivals upset you," he breathed against my hair before folding away.

~

Bekzi met me in the kitchen; he nodded after I did, silently acknowledging that my night had gone well.

Breakfast had to be started, so we went about it, making preparations while our kitchen helpers set the simple spells for the stove and oven.

"Lord Hegatt has arrived, set another place at the table," Milar appeared inside the kitchen.

I'd jumped at Milar's sudden appearance, he was straight-spined and stuffy as always, although I could read in him that he hadn't expected Hegatt until the afternoon. Somebody had folded space, horse and all, for most of the trip, so he could come riding in for breakfast. Milar disappeared quickly; I assumed it was because Helsa sent mindspeech.

Or her father had.

How is he? I sent to Ilya while Bekzi and I prepared another plate of food.

He wears a permanent scowl, so you'll have to judge for yourself, Ilya

149

replied. *Take care around him, my love. He may be of the rape and dismiss variety.*

I'll remove his cock if he tries, I snorted.

I think I'd like to watch, Ilya replied. *He comes. Let me know if help is required.*

CHAPTER 11

*L*e-Ath Veronis
  Queen's Palace
  Kell

Yes, I'd kept up with the Queen of Le-Ath Veronis. I never thought to meet her in the flesh, however.

Father, do not fidget, Rigo instructed mentally as we stood inside the Queen's palace library on Le-Ath Veronis.

Mindspeech. He'd never had it until his mating with the Queen. If I hadn't understood before that she was more than powerful, the present evidence would have overwhelmed me.

Rigo grinned after the sending, letting me know how happy he was to see I was still alive and working for the good of Hraede from the shadows. As I had no mindspeech to reply, I merely dipped my head in acknowledgement.

"Kellik of Abenott, come forward," Queen Lissa commanded.

Surrounding us was a gathering of those handpicked by Rigo and the Queen to witness this event.

I had no idea why she was determined to do this.

I was determined, as a result, not to bring the slightest harm when I took her blood. I stepped forward as commanded.

No climax. Lissa, Queen of all vampires, informed me in mindspeech as she tilted her head to expose the vein in her neck.

I wanted to argue. To tell her what she already knew, that the climax eliminated the pain of the bite.

"My blood is a gift to you, Kellik. You will take no harm from it," the Queen recited. "There are no bindings or conditions, it is freely given."

I sank my fangs into her throat as carefully as I could.

Karathia—Present

Quin

I wanted to ask Dorgus why they were moving us. I dared not. I had little to move after all, so I helped Dorgus pack Vardil's belongings.

He, Vardil, Daris and I were the only ones moving, too. Perhaps it was to ensure that at least one of the twins would survive if the other were killed.

Daris snapped at her servants to ready her things faster. It was something she could do herself with a spell; therefore, she chose to trouble her humanoid underlings with the task.

I watched as she swept down a hall with servants carrying heavy bags in her wake. I also saw in her face what I most wanted to know.

The move wasn't for safety; the plantation that held their largest drakus seed field needed additional supervision, and Vardil's employees required Vardil's presence in order to get things accomplished efficiently.

Also, housed in large buildings on a hidden corner of the same property were thousands of death machines, already manufactured and awaiting Ruther Kend's upgrades.

Deris and Daris intended a war against Karathia, and, as the machines could fire from any location while making the shots appear to come from another direction, the Karathian King's army wouldn't know where to send the spells.

These truly were death machines, and I worried that neither of the twins recognized what they might do if they were properly constructed.

Ruther Kend also wasn't aware that his wife had escaped. I still had no idea how that had happened—the driver who'd survived the crash couldn't recall what had happened, which resulted in his fiery death at the hands of Deris.

His screams and the stench from being burned alive still invaded my sleep and woke me with visions of the nightmares that had come.

Shivering involuntarily, I laid another carefully folded silk shirt in Vardil's heavy trunk and focused on my task.

By midday, we were on another world near its equator, where the rains and warm temperatures were ideal for growing drakus seed. My shoulders sagged at the first sight of this massive farm—as far as I could see the plants grew, tall and green while a light rain fell, giving life to the poisonous growth.

"Hurry, girl," Dorgus snapped. "We have to get him inside before he gets soaked."

He meant Vardil. Pulling a rainshield from the pouch of Vardil's hoverchair, I snapped it open and held it over Vardil's head while Dorgus guided the machine toward a massive plantation house.

"She can't speak," Dorgus informed the cook and her staff.

Unlike the cook who stayed on Karathia with Deris, this one had been forced to work for the twins, after they took over the plantation from one of their wealthy kidnap victims.

"Does she have dry clothes?" The cook glared at Dorgus.

"She has what she's wearing," Dorgus snapped.

"Do you pay her?" The cook's fists went to her hips. She wasn't heavy; she was tall and substantial, nonetheless.

"That is none of your business," Dorgus responded.

"Every mouth in this house is my business," the cook's voice rose. "Find clothing for her or I will."

"Fine. Do whatever you want. Dress her like a princess, if you like. It won't improve her face any."

He'd merely put into words what I'd known all along. Dorgus preferred what was pleasing to his eye. I, in my current state, was only good enough to serve him and Vardil, while staying out of his way the rest of the time.

"Someday, Master Vardil," the cook pointed a finger at Dorgus, whom she believed to be Vardil, "You'll learn that all are the same, no matter what they look like or where they come from. It's what's in their heart and soul that makes them different."

"Come." One of the cook's assistants, a young woman with a pretty smile, took my hand and led me toward the laundry. "I'll help you find something to wear."

Cook Janis nodded her approval when assistant cook Ela brought me back to the kitchen dressed in a young boy's clothing. "Gem's clothes fit her well enough," Janis turned away. I already knew that Gem was dead—he'd died while attempting to help his father when Deris and Daris arrived with the wealthy kidnapped owner in order to take over the plantation.

Gem, at fourteen, was a favorite with all the staff. His death angered them greatly, but they were helpless against the kind of power wielded by the twins.

Gem's death had been an example to them, too. Everyone else there feared for their lives as a result. Gem's father, grieving and hopeless, was taken away again while the staff was forced to bow to the whims of those who'd taken him.

Except for Janis.

She was wise, however, and understood she didn't have the strength or resources to fight those who'd taken over. It didn't mean she wasn't making plans to alert the authorities.

Every comp-vid and other forms of communication had been destroyed or locked away. She constantly searched for a key and watched for one of Vardil's employees to carelessly leave a device lying about.

Most of the household staff were watching with her.

"Don't speak, eh?" Janis said while kneading dough.

I shook my head.

"Can you read and write?"

Stepping toward her wide, wood-topped table, I hastily wrote *yes* in the flour surrounding the dough before wiping the word away.

"They don't know, do they?" Janis' voice was soft.

Again, I shook my head.

"Good."

Janis was determined to make this secret work to the household's advantage. I nodded. I, too, wanted it to work to our advantage.

~

Le-Ath Veronis

Lissa

I had no idea why I hadn't thought of it before—giving blood to all the Rith Naeri, so Rigo could send them in any direction at any time. Yes, two would always remain on Hraede to command the small vampire army they'd built, but with their ability and experience, the Order of the Night Flower could boost Rigo's spy network in many ways.

And, if I gave them a few extras along with my blood, it could prove invaluable. After all, these vampires had stood against adversity for thousands of years, and not once had they been tempted by corruption.

Kellik, well, his return was practically a miracle in Rigo's eyes, who'd imagined his sire dead long ago.

Kellik, after all, taught Rigo and the other Rith Naeri. Most would call him the ultimate spy, as no record of him had ever been made and no sightings ever reported.

When he woke, he'd be able to mist and mindspeak. Those were my gifts to him for rescuing Barra Kend and countless others through the millennia.

Soon, I'd take care of the others, with Rigo's permission and supervision. It was time the Rith Naeri took on the Alliances and not just Hraede, to keep them from falling to what I called the new super-criminal.

Vardil Cayetes had been bad enough; Vardil combined with the Arden twins was fifty times worse.

"What are you thinking, Tiessa?" Rigo asked.

He sat on a comfortable chair in a corner of my private study while my thoughts consumed me.

"Something is bothering me," I sighed. "I think I want to pay that coffin in my dungeon a visit."

Rigo frowned. "You're not thinking of misting inside the base, are you? It could be a trap, my love."

"I'm not going inside it, but that doesn't keep me from worrying about what's in there. Zaria says there's a book and a ring. Damn, I should have asked more questions about that."

"I assume it is Wellend's book—I hear from Rylend that neither he nor his father were able to find that particular volume, although they diligently searched both family homes for it."

"I think that's what it is, too, but my concern is this—what did he write in it before he died? Did he change enough laws to give the twins a clear path to the throne?"

"You worry that all of Karathia will fall in line behind those two?"

"Karathia has always occupied the dividing line between the worlds of dark and light. Yes, the wall between the two has dropped, but you don't get rid of history by knocking down an invisible barrier. What if half the planet is predisposed to follow the darkness? Most of the population is more than a thousand years old. Only five percent have been born since the barrier came down."

"Can that be—that half or more would be attracted to the darkness? Surely not, my love."

"I'm not sure of anything anymore. The twins have had ample time to make a move, yet they waited until now. Why?"

"I cannot say. Perhaps I will ask my sire to help research this when he wakes. I look forward to showing him the light half of our planet." Rigo smiled.

"Take him drinking," I waved a hand. "He hasn't done that in a while, I think."

"There are many things he hasn't done in a while." Rigo chuckled, and that was a very rare sound.

~

Karathia—Past
  Zaria

Hegatt Blackmantle not only provided the genetic propensity for Helsa's irrationality, he'd honed the inborn trait in himself as well as his daughter. I suspected that Helsa's mother, dead for more than one hundred years, died in self-defense against the two.

I'd only seen Hegatt from a distance as he shouted and ordered servants about while his things were settled in a well-appointed guest suite.

That meant I didn't see his face clearly until the following morning. What I learned from that brief, initial reading almost made me vomit.

When my gag reflex was under control again, I fired off a terrified mental message to Ilya.

Honey, Hegatt bought the plans for those death machines from someone in the Hraedan court, I whispered, as if anyone could listen to my mindspeech. *He keeps them with him, in a hidden jacket pocket, and he intends to find someone to build those things in order to take the throne for his daughter.*

Ilya was stunned by the news, as it took him several minutes to form a reply. *He wants the throne for his daughter? Not his grandson?*

His grandson isn't as malleable as he'd like, I reported. *Nor as powerful as his mother. She's a very strong Fourth-level. He's not up to that. Besides, the twins haven't reached their majority. I think she's willing to hold the throne for one of them.*

We were told not to interfere with the coup, Ilya sighed. *Wylend didn't know about this, did he?*

I doubt he had a clue, I retorted. *After all, he wasn't at the palace when things went down—he came in afterward, when everybody was dead and—wait. Who the hell took over the throne? They all say Wellend was here, and, as he wore the heir's ring, he was rightfully King. Who was at the palace, running Karathia? Nobody ever says that; they only say that after a few weeks, Wylend and his followers came in to take it back. Wellend refused to go with them and he ended up dying here—although nobody knows who killed him.*

This is the worst kind of conundrum. We're witnessing an unwritten part of history, my love, and we have no authority to do anything to help or hinder.

Yeah.

Li'Neruh Rath had been quite specific—that we couldn't do anything to prevent the coup from happening. Things—strange things—were clicking into place all around us, and all we could do was watch.

I wanted to curse.

Throw expensive vases and crockery at the walls.

I was a servant and wasn't allowed fits like Helsa.

"A snack is required in the drawing room," Milar made one of his sudden, unannounced appearances in the kitchen.

"Of course, Lord Chamberlain," I bobbed my head and turned toward the prep table. Tiny sandwiches, tea and cake would be prepared for Hegatt the murderer and his equally murderous offspring. The maelstrom rotated faster and its malicious, unblinking eye closed in to destroy us all.

Daris' Compound

Quin

"What do you mean it's in the palace dungeon?" Daris screeched.

She'd received mindspeech from her brother, and responded to the news by venting her frustrations aloud.

I understood perfectly what she meant.

Deris had scryed to search for that foul coffin, discovering it was guarded in Lissa's palace rather than an unprotected spot in Justis' glass castle.

What would they do to attempt to retrieve it? For perhaps the thousandth time, I cursed the Orb for taking away my mindspeech. I wanted to warn Queen Lissa.

Yes, she was powerful, but I had no doubts as to the depths of treachery Deris and Daris would plumb in order to get the thing back. Whatever it held, they wanted it badly, else they wouldn't have gone to such lengths to hide its true contents from Vardil Cayetes.

Poor Barc had lain, almost lifeless and in full view, inside the glass-topped coffin to taunt Bleek.

Those two—the Arden twins—didn't have the power to heal. If I still had wings, I'd have rustled them in disgust. Deris and Daris—they should be dead. *I* wanted them dead.

Why did the Orb want them alive?

Vardil was no longer a threat and may as well be dead. Why was it supporting the twins? I wished mightily to have a conversation with Zaria and Queen Lissa about this. Surely, one of them could make a guess at this twist of fate.

"Girl," Dorgus poked his head out of Vardil's doorway and hissed at me to hurry. Abandoning my thoughts, I rushed to bring the tray of food to him for Vardil's midday meal.

"I have no idea why they wanted to leave us with fields so overrun with snakes," Dorgus muttered as he placed the spoon in Vardil's hand, urging him to feed himself. "All Daris complains about is the snakes out in the fields. She wants them gone, when there is no way to get rid of them without calling attention to us. She says she can't get a spell to work to destroy them without destroying the crops, too."

I blinked at Dorgus for a moment.

Janis would know when the harvest would take place.

We desperately needed to make a plan when that happened, or both Alliances could be flooded with drakus seed.

Were they killing more troops with the drug by sabotaging food supplies?

What about the water and other essentials?

I hoped Director Griff understood what was vulnerable. Populations needed food and water to exist. With a Sirenali available to obsess those in charge, how many places could the drug be smuggled into, to poison the masses?

Queen Lissa had a term she used for such, although most merely frowned at her when she used it.

Terrorism.

I was beginning to see what she meant, because I was afraid of what could happen.

"Go amuse yourself," Dorgus waved a hand, dismissing me.

I left immediately. I had no use for a weak-spined man whose only love was for his life and that of a terrible criminal, even if Vardil Cayetes was now a drooling invalid.

If either of them had been better men, I would have offered to heal.

When will crop be harvested? I wrote hastily on a damp countertop before wiping the message away.

"Two eight-days," Janis whispered. "Daris won't go to the fields because of the snakes, so the hands will hold off harvesting as long as possible."

Where are we? I wrote.

"They didn't tell you?" Janis wore a puzzled frown. "Oh, never mind. I can see that they wouldn't. The fools." She wiped away my finger-scribbles herself. "The jungle planet of Goor-Phin. The soil is perfect for growing certain fruits and vegetables. You see that our fruit trees were torn from the ground in order to grow this foul excrement."

I nodded once in understanding. *Snakes?* I wrote in the water.

"I've never heard of so many getting so close," she bent toward me to say. "Something is drawing them here, just in the last few days."

I went still.

I knew what drew them.

The Orb hadn't taken that gift away from me; I'd been calling for help every night before I slept, hoping someone would hear me.

The snakes had come. I merely had to take stock of all our resources and with Janis' help, figure out a way to outsmart a powerful witch before the drakus seed harvest.

Don't kill the snakes, I wrote in the moisture before nodding to Janis and walking out of her kitchen.

BlackWing VII

Terrett

Yanzi, Berel and I were back aboard BlackWing VII. Caylon and Sal were still in charge, but there was a sadness in Caylon's eyes as he taught Jayna hand-fighting every morning.

He missed Zaria. His mate, Cleo, was now on-board and when no one watched, she brushed stray strands of black hair away from his face and wrapped her arms about his waist.

He held her as tightly as he dared—she was pregnant, just as Zaria said. It looked as if Cleo missed Zaria—someone she'd never met— almost as much as Caylon did.

I tapped my experiences into a comp-vid while staring out the window of the dining hall; I hoped to share my writing with Quin if she returned to us.

I dared not think that she wouldn't—as if that would pull the darkness around me and she'd never come home. I wrote now my memory of taking Quin's wings to Justis.

The Avii King gathered them in his arms and shut himself in his suite for two days, refusing meals and comfort of any kind.

Perhaps he, too, was terrified to consider the worst—afraid that it would pull it inevitably toward us. Better to keep hope alive and dark thoughts locked in the recesses of our minds.

"Tell me about Zaria," Cleo took a seat beside me and patted my hand.

She had long, auburn hair, dimples when she smiled and was quite beautiful. "Don't worry," she offered a lovely smile, "I have no jealousy toward her. I merely worry for Caylon, because he fought like a mighty, razor-finned fish against the pull of our M'Fiyah. I can only imagine the look on his face when he saw Zaria for the first time."

It is a tale already among the Avii, I set my comp-vid aside and turned my full attention on Cleo. *Caylon thought to test her. Like Ilya, he thought her weak and ineffective as a bodyguard for Quin and Prince Bel Erland. He threw a knife at her, expecting to take her off guard and graze her ribs. Instead, she stopped the knife in midair between them, and left it hanging there.*

Cleo stifled a laugh. I waited for her to regain her composure before continuing. *Then,* I went on, *as the knife was still hanging there, he stepped forward to retrieve it. Zaria had heated it so hot, it burned his hand. He dropped the knife with much surprise.*

Cleo laughed aloud this time.

He held up his hand and said, "See this?" Zaria walked toward him, took his hand in hers, treated him like a child with a skinned knee and healed it immediately. I can't say for certain, but things may have changed for him then.

"I really want to meet her. So does everyone else. I think the Saa Thalarr as a whole love her already, because she stood up to Caylon. Not many can do that." She dimpled at me.

I hope he loves you very much, I responded.

"He does—he just doesn't like to admit it," she replied. "I'm grateful for Zaria, because Caylon and a daughter," she shook her head and laughed again.

No bows and ruffles for him?

"I figure he'll have a blade already made for her before she's born," Cleo said. "We haven't picked a name yet, because he'll want to give her something that may be less than appropriate. I'm hoping Zaria will help—that she'll see the baby and know immediately what to call her."

You want Zaria to join your family that badly?

"More than I can say," she sighed. "Caylon can be a handful, at times. It will be nice to have someone in my corner for a change, where he's concerned."

I understand, I think. He can be somewhat overbearing.

"Take out the somewhat and you're exactly right," she laughed.

I smiled, because that's exactly what I'd thought, I'd merely attempted to soften the blow of my statement. *It is my hope that she and Gerrett will return to us very soon,* I said. *I wish to get to know both my brothers better.*

"Someday, perhaps you'll all have dinner with me—you, your brothers and Zaria," she amended. "So you can tell me about your pasts and how you've managed to survive all that."

It is a long and sad tale, I shrugged. *Are you sure you wish to hear it? Perhaps after the baby comes.*

"That's probably a good idea. Raffian says the same thing—in case someone needs healing."

Raffian?

"Raffian Grey."

The Master Wizard?

"Yes—he's my half-brother. He comes from a very long line of Master Wizards, descended all the way from the original Grey House wizard, who married a female Larentii."

There is Larentii blood in Grey House? That is quite enlightening, I said.

"Few knew of it, until one day, Ferrigar came, announcing that he was prepared to accept the kinship. It was his daughter, you see, long gone, of course. She separated her particles when her husband died at age one hundred twenty-nine thousand."

Ferrigar?

"Former Head of the Larentii Council—also dead. His son, Kalenegar, is now Head of the Council and also related to Grey House. He doesn't visit like his father did."

"Heads up, we have a shipwreck to investigate," Sal appeared, made his announcement and disappeared again.

"I wish I could heal while I'm pregnant," Cleo sighed. "I'll put in a call for Kevis and his father, just in case."

~

Le-Ath Veronis

Lissa

"Sal called me when they reached the ship," Winkler set a comp-vid on my desk. I looked up at my werewolf mate, who wasn't smiling.

He always smiled at me. There was trouble and I knew it. "What's on this?" I placed my hand over the small device.

"It's not pretty, but it's an example of what Deris and Daris are capable of, if they don't get their way."

"How did you get this?" I lifted the comp-vid and hesitated. If Winkler said it was awful, then it was going to be awful.

"Off a dead pirate. I doubt the Arden twins know this recording exists—probably a sick trophy taken by the pirate before he accidentally got dead while raiding the cargo ship. You see his friends left him behind—he no longer mattered. This," he nodded toward the comp-vid in my hand, "was found inside a hidden pocket. That's why Sal called me—to take a look."

I made a face as I switched on the comp-vid—someone had broken the code. It wasn't Joey, this time; I suspected Sal had notified Ashe, who'd given him the code after a brief examination.

"Ashe wanted this brought to me, didn't he?"

"Well, yeah," Winkler shrugged.

"Then watch it with me, in case I want to throw up," I said.

I was wrapped in Winkler's arms and crying as we watched Deris Arden destroy a fourteen-year-old boy for attempting to protect his father.

"I want Rigo and Kellik on Goor-Phin as quickly as they can get there," I hissed after wiping tears away with the heel of my hand. "I want an assessment of what's going on there immediately."

Kell

"You won't be able to teach him anything he doesn't know already," Rigo held up a hand as Kooper Griff, Director of the ASD and also a shapeshifter, handed ranos pistols to both of us.

Kooper had been prepared to give advice. Rigo told him what I wished to say—that I'd been doing this for millennia already.

The misting and mindspeech talents given to me by the Queen would only enhance what I already had.

"Then hear this," Kooper said to both of us. "A spell can't land on dispersed mist. Protect yourselves at all times."

"I thank you," I nodded to Director Griff. "The misting talent is new and much appreciated, I assure you."

"Send mindspeech to me or Lissa at any time," he grinned. "Rigo, always a pleasure," he turned to my eldest vampire child. "Kell, good to meet you," Griff added. "Get us intel as fast as you can. Rigo, do you want to transport, or shall I?"

"I will," Rigo agreed.

Until then, I didn't know that Rigo had the ability to fold space. We landed inside a safe house in Brepha, Goor-Phin's capital and largest city.

"The plantation is five hundred clicks from here," Rigo said, lifting a comp-vid from a drawer and pulling up a three-dimensional map of the planet. "They're supposed to be growing nannas, but as you know, they've likely uprooted trees to grow drakus seed."

"Where do you think they'll have set the perimeter?" I asked. "A Fifth-level will be able to place a larger perimeter than a Fourth-level."

"The plantation is quite large," Rigo observed. "Do you suppose Deris Arden could protect that much land? After all, he'll have to place a spell to fool the sat-bots orbiting the planet."

"Pull up that image," I said. "Perhaps we will be able to tell by making a comparison—from before the kidnapping of Wem Jordeh."

Rigo tapped dates into the comp-vid and soon two images were displayed side-by-side. Both showed well-tended nanna trees covering most of the plantation, except for one corner of the property.

"Look," Rigo breathed, pointing toward that corner on the current sat-bot map. "This area looks overgrown. I can't imagine the employees would allow that to happen, especially since they were tended before." He drew a line with his finger between both maps.

"I would imagine," I said, "that this may be an indication of the extent of Deris' power. However," I studied the corner of the Jordeh farm opposite that of the neglected nanna trees, "Does that mean that he's protecting something else all the more fiercely here?" I pointed to the corner in question. "You see the other corners are equally protected, I believe."

"You're right. I suppose we should thank Wem Jordeh for leasing property that comprises a huge square," Rigo observed.

"It's the permits and laws of Goor-Phin," I said. "They determine which land and how much may be leased to anyone wishing to grow crops, in order to regulate the cutting of native trees and plants. Goor-Phin's Council is partial to squares and rectangles."

"That protected corner is covered in nanna trees—in both images," Rigo frowned. "Might there be something else there, besides nanna trees or drakus plants?"

"Curing sheds, perhaps, for the drakus seed?" I asked.

"Possibly—the seed is more valuable than plants, and to have much of it concentrated in one place, perhaps," I agreed.

"If we go, we should remain mist," Rigo said. "I say we check the overgrown corner first, and then follow the outside perimeter to the opposite side, perhaps?"

"Agreed. Take us there, child. I wish to see this with my own eyes."

CHAPTER 12

*G*oor-Phin
        Quin
        Two eight-days until harvest. Something about that amount of time troubled me. As if a terrible day of destiny loomed, and I had no idea what would come or how to prepare for it.

Dorgus ordered Vardil's employees about, although three were in the plantation infirmary suffering from snakebites. These snakes, native to Goor-Phin, weren't the most poisonous, but untreated bites could lead to death.

I doubted the plantation medi-unit had treated this many snakebites in fifteen sun-turns. I hoped the snakes had gotten away afterward; I had no sympathy for Daris' or Vardil's scum. At times, I was grateful I wore another face—it kept me at a safe distance from several, who'd already forced themselves upon some of the plantation workers.

Those rapists could no longer function properly and likely wondered what had happened. I'd made sure of it, employing the least amount of ability I had. I considered removing certain parts by starving the blood supply, but felt that could lead to trouble if Daris got involved and went searching for a cause.

In the interim, I was resolved to do whatever I could against these usurpers, while they looked in every direction but mine.

~

"I need someone to go with Alys to the big sheds," Janis sighed as she placed containers of food into a hovercart. The device worked much like a small wagon, except it hovered above the ground and was much easier to pull. Janis wanted me to help feed the captives in the sheds.

That meant Sirenali. I was worried immediately—I had no idea whether they'd been mistreated or needed healing, and wondered if I could get away with doing something for them if it were needed.

Alys, the assistant who'd given me clothing, would go with me. I felt I could trust her and Janis, but considered that others could be present, which would prevent me from acting.

I'd already done my duties for Vardil and Dorgus' midday meal and, as usual, Dorgus dismissed me because he didn't want to see my face. I offered my services to Janis until Dorgus called for me again.

Janis was relieved that someone was available to go with Alys. The other kitchen helpers were serving Daris and her crew on the back patio by the massive swimming pool.

"They don't eat much—I don't think they can," Alys explained as we drew the hovercart behind us.

The path to the big sheds was a long one; half a click at least and took some time to walk the distance. Paved with decorative brick, it was a comfortable walk, at least, with flowering shrubs growing alongside.

If I'd still had my wings, I would have flown over the plantation to take stock of how large it was and the size of the drakus seed harvest, so I might pass that information to someone else if given the chance.

"I don't know what all those machines are for," Alys whispered as we walked through a side door into the largest shed. "But they have thousands of them."

My breath stopped as if I'd run into a wall the moment we were inside the shed. Where equipment, crates and vehicles were once stored in anticipation of nanna harvests, the floor was now covered by cylindrical machines, their four legs tucked against a central core and folded much like a grasshopper's would be.

A conical sort of head, with sensors all around the base, sat atop each machine, and they frightened me—I envisioned electronic eyes opening to stare at anything that approached.

Each leg was equipped with sharp, finger-like grippers, capable of carrying it over any sort of terrain.

I imagined they could fly, too, similar to the hovercart Alys and I pulled behind us. These things held death in their sleeping eyes; I could only tiptoe past them, afraid that too much noise could wake them and the Alliances would be doomed by my carelessness.

"I sometimes think of turning one on, just to see what it will do," Alys sighed.

I broke my self-imposed silence, then.

"Never, ever, wake one of these, unless you want your planet to die," I whispered, shaking my head at Alys. "They are made for one purpose only, and that is to kill."

Alys' eyes grew round as she gaped at me—not because I spoke, but because of the dire warning in my words.

"Is that what they came for, and not just the drakus seed?"

I motioned for Alys to move along, worried that these silent machines could be listening. "Yes," I whispered, making myself smaller and moving alongside the wall as I followed Alys' lead. "The drakus seed is just a distraction, I think. These—Vardil and the others mean to destroy worlds or take them over, with these machines as their soldiers."

"Can't the ASD do something?"

"The ASD has no idea where they are," I mumbled. "Don't say that again—anyone could be listening."

"I was scared already," Alys muttered. "Now it's worse."

"Where are they—the ones waiting for food?"

"Inside the supervisor's office," Alys said and led me toward the opposite corner of the massive shed.

Inside, we found no supervisor. Instead, there were four Sirenali, mute, sick and pitifully malnourished.

"Say nothing of what you are about to see," I said after checking the room for cameras or listening devices.

Each Sirenali was manacled and chained by his neck, arms and ankles to a metal bar on the wall.

Perhaps a vampire could escape these shackles by pulling them apart, but the Sirenali had no chance.

"What are you going to do?" Alys whispered as we set containers of food into eager, waiting hands.

Janis was feeding these well, but they had much ground to make up. Who knew where these poor souls had been before coming to Goor-Phin?

"I will not harm you," I said, placing my hands on the Sirenali who was worst off. Terrible sores covered his neck, wrists and ankles where the shackles chafed.

"Watch the door and let me know if anyone comes," I said as I set about healing the first of my four patients.

Le-Ath Veronis

Kell

"There are thousands of those machines in the sheds here," Rigo pointed at the three-dimensional map in Kooper Griff's private office. Lissa, her mates Gavin, Winkler, Drake and Drew were also present, to hear what Rigo and I had to say concerning our visit to Goor-Phin.

"And no idea what kind of spells Deris has placed around them. They could scatter and destroy the population, or be flung elsewhere, and we'd be hunting them again," Lissa snorted.

"Deris is not there, Tiessa. Only Daris. If we move in, he will be warned and they may have more of those terrible devices elsewhere. This is a trap, no matter how you view it," Rigo spoke to Lissa.

"Yeah, I get that," Lissa rubbed her forehead. "Was there any sign of —you know."

"We did not see anything of her, but we only misted quickly through the main house and the largest shed. We left many things unchecked, as we worried that something could be triggered the longer we stayed."

They searched for the winged girl, I knew, except she no longer had wings. The moment I had time to myself, I intended to do research and ask many questions. I imagined the werewolf or Lissa's Falchani mates would be more easily approached; Gavin's hooded eyes and stone face told me he would not be as cooperative.

Ask Justis, King of the Avii, too, Rigo sent mindspeech. He knew the expression I wore; the one that said I did not have sufficient information. *Lissa can tell you much; the girl is mated to her grandson.*

You know me well, child, I returned. *I must be properly informed if I am to be at my best in this.*

We will find her—we must.

~

Goor-Phin

Quin

I wished mightily for the return of my own mindspeech, so I could communicate with the Sirenali I'd just healed. They'd cleaned their plates after the healing; the sores were all but gone and the malady keeping them ill and incapable of mindspeech had been eliminated.

The youngest was probably less than eleven turns in age, and all hope had died in his eyes before I'd come. Now, there was a slight gleam, as if he dared dream of a life other than the one he presently had.

"We must go," I nodded to them as Alys and I gathered containers and placed them in the hovercart. "I will ask that you be fed even more so you will regain your strength," I added. "Be safe. If you are ever unchained and can safely get away, run. The snakes will not harm you."

Alys, her eyes revealing her growing terror at the mention of snakes, shivered as she closed the hovercart for the journey back to the plantation house kitchen. I had less than two eight-days to devise a plan to save many, and my fear was that I couldn't even save myself.

~

Avii Castle

Kell

"My King, this is Kellik of Abenott," the Blue-winged librarian introduced me to Justis, Red-Winged King of the Avii.

Justis stood at a large window in his suite, his face toward the light and his back, stiff and uncomfortable, turned toward me.

I read his troubled stance easily. His love—the winged young woman called Quin, was missing. He was terrified we wouldn't find her alive—if we found her.

I'd already studied many images, including those of her with long, blonde hair interspersed with streaks of gold, copper and silver, and wings to match.

Then, I'd studied the images of her with dark hair, eyes and wings. Both images were striking, and, unless one looked carefully at facial features, they appeared to be two different people.

I will say this much; the blonde looked somewhat younger and coltish, as if she were unsure of her place in the world. The other showed someone in charge of herself and of the place she occupied.

"What do you wish to know?" Justis' back was still turned toward me.

"I want to know her familiar gestures. What she prefers to eat or wear. The way she moves—when she walks and works. These things might help me identify someone who may have gone through another change in appearance."

I saw him stiffen; he hadn't considered that Quin could not be easily recognized by those who knew her best, unless they watched carefully.

"I can help you." A Larentii appeared from nothing. This was something I hadn't considered—that Quin was mated to this one, as she was to several others.

"I am Daragar," the Larentii's bright-blue eyes half closed as he gave a slight bow. "I can recreate visual images of Quin—eating, sleeping or any other activity you think may be important. Should you find her, you will have the favor of the Larentii from now on."

It isn't often that I am astonished by anything. Daragar's promise rendered me speechless with wonder.

~

Karathia—Past

Zaria

Hegatt pretended his concern was for King Warlend.

It was anything but.

He wanted to hide his machinations from the King; therefore, it was his intention to be as solicitous as possible.

I wanted to call him a two-faced, scheming bastard, even if he should have been my maternal great-grandfather. Frankly, I wanted to spit on him and Helsa, who would have been my grandmother.

Hegatt and Helsa shouted at servants and drove them before their anger as Helsa's palace was readied for the King's visit. He was scheduled to arrive the following morning on his birthday and be greeted by family, two of whom pretended to love him.

As Wallend still hadn't arrived with his wives and twins, I couldn't say how they felt, although I dreaded their arrival later in the day.

Bekzi and I marshalled our assistants in the kitchen, preparing what we could in advance while rugs were beaten, silver and gold polished until it shone, everything was dusted at least twice and crystal decanters and wineglasses were made spotless, awaiting the King's visit.

Milar, blessed with a Third-level talent, appeared here and there throughout the palace, overseeing every activity and doing some shouting of his own.

Yes, I understood that he warmed Helsa's bed on cold nights, although he did it for favors and not because he truly cared for her.

I despised him for his duplicity, and hoped that somewhere in the recesses of his mind he realized that Helsa wouldn't leave him a single copper when she died.

When she died.

While Karathia didn't have anything equivalent to a national newspaper, I did consider that I might read of her passing in the Archives with something akin to a smile.

Hegatt—well, when I considered his death, I also considered doing a celebratory dance of some kind. I looked forward to seeing Warlend, so I might understand his thinking when he took Helsa as his second wife.

Helsa and Hegatt were so overwhelmed with their particular insanity and greed that I couldn't get the full history of the marital alliance from them—not from Warlend's perspective, anyway.

Poor Wellend—he didn't have a clue, since his parents hadn't confided anything to him through the years.

Wallend is here, with his wife and the twins, Ilya warned. *Deris has already set hay on fire as a prank and Daris is arranging her hair and asking her mother which style is better to meet with Hegatt.*

Are their parents attempting to control them?

Deris is already a stronger warlock than Wallend, so nothing from him. His mother warned him not to hurt the horses, but that's it. They're coming toward the house. Get ready.

Perfect. The only thing worse than spoiled brats was powerful, spoiled brats with no parental control.

"We need extra sandwiches, tea and cake," I announced to the kitchen staff. "Prince Wallend and his family have just arrived."

The kitchen felt like a place of solitude with all the activity going on throughout the rest of Helsa's palace, until the moment Deris chose to visit.

Filth here, Bekzi announced as he chopped vegetables for the evening meal.

Deris strode in with a swagger, dressed in the finest brown velvet jacket and pants, with a cream silk shirt and knee-high, calfskin boots.

"I hated the cake you served at tea," he said, his back half-turned toward me. I could still see his face, however.

Lie.

I watched as he studied the shelves of canisters, jars and sealed containers of spices, sugar, salt and other cooking supplies near the massive cooking stove.

"You have to be punished for such shoddy work," he turned his full face on me, then. Everything on the shelf exploded as the spoiled fucking brat disappeared with a laugh.

"No, stay back," Bekzi cautioned the others as I surveyed the mess.

The mess I could fix.

Deris had fired the first volley at me. I saw what I'd expected to see in him—contempt for those he considered less than himself. The only person he had any sort of respect for was Hegatt, and only because Hegatt was currently stronger than Deris and didn't put up with any rudeness from his grandchildren.

With a sigh, I employed power to put everything back to rights in the kitchen, watching in grim satisfaction as the smallest jar of the most expensive spice dropped into place at the last.

Not even a dusting of flour was left on the kitchen floor afterward. It would take a Fourth-level talent to do what I'd just done—to the extent I'd done it. "I hope you all know to stay quiet," I turned back to our helpers, then.

All three nodded silently. They were just as helpless as the rest of the staff and understood their employment, as well as their lives, could hinge on that reserve.

Going back to work on the evening meal, I considered what else I'd seen in Deris Arden before his abrupt exit.

He thought himself special. Not because he was the son of a Prince and a potential heir to the throne.

No.

He thought himself heir to a prophecy—a prophecy he hadn't been allowed to read as yet.

The strongest of tornadoes will lift trees, homes, debris and even soil into its whirling vortex, rendering it so dark you can no longer see what is churning inside it. Bekzi, Ilya, Gerrett and I were watching the storm come toward us, with no idea what it would batter us with before it swallowed us, too.

"Go back to work," Bekzi ordered our assistants. "We make good food. Nobody else say different."

He was angry; I could hear it in his voice.

Our three assistants felt defeated. This was just one more insult in a long line of insults hurled at them by one who thought himself more than special. One who went out of his way to belittle those about him, even if it took lies and violence to achieve that goal.

I wondered if Daris believed the prophecy, too, both now and in the future, and worked at her brother's side to ensure he was given his due.

I hoped Warlend knew the prophecy; if he didn't then I had digging to do. Cooking for this family left little time to search quietly through family history to find something so small, it could be a single sentence in one of many, massive volumes in Helsa's library.

Wellend didn't know it—I'd seen him already and there was nothing concerning a prophecy in his eyes.

"Have you seen Deris?"

Wallend appeared in the kitchen, making me jump.

Turning toward him, I blinked as I read what he was in seconds.

An angry, angry man.

Who knew of the prophecy.

It was written in Warlend's book, after all.

The last living Q'elindi had given this prophecy to Warlend's father, before setting off a spell to end his life of serving Worlend.

Your son's son will father a child who can rule Karathia better than any other who has come before, the Q'elindi said.

Wallend had been allowed to read Warlend's book, as he'd fathered children.

Wellend, whose wife remained barren, had not been allowed to see it.

Hegatt and Helsa knew of it through Wallend, but Deris couldn't take the throne before he gained his majority at twenty-two.

Perhaps Hegatt wanted to jump the gun and put Helsa on the throne first, then allow Deris to take over once he was old enough.

Eight years would be more than enough time for Deris to refine his talent for torturing people; his father and grandparents believed that Deris was destined to be a king like no other.

He would be—it just wouldn't be to their liking.

Wallend didn't know about the coup; that plan had not been hatched, yet.

I wondered why.

Two eight-days remained before the date came as recorded in history and reported by those who'd survived.

Le-Ath Veronis

Lissa

"My father had some skill at drawing; my talent is less," Kellik informed me as he handed a comp-vid to me. On it were his renderings of the machines he and Rigo had seen on Goor-Phin.

"Was your father a vampire too?" I asked. Rigo told me that Kellik was turned by his own grandfather, who was long dead.

"No. My father—there are records in the Hraedan archives," Kell shook his head. "My father hated my grandfather's teachings. He loved money more than he loved his family, and often left my mother and me alone while he attended court."

"So your mother is your grandfather's daughter?"

"Yes. My father married into the family. I believe Mother regretted her decision to marry him many times. Eventually, my father was accused of treason and died in his cell by his own hand."

"Treason?"

"Selling secrets against the crown," Kell shrugged. "He was caught before he could cause a great deal of damage."

"Do you know what secrets?" I asked. Something bothered me about that revelation, but I couldn't say what.

"Those were never publicly disclosed; the trial was private rather than open and only a handful of the King's most trusted advisors attended, that's how sensitive the situation was."

"I understand," I said, although I worried just the same. I would have to speak with Rigo about this, just to see when the plans for the N'il Mo'erti were removed from the King's treasury on Hraede and hidden by the Rith Naeri.

I pitied Kell, too, if he ever learned what his father may have done. Kellik was honorable in every cell of his body. Learning that his father may have been responsible for this sort of betrayal could bring harm.

"I see you've figured out my family secret," Kellik's smile was sad. "My father did perhaps the worst thing any Hraedan can do, and sold out not only his own people, but those of the Alliance, too."

"Are those his drawings?" I asked, reaching for my own comp-vid in a desk drawer.

"They are mostly his drawings, Tiessa," Kellik dipped his head. "A few things have changed, and I know those things are not my father's handiwork."

"You've seen them already?" I blinked in surprise.

"Rigo showed them to me. You forget, Tiessa, that we are the ultimate spies. Very little will get past us."

"Tell me which parts are not your father's drawings," I pushed the comp-vid across my desk. "This way, perhaps we'll know what it is that Deris and Daris seek in changing those machines."

"This," I pointed to one component in the machine's schematics. "It looks to me as if this should have been larger—as if something were left out."

"That's the computer brain controlling the machine," I whispered.

"And these, here," he pointed to a drawing of the power cells that kept the machine working, "These have been changed, but I cannot say how. Also, this," he indicted the weapons system. "This has also been altered in some way."

"You know all this because you know your father's hand at

drawing," I shook my head. "You have a very, very good memory, Kellik of Abenott."

"It has served me well," he dipped his head to me. "I would give my life to see these machines destroyed forever."

"I want those machines destroyed, too," I sighed. "But I don't want it to take your life. We need you, Kellik. Now, perhaps, more than ever."

"Then call me Kell," he smiled. "My closest friends do, and I prefer it."

"Thanks, Kell," I said. "Are you hungry? Might I interest you in lunch?"

"Ah, food. I'd forgotten what a pleasure that was," he grinned. "Yes. Lunch will be good."

~

Tulgalan

Bel Erland

"Rigo says they didn't see Quin on Goor-Phin, but they didn't go everywhere on that plantation—it's enormous," Granddad said. "We do know that only Daris is there, likely overseeing the drakus seed operation and protecting the army of N'il Mo'erti stored there."

"So we know Quin was on Hraede, but she could be with either Deris or Daris, now. Why would the Orb send her to those two, without letting her get rid of them, somehow?" I asked.

"We don't know or understand the Orb's ultimate intentions," Dad said.

We'd sneaked away from Karathia and now sat in a private room at Dees, where Mom was supposed to join us for dinner. Drinks and appetizers were set on the table for us, but we'd barely nibbled and sipped while we discussed the current status of the twins. At least we knew where Daris was, but things were pointing to the fact that Deris was the more dangerous of the two.

Corolan, who often disguised himself as Dad, had taken up residence in Dad's private suite so nothing would seem amiss.

The private room here was spelled against intrusion or listening devices as we held our discussion. "We're here," Mom arrived with Farzi and Nenzi. Nenzi gave me a huge smile and a hug before sitting next to me. Farzi tousled my hair and sat on my other side so Mom could sit with Dad.

"What's going on?" Mom asked after Dad kissed her—maybe longer than normal.

"We know where Daris is, but not Deris," Granddad said.

"Where's Daris?" Mom's eyes are green—she inherited them from her grandfather. Mine are deep brown; I'd inherited them from my grandfather. Her green eyes were trained on Dad and Granddad.

It didn't matter that Uncles Farzi and Nenzi were here; they'd never give this information away.

"On Goor-Phin," Dad said, lifting Mom's hand to kiss it. "The intel we have was gathered quickly, so we don't know whether Quin is there or if she's with Deris, wherever he is."

"Strange that the twins split up now," Mom said, reaching for a breadstick. Nenzi pushed the basket toward her so she could reach it easier.

"We know what Daris is doing, protecting a huge plantation filled with drakus seed plants and sheds filled with N'il Mo'erti," Granddad grimaced. "We don't know what Deris is doing, wherever he is."

"What are Kooper's plans for the N'il Mo'erti?" Mom asked before crunching into the breadstick. "Mmm, cheese crusted—my favorite," she mumbled.

"They're still working on that," Dad said. "Everybody's worried that this may not be the only cache, and if that location is taken, it may release chaos on the Alliances."

"So we're watching and waiting? Is that it?" Mom shook her head.

"That's pretty much it," Dad declared. "BlackWing VII has found six more wrecked freighters, with nobody alive on board and the cargo taken, just like before. Those ships were loaded with everything from preserved foods to comp-vid components."

"We can't infiltrate the Goor-Phini plantation?" Mom asked.

"There are spells to prevent unauthorized visitors, you can count on that," Granddad huffed. "It's clear enough that Deris placed a shield over the entire place; sat-bot images confirm that."

"Both he and Daris have placed a disturbance spell on the property unless I miss my guess," Dad nodded.

"What about snakes?" Farzi asked.

"What?" The rest of us turned toward Farzi when he spoke.

"Same spell for animals, or just people?" Farzi continued.

"I would imagine that it's for people," Dad began, then stopped as the implications came to him.

Deris and Daris were looking for humanoid infiltrators, in all likelihood. There were snakes aplenty on Goor-Phin, in addition to other animals—small and not so small.

"Snakes get in," Farzi shrugged. "Shapeshifters too, if they look native."

"Why didn't we think of that before?" Granddad scooted his chair back and stood. "Yes," he slapped a hand on the table while a slow smile spread across his face. "I'll be back," he said.

"Tell Mom I said hi," Dad grinned.

CHAPTER 13

*L*e-Ath Veronis
     Lissa
     "I believe the reptanoids will all volunteer—except Bekzi, who's with Zaria, wherever she is," Erland said.

Kooper, Rigo, Kell, Winkler, Gavin, Drake and Drew had come to this emergency meeting, to discuss the possibilities of sending shapeshifters onto the Goor-Phini plantation.

"Sorry we're late," Merrill arrived with Kiarra and Adam.

"We're discussing sending shapeshifters to the plantation on Goor-Phin," I gestured toward extra seats in my library.

"That's a really good idea," Kiarra nodded as she took a seat between Adam and Merrill.

Merrill winked at me as he took his seat. More than anything, I wanted to take a few days off to spend with him at NorthStar, but I dared not. Too many things needed my attention, and thousands of N'il Mo'erti, coupled with Quin's kidnapping by the Orb topped that list.

When did drakus seed and poisoned planets take a backseat to something even worse? I sent to Merrill.

My love, don't fret, he returned. *We'll sort this out.*

Baby, stop worrying, Winkler broke in on the conversation. *I just found out wolves are native to Goor-Phin.*

In the jungles? Honey, no, I responded. *Wolves are much farther north. It's mostly snakes and jungle cats in that area of the planet.*

Then you'll let Caylon Black go and force me to stay home?

I'll let you coordinate from the capital city. How's that? Rush and Rachel have volunteered to go, I added. *A lot of the animals in the area are black.*

Even the lions?

Yeah—they have black lions there. That's why those two are going.

But what about black dogs?

Honey, if you can look like a black dog, then blessings upon you, I said. *Just keep the line of communication open, in case I need to come in as mist with Rigo and Kell.*

Did you know Kell can fight with blades? I watched him spar with Dragon this morning. Dragon nodded his approval halfway in.

Honey, everybody is staring at us, because they know we're having a private conversation, I said.

"Sorry," Winkler held up a hand and grinned. "Just pleading my case to go with the others."

"You come?" Farzi asked. He'd welcome Winkler's presence, I could tell.

"Yeah," Winkler barked a laugh.

"When we go?" Nenzi asked. "Yanzi look for Quin."

"We know when drakus seed ready," Farzi added. "Scout first, then make plan."

"Two days and we go on a scouting mission," Kooper said. "That will give us enough time to coordinate everything and place a team in Brepha. Perhaps we will locate Deris during that time, enabling us to make a move on the Jordeh Plantation without fear of reprisal."

"I wish we had Zaria here," I whispered. Kell and all my mates who were present dipped their heads in agreement.

Goor-Phin

   Quin

Daris was irritated about something. Her braided hair coiled tightly atop her head, as if it were a snake preparing to strike. Two servants had been assaulted for not getting out of her way fast enough.

Like her grandmother, her angry visage informed me. That displeased her, because she'd known that her grandmother wasn't completely sane.

She didn't know how her grandmother died, either, so I couldn't see that in her—only that Helsa died under unusual and terrible circumstances, according to records and tales.

Her great-grandfather—she had no records or tales that spoke of his death. Those things angered her—that they were dead and she could be turning into what they were—mad fools.

She'd been in her late teens when they died, and her only experience was one of being rushed away by her father while her mother stayed behind at the family home to fight off those determined to kill them.

That, in turn, had resulted in her mother's death.

Less than six moon-turns later, their father was also dead; killed in a dispute at a bar, where he'd gone to drink.

The twins had been on their own since they were eighteen.

There was more, but it disgusted me. How they'd survived by hiring themselves out to the worst criminals, their only thought the money at the end so they could build an army to take what they considered theirs—Karathia.

My small plans to throw the plantation into chaos were taking shape, but so many things could go wrong. Instead of rescuing innocent lives, I could end up killing them with poor strategy. Janis, Alys and the others could die as a result.

Caylon and many others would know what to do—they were masters at strategy. I wished for their talents as I considered my plan and what, exactly, could go wrong once it was employed.

"I'd better find that comp-vid," Daris shouted. By this time, the entire plantation could hear her. "I'll kill you all if I don't."

Oh, no.

Had one of the servants taken one?

"Here, Lady," a servant rushed in with the comp-vid. "It fell behind your night table. It is not lost, as you see."

With trembling fingers, the poor soul held the comp-vid out to Daris.

I stared, unmoving, as several thoughts flitted across Daris' features. Mistrust. Anger. Doubt.

The last one was accompanied by the thought that she was becoming her grandmother at an ever-increasing rate. She should have known to have someone check behind the night table already.

What if they stole it and are claiming it fell there, to test me?

I heard her thoughts clearly, as if she'd spoken them aloud.

Daris had mindspeech—it made sense that she would.

Turning toward the servant, her face twisted in rage, Daris launched the spell before anyone could even whimper in horror.

The servant died, burned to death in seconds by the spelled fire she'd created.

Tears blurred my vision as I ran from the room.

My eyes accused Dorgus and Vardil as I delivered their evening meals; Daris had shut herself inside her suite and had dinner brought to her.

I was grateful I wasn't the one charged with that particular task.

Dorgus ignored me as he made Vardil comfortable before helping him eat his meal first. Perhaps that's when the idea sprouted in my mind and took root—I wasn't in a charitable mood and more than tired of watching innocents die on the whims of a witch slowly going mad.

The more I considered the idea, the better it sounded to me.

Yes.

I would heal Vardil Cayetes, then watch Dorgus, Vardil and their employees fight with Daris while I called in all the snakes and attempted to get the servants out of the house.

The only thing I didn't have planned was getting the Sirenali out of their chains so they could run away with the others.

Without the Sirenali, Vardil and Daris would be visible to those with *Looking* skills. I hoped those who'd escaped would be rescued, then. I understood that the ASD could be watching, but with the illusion shields Deris and Daris had erected, they probably couldn't look past the nannas they saw on their mundane devices.

Yes, I would heal Vardil Cayetes.

When I found a way to release the Sirenali.

Karathia—Past

Zaria

I saw and heard what Gerrett saw and heard. Deris held back whenever his grandfather wasn't looking. Whenever Hegatt took his eyes away from his grandson, Deris set the tablecloth on fire, then doused the flames with power whenever Hegatt sniffed, searching for the source of burning cloth.

Deris ducked his head and snickered whenever Hegatt frowned at his inability to locate the smell or the fire.

Suddenly, Deris went stiff, his head lifted and his eyes widened.

Hegatt had finally figured it out and sent scathing mindspeech to his misbehaving grandson.

Wellend, sitting at the other end of the table, bit back words and kept eating.

Wallend, who'd been having conversation with his wife and Helsa, ignored the entire incident.

Daris, on the other hand, watched Deris the whole time with hero-worship in her eyes.

Birds of a feather—isn't that what they say? Gerrett sent to me while pouring more wine for Helsa.

I can't say that dinner with the Blackmantle-Ardens is ever a pleasant experience, I replied. I couldn't really say which was worse—watching Helsa have a fit or seeing Deris destroy a hand-woven tablecloth trimmed in lace made by the finest lace makers Helsa could find.

He psychopath, Bekzi broke in. I'd allowed him to see what I was seeing through Gerrett.

Honey, I think he's more of a sociopath, I mentally sighed. *Either way, it's not good for the rest of us.*

We clean up after anyway, Bekzi lifted my hand and kissed it.

He and I were in the kitchen; poor Gerrett witnessed everything firsthand while filling empty wine cups in the dining hall.

I honestly hoped things would be different when Warlend arrived; I didn't want to watch Deris burn Helsa's palace to the ground, merely because he held the ability without the restraint of an inconvenient conscience.

Wylend, Warlend and Wellend's two wives arrived together the following morning. Helsa and Hegatt pretend-bowed to Warlend; Palia and Titia pretend-kissed Helsa and Hegatt. Wylend stood by, his eyes hooded so Hegatt and Helsa couldn't see the contempt he held for both.

Warlend didn't pretend-kiss anybody, including his wife.

"We have tea and cakes in the library," Wallend announced. He'd arrived late with Valia and the twins in tow. He didn't pretend to acknowledge anyone else—only his father.

Bekzi and I, taking up as little space as possible at the back of the hall, nodded to Gerrett and three other servants to run upstairs and serve the family and guests once the King arrived in the library.

What you see in Warlend? Bekzi asked as we made an extra pot of tea in case it was called for. Three had been sent to the library already, with a warming spell placed on each silver pot so it would be the proper temperature when served.

187

He has an announcement to make, and I doubt it will be to the liking of Hegatt, Helsa or Deris, I responded.

Bekzi blinked at me for a moment. *We not know this yet?*

You don't, I heaved a mental sigh. *Things are about to get weird.*

What's going on? Ilya sent.

Honey, the fur may fly before the day's out, I said.

BlackWing VII

Terrett

Yanzi asked me to come to Goor-Phin with him, to search for Quin. I'd agreed before he finished the question.

I would go anywhere and do anything if it meant we might find her; a preliminary scouting party hadn't seen her, but by their own admission, they hadn't searched the entire plantation.

Yanzi and I intended to do just that. He would go onto the plantation as a lion snake; I would provide the shield to protect others from the scrying of homicidal Karathians.

They wore a tracking device so the ASD could find them—that's all they needed. Morrett was still aboard BlackWing VII to conceal the ship from prying evil. Already my brother was endearing himself to me. I hoped he, Gerrett and I could have a private meal soon and talk about our pasts—all were different and yet alike in certain ways.

I had family, something I could never claim before.

If we could only find Quin, my life would be complete.

"You take," Yanzi walked into our shared suite at the safe house and handed a pistol to me. I blinked—it was a ranos pistol, provided by the ASD.

"You know how use?" Yanzi asked.

Enough to protect myself, I said.

"Good. Protect. You. Quin. Anybody else who need."

I have three brothers, I clapped Yanzi on the back with my free hand. *Brother, are you interested in a drink?*

"I interested," Yanzi grinned. "Beer?"

Whatever you want, I'll buy, I agreed.

"Did somebody say beer?" Winkler stood in our doorway.

"We say beer," Yanzi laughed. "You come. We sick wolf on bothering drunks."

Winkler threw back his head and laughed.

Karathia—Present

Morid

I'd been forgotten by all except Norn and Gale. Somehow, they'd found a hidden door in the corner of a storeroom where my cage had been left. With crates, boxes, old furniture and rolled up rugs all around me, I figured I'd been left there to rot with the rest of it.

Gale and Norn found me quickly, much to my surprise. The girl who'd helped them smuggle food and clothing to me on Hraede was gone; she'd been sent with Daris to an undisclosed location.

I imagined it was to serve Daris' underlings while she saw to another important facet of their operation.

Gale told me I was on Karathia, which troubled me greatly. A coup was in the works, yet I was helpless to warn anyone.

"Food package," Norn quietly passed the container through the bars of my cage. "Toiletries," he pushed the larger package Gale had carried through the same narrow opening. "You have a change of underclothes and wipes in there; we'll bring a full set of clean items tomorrow," he promised.

"Thank you. I can't say how much I appreciate this," I mumbled, opening the container of food.

"We understand," Gale said. "We're hoping for a way out of this soon. Until then, we'll do what we can for you."

I nodded; the scent of the food almost drove me wild with hunger. They could only feed me once a day without someone getting suspicious, and it never occurred at the same time of day.

Wise of them, but their strategy left me with a growling stomach most of the time. No, I wasn't complaining—I would have been grateful to have crumbs. Instead, I received a generous meal on most days and blessed them for getting that much to me. As yet, I had no idea how they managed, but my stomach and I thanked them every day.

Biting into the sandwich first, I chewed and contemplated the effect a coup would have on the planet and the Campiaan Alliance, because Karathia was one of the most important member planets of that Alliance.

If it were taken over by recognizable criminals, I anticipated that Campiaa would close Karathia's membership immediately, leaving it to Deris and Daris' lawless machinations.

That meant they'd likely allow warlocks and witches to hire out to whomever paid the most while charging stiff fees for the privilege of working offworld.

On the other hand, all legal imports would cease, seriously limiting the food supply until the black market extended its hand and offered whatever Karathia wanted—again for a premium price. I wasn't sure the twins had thought this through well enough to realize what sort of weight the throne brought with it.

One cannot rule a planet if that planet starves its citizens, levies taxes too heavy for them to bear and drives them to flee elsewhere; I'd seen it happen before, when lives were threatened after they refused to cooperate.

I'd lived on too many lawless worlds not to know better; Father could never house his family on an Alliance world because of his willingness to associate with criminals.

Bite. Chew. Bite. Chew.

My life had dwindled to the constant hunger for food and small comforts.

∾

Goor-Phin
Quin
Every day, I helped Dorgus lift Vardil from the water of his bath.

Dorgus insisted on bathing Vardil himself; he only needed help getting the man in and out of the tub. Once Vardil was dressed, exercised and the suite cleaned, I carried food and other necessities for them.

Aside from that, Dorgus dismissed me. I used my extra time to help Janis, where I had a new task each day—carrying food to the Sirenali in the large shed.

Each time I made my way to the shed, I searched for tools or anything else casually left behind by those who tended the fields or repaired equipment. Whatever might get those chains off the Sirenali would be welcome.

So far, I'd found nothing.

Still, I was determined to do something to get them away; I couldn't leave them behind to die as Daris intended.

Karathia—Past

Zaria

Warlend has been in a meeting most of the afternoon with Wellend, I informed Ilya when he asked. *The others are restless—Deris has set furniture on fire in the library,* I added.

I'm worried, Ilya admitted. *Wellend's wives are out for a ride and haven't returned yet; I sent two stable boys with them, just in case.*

Is that unusual? I asked.

Probably not, but something isn't right—even I can feel it.

I'd felt that way for days. I suppose I could be forgiven for wanting his arms about me. Too many things were beyond control, once Warlend arrived.

Where's Wylend? Ilya asked.

Last I heard, he was cleaning up Deris' mess in the library, I said. *He hasn't reprimanded the boy, but he wants to—I can see it clearly in his face.*

I wouldn't just reprimand—I'd lock him up and see to it he couldn't use his talent again until he'd gone through extensive therapy and proved himself

191

safe to walk free again, Ilya returned. *If that never happened, then I'd burn the talent out of him.*

You can do that?

It takes a majority of the King's Council to do it, but it can be done—as a last resort, you understand.

Yes, but has it ever been done to a member of the royal family?

Not to my knowledge. I'm surprised you haven't heard of this—you know everything else, Ilya said.

I guess I've never seen it in someone, or read it anywhere, I replied.

Ah. That makes sense. Don't let it worry you, cabbage. Keep me informed.

I will.

"Not worry," Bekzi gave me a swift hug. "We get through."

An announcement will be made at dinner, Gerrett's mindspeech interrupted us.

"Honey," I turned to Bekzi, who placed the finishing touches on the King's birthday dessert, "I hope they eat that, it looks delicious."

He leaned in to kiss me. It was a good kiss and I'll admit, it left me wanting more.

"You get more," he grinned. "Later."

I saw Wallend shortly before dinner. He was angry that he'd been left out of the meeting between his father and older brother. Wylend, who'd dropped by the kitchen for a glass of wine, was curious but not angry about being left out of the meeting.

I could see he'd resigned himself to things of that nature and, as he lived in the King's summer palace most of the time, the doings of the King and Prince-heir didn't affect him that much.

He missed Erland; I did see that. He'd asked Erland to come with him, but Erland despised Hegatt, Helsa and the twins, so he'd refused the invitation. I sympathized with Lord Erland Morphis completely; those people should have been related to me and I despised them, too.

"The food has been lovely," Wylend turned back to tell us before he carried his full wineglass out of the kitchen.

"Thank you, Prince Wylend," Bekzi and I dipped our heads to him.

~

Goor-Phin

Quin

"One dead from snake bite," Janis whispered as I helped her slice a roast for the evening meal. "Not one of ours," she added. "Died fast, from what I heard."

I shrugged indifferently. I didn't care that Vardil's or Daris' criminals died. All of them had innocent blood on their hands. If this kept up, however, Daris would have to bring in more of Vardil's scum to fill in for those lost.

Should Daris keep killing off innocent servants, I imagined she'd have to search for more of those, too.

It occurred to me, then.

One of Vardil's criminals likely had a key to the Sirenali's chains.

If he died of what appeared to be natural causes in his sleep and the keys were borrowed and then replaced, who would be the wiser?

"Alys says you speak—when necessary," Janis whispered as she laid slices of roast carefully on a platter.

I nodded and cut another slice off the carefully prepared roast. Janis was an exceptional cook. I hoped she and I survived; I knew of many who'd hire her in moments on my recommendation alone.

"Who has the keys—to the chains on those in the shed?" I mumbled my question.

"I can find out for you," Janis nodded and laid the last slice of roast. "There, hand that platter to Felk to take to her majesty's table."

~

Karathia—Past

Zaria

At least Warlend waited until the meal was eaten and dessert served and devoured before making his announcement.

What surprised me is that he called in all the servants to witness it, and included one or two members of his Council that he'd invited to dinner.

What's this about? Ilya's eyes met mine as all servants who weren't already in the dining hall to serve the family, gathered in the hall outside the kitchen. We'd go in together, as requested, lining the walls of the dining hall while we witnessed whatever Warlend was about to say.

I have no idea, I replied to Ilya's silent question.

Whatever the announcement was, it was Warlend's way of saying that there were too many witnesses; therefore, there would be no argument from family concerning his announcement.

Spelled globes of light floated above the table, bathing the long room in soft light. The table still looked pristine—except for the space around Deris.

He'd taken up burning the tablecloth again. The boy thought he'd gotten away with it, but I saw in Wellend's eyes that he'd been watching his nephew the whole time.

What else I saw in Wellend's eyes made me smother a gasp. It made me afraid to see what was in Warlend's determined gaze.

Honey, I sent to Ilya. *I think we're about to hear what instigated the coup.*

Bekzi, who stood beside me, grasped my hand in his; he'd overheard our silent exchange. He was worried, too.

~

Goor-Phin

Quin

Tall, sturdy Morth was the key holder. I didn't mind taking him— he was one of the rapists I'd kept from harming others after my arrival.

He'd killed or raped too often for me to feel any sympathy for him; his death would be an easier one than he deserved, too.

It would be simple enough to pass his death off as a difficulty of the heart, as he'd neglected to visit the med unit once his cock refused to rise. I suspected that nobody would miss him, either—he was a difficulty for all on the plantation. Why Daris brought him with her remained a mystery.

～

Karathia—Past
  Zaria

As required whenever the King pronounced law or judgment, all others stood while he sat.

Hegatt didn't like it at all, while Deris cooked up more deviltry behind hooded eyes. "Say it so we can have drinks in the library," Helsa demanded. Warlend turned toward her.

"You will wish back those words," he began. "My decree is thus; today, upon my birthday, I wish to give a gift rather than receiving one. I, Warlend, King of Karathia, am abdicating my throne in favor of my son and heir, Wellend Arden, Crown Prince of Karathia. It has already been recorded in both our books. All that remains is for Wellend to remove the Heir's ring, as it will select his successor."

Deris, who'd been ignoring everyone in favor of devising his next set of torturous plans, perked up immediately.

"My King," Warlend rose and dipped his head to Wellend, who smiled genuinely at his father. Helsa's eyes grew round and greedy as they settled on the Heir's ring on Wellend's right hand.

Hegatt blinked in anticipation as Wellend pulled the ring from his finger and set it down in a clear space before him on the table.

They knew the ring would go to Deris. It would choose the designated heir of the prophecy.

All along the walls of the dining hall, servants held their breath— not in anticipation like Deris' family—no. They held their breath in dread, because the Heir would be someone who could and probably would destroy Karathia.

The ring, pale gold with a Tiralian crystal setting surrounded by smaller black diamonds, set on the table for only a moment before rising on its own in the air.

Deris' mouth formed an O, he expected the ring to fly in his direction. He held out his hand for it to come to him.

At eye-level to most at the table, the ring turned three times, as if it were taking stock of all present.

Helsa shrieked when the ring disappeared in a sudden flash of light.

"This is as I expected," Warlend snapped at Helsa as he watched his trunk being readied. He didn't want to spend the night under Helsa's roof. Wellend, named King before all in attendance, had already taken his two wives and left for the Palace.

"That ring belongs to Deris," Helsa hissed.

"No, wife, it does not. There is more to the prophecy than even you know, and Deris does not fit the full description. Take care from now on; you have a new King who has no illusions as to what your grandchildren are. In my mind, it will not be difficult to convince the Council that their power needs to be removed."

I saw and heard all this through Gerrett, who helped pack Warlend's things. Wylend had left Helsa's palace with his brother, although I'd seen disappointment in his eyes that the ring hadn't come to him.

He had to be a suitable choice—after all, he'd sat the throne after those who'd instigated the coup had been disposed of. What concerned me most about Wylend was why he hadn't told anyone this part of the story—that his father had abdicated in favor of Wellend, or that Wellend was King when the coup happened.

There was more to this story, and I waited to see how it would unfold.

"There is one more thing," Warlend said before turning to leave. "I'm taking both head cooks with me to the Palace—at the King's insistence."

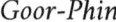

Goor-Phin

Quin

Morth was dead and I was halfway to the shed housing the Sirenali when the drakus seed fields exploded around us. I saw the Orb as it flashed briefly before my sight. Not only was it responsible for the drakus plants' destruction; it flung everyone on the plantation to another world in the blink of an eye.

CHAPTER 14

Quin

uin

Daris wasn't happy, of that I was certain. Half the night, the Orb hovered over her head, issuing orders in mindspeech as the rest of us scurried to make our new surroundings comfortable for the angry, Fourth-level witch.

An abandoned palace was our new home, and I hoped with all my might that it would be temporary.

I was finally beginning to understand the Orb's motives, however, and they frightened me.

Yes, it had appeared to serve good, as long as it searched for the one responsible for Siriaa's destruction. The Orb, connected to Liron the god, was set to protect Siriaa or avenge it if it were harmed.

Vardil Cayetes was no longer a threat; therefore, the Orb considered him dealt with. Its real objective had come to the fore and it had found the likeliest of servants to effect that goal.

It intended to destroy the Alliance—if not all living worlds.

The poison wasn't working fast enough, I suppose. Scientists were desperately searching for a cure for the foul creatures every moment, which could spoil the Orb's plans.

The Arden twins, with their N'il Mo'erti and penchant for causing

198

pain and death, were a better method of killing everything. Not only was I a servant to the Orb's whims, the Arden twins had become its pawns, too.

Perhaps the Orb hadn't realized that I opposed its objectives. I imagined it might kill me easily if I made that fact clear.

I didn't object to my death, as long as I did my part to free the Alliances of the Orb's machinations and conspiracies. How I wished at that moment that at least one of my mates was with me, to help me muddle through this terrible conundrum.

Le-Ath Veronis
Lissa
"We barely got out of there with our lives," Winkler paced like a caged wolf inside my suite.

"What set it off? Do you know?"

"No idea. Bekzi admits to biting someone who came too close, but that was easily explained—there were snakes all over that plantation. The moment we got within sight of that storage shed, the whole place went up like fireworks."

"This worries me," I sighed.

"In what way?" Winkler stopped pacing and turned nearly-black eyes on me.

"I doubt Deris or Daris were looking for anything in the animal kingdom. That doesn't keep the truly powerful from knowing when something touches the ground in a certain area—if they're looking for that particular contact," I said.

Winkler held his breath for a moment as he considered what I'd said.

"You mean it was waiting for something to pass a perimeter that wasn't exactly native to the area?"

"I think that's precisely what happened."

"But who or what would do that?"

"Who or what would kidnap Quin?" I rose and headed for the

window. I merely wanted to reassure myself that Lissia and the rest of my planet was safe.

"You think the Orb had something to do with this? So far, it appears to be on our side," Winkler argued.

"Until our common goal is no longer a common goal," I pointed out. "Remember, Liron created that thing. Man, I wish Zaria were here."

"What would Zaria do that we can't?" Winkler growled.

"She's the only one who's ever come face-to-face with Liron," I said.

"You're joking," Winkler began.

"No. Zaria Keppler is just a name she used this time. I hear that it's appropriate, although I don't really understand how."

"You're talking in riddles," Winkler accused.

"Honey, this isn't information to share with just anybody. Keep this secret—not just for me, but to protect her life. Possibly the lives of who knows how many others, too."

"Where the hell is she that you can't get to her?" Winkler exploded. I understood then that the plantation explosion affected him more than he'd let on.

"Where Hank Bell put her," I snapped. "And he's not telling anybody."

I hadn't seen Winkler this angry or upset in a very long time. For a century, at least. He didn't like being kept in the dark. I didn't say it, but I liked it as little as he did.

~

Karathia—Past

Zaria

I was more than grateful that Warlend allowed me to take as many of the staff as I wanted with me to the Palace.

It left no eyes and ears behind to watch Hegatt, Helsa and the others, but I knew them well enough by this time to understand what their endgame would be. I just didn't know who or what they'd send against Wellend, in order to take the throne.

"Son, they're here," Warlend announced as he led my bunch into a private interview with the new King.

The private study of the King had changed greatly over the years; it looked far different in the future where I'd first seen it. I suppose the coup had destroyed much of what surrounded Wellend at the moment, although the space was well and richly appointed.

"I see we have extras," Wellend said. "Madam cook, tell me what these can do for me." He swept a hand toward Gerrett and Ilya.

"My King," I dipped my head, "Gerrett can act as your valet; although he is silent, he has exceptional taste. Ilya," I nodded to Ilya who had arms crossed tightly over his chest, "He is perhaps the best bodyguard you will ever have."

My words caused Ilya to frown at me. Not only had I asked that Gerrett remain close to Wellend, keeping him away from scrying eyes, I'd asked that Wellend accept Ilya as a bodyguard.

Ilya saw that as interfering in the coup. I was about to tell him otherwise.

"Are you trained as a bodyguard?" Wellend's eyes settled on Ilya, whose muscles bulged as his arms shifted into a tighter stance.

"Yes," Ilya answered truthfully.

"Good. I'll watch you spar with my captain of the guard tomorrow morning. Father, would you like to be there?" Wellend turned to Warlend.

"Very much. Nothing gets past Braven."

Too bad Bekzi and I would be stuck in the kitchen. I wanted to watch Ilya make short work of the captain of the guard.

Do your best, I sent to Ilya. *Trust me, we won't interfere with the coup when the time comes.*

I wasn't lying to him—we wouldn't interfere. That didn't stop me from doing what I could *before* the coup happened.

Or after, for that matter.

Goor-Phin

Quin

When next I saw Daris, I could see she thought her mind was slipping. It was, but not for the reason she feared.

Only she and I could see the Orb, as it floated above her head most of the time. I'm sure she imagined the voice in her head as one indicative of madness.

It had shut me out of much of its communication, so I had no idea what it ordered Daris to do.

Perhaps it found her more malleable than her brother, as it hatched its plan to destroy whatever it could.

I worried that the time would surely come when it would order me to do something against my conscience. I could only refuse to do its bidding; I had no power over it, after all.

Without my mindspeech, I couldn't say good-bye to any of my mates when it killed me.

Liron loved Siriaa, likely because he'd created it. The Avii worshipped him as such. Even the capital city of Fyris was named after him.

At the end, however, he'd been just as bad as any other rogue god; one who'd been charged with the duty to kill everything.

He'd only intended to keep Siriaa alive.

Strange that it was the first world to die of the poison within its depths. Its death, in turn, looked to cause most other worlds to die, too; slowly, as Fyris had been dying.

Before Vardil Cayetes reached out his hand and hurried things along.

That stopped me for a moment.

If Vardil were whole and sane, the Orb could be distracted for a moment as its previous target reappeared.

Daris, too, would be distracted, as she fought, perhaps, with Vardil for control of his empire.

My original plan was back in motion; I merely had to discern where they'd hidden the Sirenali so I could free them before I died.

~

Karathia—Present

Morid

V'ili, bent over at the waist, stared at me through the bars of my cage. Struggling to hide any emotion, I refused to meet his eyes with my own. I lowered them instead, in a subservient gesture.

I prayed he'd leave me alone as a result. V'ili's whims were irregular and unreliable at best. He'd just as soon order someone to kill themselves while he watched in pleasure.

He'd been gone for two eight-days; I had no idea where and was afraid to know why. Wherever V'ili went, chaos followed, and many tales of his exploits were too horrifying to bear.

He liked women.

Worse, he enjoyed killing them in unusual ways, once he'd had his fill of them. I can't say how often I prayed that he'd find one who could plant a knife in his back before he had time to place an obsession.

I assumed that was only a daydream for me—imagining his death at the hands of one strong enough to deliver it.

"Hmmph." V'ili was done looking at me and walked away. I waited until he was out of my storeroom to breathe a relieved sigh.

The small, hidden door behind my cage creaked open; Gale set a container of food on the floor before climbing through the narrow space.

"Don't worry; he's headed for the dining hall," Gale handed the container to me. "Norn is watching him carefully."

"Thank you," I allowed my shoulders to slump, only realizing then how tense I'd become.

"Things are becoming critical," Gale whispered. I accepted the fork he handed through the bars and dug into the food while listening to his news. "Deris is almost crazed by a message received from his sister, although we don't know what it is, yet. Kend is still working feverishly on the machines; Deris threatened to turn his wife over to V'ili if he doesn't."

"I don't think Deris has Kend's wife. Not anymore," I said. "Something happened on Hraede. I hope the ASD found her before she could be delivered to Deris for torture and death if Kend didn't move faster."

"What about his children?"

"I don't think they've threatened him about that lately. I hope that means they're no longer captives, too. Of course, all this is speculation at this point."

"If we are ever able to get away, it is our desire to bring you with us," Gale whispered. "Norn will bring fresh clothing and wipes later."

I'd wolfed down the food, so I handed the fork and container back to Gale with a nod of thanks. Truthfully, I wanted to weep at their generosity.

"We'll keep you informed as best we can," Gale said and disappeared through the small doorway, carefully shutting the invisible door behind him.

~

Goor-Phin

Terrett

Yanzi, Farzi, Nenzi and I stood at the perimeter of the burned drakus seed fields, surveying the damage.

The plantation house and shed were smoking ruins, but they'd been emptied before the blast leveled and burned everything.

Not even a bone was found, except for the skeletons of snakes littering the perimeter. Somehow, most of them had escaped—these bones were of the last few that didn't reach the boundary in time.

"Sad," Farzi shook his head. He and his brothers felt a kinship with these—they were snake shifters and weren't threatened by other snakes.

"This terrible," Yanzi whispered. "We not find Quin. I think she here. With these," he swept out a hand. "They mostly not get near humans. Quin—she draw them, I think."

"There's been no word on where they went," Caylon arrived with

Sal and Jayna. "The ASD is scrambling to locate those death machines again. We should have blown the whole property the moment we discovered them here." He shook his head, his gaze dark as he surveyed the plantation.

ASD hovervans could be seen in the distance, floating above specific sections of the house and sheds. The drakus plants in the fields were destroyed well enough that no usable seed remained. All of it would be sifted anyway, by agri-bots programmed to search for anything dangerous.

Caylon flexed his arms; I watched the tight muscles move beneath the black shirt he wore. Not only was his skin darker than most Falchani, I imagined his thoughts were dark as well.

He worried about Zaria, as I worried about Quin.

We'll find them, I sent to him. *We have to.*

An imperceptible nod was his only response.

∽

Karathia—Past

Zaria

"Madam cook, what is for dinner?" Wellend appeared in my kitchen, wearing a smile.

"Are you hungry?" I asked. It was past midday, but still not time for tea.

"Perhaps a little," he grinned.

"Sit. We'll make something for the King," I nodded and returned his smile.

"I feel as if I'm being naughty, sneaking into the kitchen between meals," he laughed.

"I believe that is royal prerogative, my King," I said and set about making small shrimp salad sandwiches for him.

"Ah, there you are," Warlend walked in while Wellend ate.

"Sir Regent, may I interest you in dainty, shrimp salad sandwiches?" I asked.

"Leave out the dainty and I'll eat," he said.

"My King," a servant walked in as I set a small plate of food in front of Warlend. I went still for a moment after reading him; I had to remind myself to set the plate down as if nothing were wrong and this one weren't Hegatt's spy inside the palace.

"What is it, Brill?" Wellend turned to ask.

"Ah. Sorry, I forget myself. Sir Regent," he turned to Warlend, "When should we prepare for the coronation? Many Nobles and the Council are asking so they might bring their wives and husbands."

"I've never known you to be so eager for a celebration," Warlend lifted an eyebrow at Brill.

He wanted to know, because Hegatt was plotting already. Brill, a minor noble, had worn out his welcome at court, yet insisted on staying on in a guest suite at the King's expense.

"We will decide later—when we've finished our meal and conversation," Warlend said.

I realized then that Hegatt was seeing through Brill's eyes. I wanted to sear his brain for it, but considered that the connection could be useful. Whenever Hegatt looked through Brill's eyes, I could see into Hegatt's mind.

He'd invited someone to Helsa's palace.

Someone he should have kept far, far away.

Marid of Belancour was ensconced in a suite at the back of that house. It was too much to hope that Deris would set Marid's suite on fire and drive him away.

I hesitated to mention Marid to Bekzi, Gerrett and Ilya. It troubled me greatly that a warlock would invite a wizard to help plan a coup.

Until I recalled that a wizard had made the Heir's ring.

Hegatt, Helsa and all others had watched as the real Heir's ring disappeared. None of them knew where it was. Was Hegatt asking Marid to help find it—or was he asking Marid to construct another?

One with a red stone.

Tiralian crystal wasn't easy to get, and the red stone in the ring I'd seen certainly wasn't made of that precious substance.

I imagined it to be a ruby or a plain diamond, spelled to become red. Was Hegatt asking Marid to construct a ring that would only allow his heirs to sit the throne? What about the plans he carried for the death machines?

He didn't have time to construct any of them to assist in his coup.

Something needed to be done and I had very little time to determine what that could be or how to accomplish it, once my plan was formed.

More than anything, I wanted to go to Wellend and tell him everything.

I couldn't. The one who'd placed me here could jerk me away just as fast, and I didn't have time to argue with him about the necessity or the propriety of my actions.

The days were dwindling about me, while the raging storm moved ever closer. In this case, seeking permission or forgiveness was equally as dangerous.

Le-Ath Veronis

Lissa

Kaldill Schaff stood in my study. He looked worried.

Anytime the Elf King looked worried was a time for everybody to feel worried.

"What is it?" I asked.

"I need Quin's wings," he sighed and dropped his gaze. "I must attempt to find her."

"You'll have to ask Justis," I began.

"I know. I fear that what I may find will be worse than not knowing," Kaldill said. The green of his eyes, normally clear and pure, was dark with terror.

He feared for Quin's life.

Somehow, I got the idea that wasn't all he was worried about.

"You think the Orb is involved in this, too, don't you?" I rose from my seat and stood, as if that could prepare me for Kaldill's answer.

"I do. All along I've been concerned, but as it hasn't actually threatened Quin's life before, I banished it from my mind. You and I know a rogue god, whose full intent we do not know, created it. That book Halthea destroyed—I fear it had something to say on the subject. I curse her footsteps and her flights upon any world."

I blinked. For an elf to curse someone's footsteps upon any ground —it was a violent curse, although it sounded so benign.

Coming from Kaldill, it was anything but. To also curse her flights —he may as well have sentenced her to a terrible death.

Too bad she was already dead.

"Do you think you could read it? The book, I mean," I said. "Gurnil says none living on Siriaa could read the text. Quin probably could, but only because it involved her in some way."

"The Larentii can read it," Nefrigar appeared. "It does mention Quin, in such a way that I do not deem it fitting to ever show her. It also mentions another," he said. "For that reason, too, we will never freely show the book to Quin."

"Who?" Kaldill and I spoke at the same time.

"Corinne," Nefrigar replied, his voice flat.

"The only person I know who's ever seen Liron, face-to-face," I mumbled.

"Exactly," Nefrigar nodded. "The book gives specific instructions to Quin should she ever see this female Larentii, who is described perfectly in its pages."

"She's supposed to attempt to kill her, isn't she?" Kaldill guessed.

"That is the book's instructions," Nefrigar replied. "The Larentii were unconcerned, as we believed Corinne dead for centuries. Until Zaria appeared."

"May the stars and the Mighty be merciful," I breathed.

"What are we supposed to do about this?" Kaldill demanded.

"I know not," Nefrigar sighed.

∼

Avii Castle

Justis

"I would not allow anyone else to touch them," I whispered as I opened the glass case containing Quin's wings. The Elf King had asked, therefore, I allowed this.

"I merely need to take another feather," Kaldill nodded to me. "From the other wing. With the one I already have, perhaps they will guide me to her."

"Find her, Lord Elf," I muttered. "Please."

"I will do what I can."

I watched as Kaldill gently plucked a downy feather from Quin's left wing and then held it gently on his palm. "Yes, this will be enough," he sighed before nodding to me and disappearing.

Cloudsong

Quin

"Where are we?" I hissed my question softly, so only Janis might hear.

"Cloudsong," Janis mumbled as she and I peeled potatoes to boil for dinner. "I only found out last night. The whole planet is deserted and we're stuck in a castle that could fall down around us at any moment. Don't worry, your silent friends are safe. Stuck in a cage in the old stables, or so I hear."

My shoulders sagged in relief. I'd be forced to search for another key, but I still had some time.

Time to set the Sirenali free and heal Vardil Cayetes. Time (I hoped) to get the others away when the battle began between his people and those loyal to Daris.

I had no idea what role the Orb would play in all this, or whether it would attempt to stop me at any point until I deliberately refused to obey its command.

"I think Yark holds the key this time," Janis interrupted my thoughts.

"Thank you."

～

Le-Ath Veronis

Lissa

"Sweetheart?" Merrill's fingers brushed hair away from my face.

I'd been asleep when I heard his voice.

"Honey, let me sleep," I mumbled and attempted to turn over in bed.

Wait. I hadn't gone to bed with Merrill. Gavin was on the other side. I was awake immediately.

What's wrong? I sent in mindspeech as I misted both of us out of my bedroom, leaving Gavin snoring away on his side.

"Half of the capital city on Wedeb II is dead and many others are ill. They're calling for medical teams from other cities and help from the ASD. The city was poisoned. I think it may be drakus seed," Merrill said aloud when I set him down in the hallway outside my suite.

"How?" I was still struggling to wake.

"I've sent mindspeech to several others—get your group together and meet us in the library in an hour." Merrill leaned in to kiss me quickly. "Hurry, my darling. Other cities may be in danger."

～

Kellik

"It wouldn't be difficult," Rigo paced in Lissa's library. "I'd say the Arden twins have been making fools of all of us, all along," he added.

"What are you talking about?" Kooper Griff demanded.

"We've only been concerned with the ships they've captured. Those are easy enough to spot—once they're stripped and abandoned. What if many others are boarded, obsession placed while cargo is tainted with drakus seed and then the ship is sent on its way?"

"How long would that take? To stop a ship and poison the cargo?" Lissa asked.

"Not long, if you had a wizard or warlock with you to employ power in distributing the seed into sealed cargo."

"The ship's chron-bot cannot be compromised," I said, causing Rigo to turn in my direction. "They have built-in safeguards. They record speed variations, in addition to stops and starts. I believe this wizard or warlock would have to be more powerful than any I've ever seen to change anything within the mechanism. Perhaps we should study ship's chron-bot logs to determine whether there were any unscheduled stops."

Kooper rose and began speaking into a communicator, giving instructions to a crew elsewhere.

"Check them all," I heard him say. "Pull the cargo manifests on any with unscheduled stops. Let me know what the drakus seed was in and backtrack those shipments to Wedeb II."

"We have it, sir—ground-up drakus seed was substituted for chemicals to treat the city's water supply."

"Deris," Lissa hissed. "He did this. Is the Governor of Wedeb II available? I want his ass in Kooper's office now. We need to know if he received a letter from a certain criminal we all know and never loved."

Lissa

Piik Guld, Governor of Wedeb II, slumped in his seat as Kooper questioned him. I hovered as mist in a corner so I could listen to the conversation. Kooper knew I was there; he'd already sent mindspeech twice during the questioning.

"Where's the letter now?" Kooper demanded.

"Please—I had no idea it would be this much devastation," Piik warbled. "They threatened me and my family. Said I'd never hold office again if I didn't pay them—and allow one shipment to go unchecked."

"So here we are, you're out the money and you'll still never run for office again—unless it's for representative of your prison cell block," Kooper hissed. "You could have sent that letter to the ASD, yet you did not."

"My family," Piik cowered.

"Your family is being cursed by every remaining citizen of your planet," Kooper half-shouted and flung out a hand in anger. "For killing *their* families."

I couldn't help wondering how many other Piiks were out there, agreeing to the same thing and now waiting, once the news of Wedeb II reached them, for the shoe to drop in the form of mass murders on their worlds.

Kooper, we have to take this to the media, I said. *Quickly. Before millions more die.*

What if they don't come forward? It'll put unnecessary pressure on those who never received correspondence from Vardil Cayetes. You and I know he's an empty shell and a cover for the twins. Are you prepared to release that information?

Kooper glared at Piik while we held our silent conversation. *I'll hold off until you're done here, but we have to disseminate the information,* I said. *I'm leaving so I can talk this over with some of mine. Let me know when you can join us.*

I will, Kooper replied.

I folded space while Kooper continued his questioning of Piik Guld.

"Most space stations are set up for drug detection—general drug detection," Rigo pointed out. We were having lunch in the library while all my mates and a few extras gathered there to discuss the problem. "If drakus seed is combined with chemicals, as in this particular case, it will slip past the detectors we have."

"We don't have the manpower to open and test every single crate or box that comes in on every freighter on every Alliance world," Drake observed. "The ASD and CSD are overwhelmed as it is. Drew and I checked numbers just this morning."

"So far, I've noticed that they haven't attacked the CSD," Aryn pointed out, his voice dry.

"They're working on this," I snapped at him. "I had a long conversation with Teeg earlier."

I didn't say I had a long conversation with Gavril, my son, and Tybus, his stand-in. Both ran the Campiaan Alliance under the same name and guise—as Teeg San Gerxon.

"I have a theory about that," Kell said, his voice soft.

"What's that?" I turned to him. I'd discovered the man was a walking encyclopedia of information.

"What is the Arden twins' ultimate goal? What are they working so hard toward?"

"The Karathian throne," Erland replied immediately.

"Very good. Now," Kell continued, "Which Alliance does Karathia belong to?"

"The Campiaan Alliance," I said. I hadn't quite figured it out, yet, but Kell was making a valid point.

"Now, I know the Campiaan Alliance won't interfere with the succession of monarchy on any of its worlds—it lets those worlds decide that for themselves," Kell said. "Therefore, Karathia, should it be taken by one royal faction over another, will have no interference by the CSD. Then, once a new regime—I'm only making a supposition, Lord Morphis," he held out a hand to stop Erland's protests, "As I said, once a new regime is in power, it is their decision whether they will remain a member of the Alliance. Isn't that true?"

Erland went still. I could tell his mind was working furiously, however.

"Should they choose not to remain a member of the Alliance, they could set themselves up as a separate entity, selling spells, spelled objects and weapons of war to anyone with enough money to buy. Is that not right?"

I was no longer watching Kell; I watched my Karathian warlock mate instead. Deris and Daris may have originally intended to use the machines to take Karathia for themselves. Something had since changed. They still wanted Karathia; it would line up with the new plan—to sell those war machines to anyone who could afford them. Non-Alliance worlds would be flooded with the deadly devices, all of which could ultimately be pointed toward the Alliances.

"We should have blown that plantation to bits the moment we found it," I whispered.

We no longer knew where those evil things were and, if my suspicions were correct, the Orb was now involved. The God Wars weren't truly over; they still had one last ace to play and it could change or destroy everything.

"The Orb is calling the shots, now," I said.

"What?" Gavin stood and blinked at me.

"The Orb is calling the shots," I sounded half hysterical. "It's telling Deris and Daris what to do. Oh, my God."

"Remember when Vardil Cayetes and his family were the worst we had to deal with?" Winkler handed me a glass of wine. We sat in a private bar inside The Chessman, Adam's casino in Casino City.

My Falchani twins had invited me out for a drink after a less than productive day of playing *what if*.

Winkler and several others chose to come with us.

Adam, Kiarra and Merrill arrived with Reah, Edward and Gavril. Tybus was watching after the Campiaan Alliance tonight. When Trajan and Trace walked in, I understood we also had the ear of the Mighty Hand.

Kooper rose from his seat to greet Trajan. Those two were mated to Bree; did we have her ear, too?

"Please, let's not talk shop," I breathed a sigh. I wanted to be drunk enough that I could get the vision of the Orb out of my mind.

My guess was that the Orb had taken over when it kidnapped Quin.

Quin. I was terrified for her. Would the Orb destroy her if she refused to do as it said?

Somehow, I doubted she'd turned out as the Orb intended. She'd developed her own independence and had fought too many battles for the right reasons instead of the wrong ones.

A collision of sorts was inevitable between those two, and we had no idea where either were or how to stop it.

Zaria, too, had been taken from us. Was there an underlying reason that we just didn't see? Was a Mighty plan in the works—one I wasn't aware of?

You still have something the twins want, a voice whispered in my mind.

I did.

The glass-topped coffin lay in my dungeon. It contained a book and a ring, according to Zaria.

How did she know that? I hadn't been inside the base of the thing —only the glass-enclosed top, in order to rescue Barc.

How did Zaria know what was in the base?

Where had she been—for the past few centuries? Corinne/Zaria. She'd separated her particles on Earth.

Who could have brought her back? There was only one answer, so that was a rhetorical question.

My sister Breanne was the Mighty Heart. Of the original Three/One, only she could *Change What Was.*

Did she also know to alter Corinne's appearance, so she wouldn't be recognized as anything other than a Karathian witch?

I held my breath for several seconds before releasing it.

Quin wasn't what she'd been designed to be.

Zaria was alive and no longer appeared the same as before.

Two small weapons had been positioned against a wealthy, well-equipped army of evil.

They were the rock in David's sling.

Would it be enough to kill the giant?

I had no idea.

CHAPTER 15

*K*arathia—Past
        Zaria

"Madam cook," the corners of Wellend's mouth curled upward as I set the tray on his desk.

Scattered across it were papers and records; his first day of hearing grievances as the King had arrived. He hadn't come to breakfast, so breakfast had come to him.

"Tea," I set the cup at his elbow, as he liked it. "Protein, to get you through the day," I pointed at the omelet. "The strawberries are just to keep you in a good mood."

"I need to be kept in a good mood?"

"I think Brill can destroy anybody's good mood," I said.

"Brill should go home," Wellend grimaced.

"Not just yet," I said. "Give him an eight-day or so, then send him on his way."

"Do you have a moment?" Wellend surprised me with the question.

"Everyone has a moment for the King," I smiled.

"Good. Sit down," he said. "Tell me, from a cook's perspective, how I should handle this dispute between two warlocks who provide the same spells in their village." He handed a paper to me.

"Are they here now?" I asked.

"Yes. I'm making them wait, because I have no idea how to settle this. They're both of an equal talent, and both get support from their customers."

"I'd like to see them," I said.

"Why?"

"Because I'm the Q'elindi you've been looking for," I laughed.

"Where have you been?" Ilya demanded when I appeared inside my tiny bedroom to change clothes.

"Serving the King's breakfast, witnessing a few disputes and then having a conversation with Warlend and Wellend. Don't worry, Bekzi is handling dinner just fine. He's herding those people in the kitchen around, and they're getting out of his way as if they understand he's a dangerous snake," I said.

"Where did that outfit come from?" he asked, crossing arms over his chest.

"I had to alter my cooking garb when I witnessed the first dispute," I sighed, letting the black silk gown drop to the floor.

"I can't believe you made me spar with the captain of the guard," Ilya huffed. "He needs to up his game if he expects to protect anybody —with spells or with weapons."

I stopped halfway through kicking off one black silk flat to stare at Ilya. "I need to see him," I breathed.

"I can arrange that. You haven't kept up with your sparring sessions. Want to go a round with Captain Horel?"

"Only if it's a battle of wits," I kicked off the second shoe before bending down and searching through my small trunk for something suitable to wear in the kitchen.

"He couldn't argue his way out of a game of riddles with a gnat," Ilya huffed.

"Now see—I knew you had a sense of humor hidden away somewhere. You should bring it out more often. I like it," I straightened up and pointed a finger at him.

"You shouldn't go about without clothing very often, it makes my cock hard," he pointed a finger at me.

"Oh, honey, I can fix that," My hips swayed as I walked toward him.

"I sure as hell hope so," he muttered and folded me into a hug.

∽

I saw Captain Horel the following morning at breakfast. He and Ilya were invited by Warlend to eat with Wellend while they went over plans for the new King's security detail. Warlend, who was also present, winked at me as I filled his cup with tea.

It had only taken a brief glance at Horel to determine that he and Brill were coconspirators with Hegatt.

Easy enough to bring a coup to fruition if you had a spy and the Captain of the King's guards in your pocket, as Hegatt did.

Horel was a high Level-three warlock; Ilya had shown him what a guard should be capable of and barely broke a sweat when they sparred together.

I worried, therefore, that Hegatt would target Ilya, in order to ease his way to killing the King.

My plan was undergoing refinements as a result; there wasn't any way I'd willingly place Ilya in danger. I'd already seen him overcome by treachery and I vowed never to let that happen again.

Horel is in deep with Hegatt, just as Brill is, I sent to Ilya. *Watch your back every moment with him,* I warned. *If he thinks you'll be a threat to their coup, they'll want you out of the way first.*

Should I thank you for placing my life in danger?

If you want. It's a gift. You don't have to get me anything, I replied.

Oh, I have something for you, all right.

Honey, I'll do everything I can to protect your ass. And the rest of you, too, I said.

Right.

Am I hearing some attitude? I asked.

Call it whatever you like. You're going to suck me into this coup no matter what, aren't you?

I never said that. In fact, if you want to be absent the day of the coup, feel free.

And make me look like a fucking coward?

Look, you can't be uninvolved if you're here. The entire planet is involved. Unless, I hesitated.

What?

You know Wallend is going to run at the first sign of trouble, don't you? I figure he'll take his kids and get the hell away, leaving his wife to fight his battle and die in his place. What if Warlend or Wellend sends you to find him?

I can live with that.

Good. I'll try to make that happen.

Don't get too close to them, they're marked for death, Ilya reminded me.

You have to spoil everything, don't you?

Cabbage, don't cry. Please.

I walked out of the dining hall after setting down the pot of tea I carried. The other servants could ensure that cups were filled. Ilya had upset me and I wanted to be alone.

Cloudsong

Quin

Dorgus was angry. As he couldn't see the Orb hovering over Daris' head, he thought her insane.

He was very close to being correct anyway, without the Orb's presence. She'd announced that Deris would be paying a visit, and everyone had to work to make the ruin of a castle presentable for her brother.

She'd gone so far as to call him the King of Karathia.

I wanted to laugh in her face.

Deris knew nothing of what being a King entailed, other than ordering servants to do his bidding and see to his every whim.

His ignorance was much like Daris', who expected to be named Deris' Regent when they took the throne away from Rylend Morphis, Bel's father.

I wasn't sure I'd ever felt such revulsion in my heart before, but that sentiment was growing. Bel, his father and grandfather were dear to me and treated me as family. Whatever it took to keep them safe, I would do.

"Hand me the powder, girl," Dorgus snapped. Vardil's privates were chafing; therefore, Dorgus would see to that and anything else Vardil needed.

It wasn't difficult to feel contempt for both.

The moment I could, I intended get the key away from Yark, who had hidden it away from the others.

He couldn't hide it from me, though. I knew it was kept in a hollowed-out leg of his bedframe. The key to his suite, however, stayed with him at all times. That, ultimately, would be a more difficult task.

～

Karathia—Past

Zaria

The obstacle I attempted to deal with as I put soup together for dinner was that of the plans for N'il Mo'erti that Hegatt kept with him. He even slept with the drawings—I'd seen that in Brill's eyes.

Foolish, foolish Hegatt, who had no idea he was watched carefully by a Q'elindi on the other end.

Cabbage, I'm sorry. A red rose dropped onto the table beside the stove, where I worked. This rose wasn't a long-stemmed beauty from a hothouse. This one was lovely, scent and all, on a short stem with small leaves and a slender twig studded with thorns.

Ilya had employed a spell to round off all the thorns. There would be no pricking of my fingers when I lifted this one to sniff.

Thank you, I replied, tucking the flower into the breast pocket of my cook's jacket. When he didn't respond, I went back to chopping celery for the soup. As I worked, I wondered who'd designed and built the first N'il Mo'erti, and how they'd communicated with those things in order to get them to do as they asked.

Certainly something to consider, I thought as I added those plans to my growing list of things to do.

"Smell good," Bekzi carried steaks into the kitchen. He'd gotten them straight from the butcher, who'd brought them to the back gate of the palace. "Good steak, too. We do fine dinner tonight."

"Wellend likes his medium rare," I said. "Warlend a little less done than that."

"We fix with good sauce," Bekzi nodded. "They like."

I couldn't help thinking that in an earlier existence, it would have been Ilya making steaks or the best Italian I'd ever eaten. Now, it was Bekzi who was a master cook. "Honey, how about a kiss?" I said as Bekzi set the crate of wrapped meat on a nearby table.

"You get kiss." He grinned and walked toward me. *You get snake in your bed tonight*, he added mentally as his mouth covered mine.

I broke the kiss when I laughed at his sending.

"Honey, remind me to get hot and sweaty with you again as soon as possible," I leaned in to give Bekzi a kiss.

"You sleep now," he pulled away to nuzzle my chin. "We have sex again soon," he promised, dropping his head to my collarbone and planting a kiss there. "Breakfast come early. We cook, remember?"

"Yeah. If we survive this, I want a vacation," I grumbled.

"I take. You like," he pulled me close and settled my head on his shoulder.

"Sounds good." I closed my eyes and shifted into a more comfortable position. It did sound good. I just had a shitload of things to do before that could happen.

Le-Ath Veronis

  Lissa

"Of course he can stay here. Master Morwin will be happy to have a pupil again," I said. Bleek and Barc sat inside my private study, Barc kicking his heels, Bleek looking somewhat uncomfortable.

Bleek wanted to go with Caylon and several others to hunt for Quin, but the conditions in some of the areas they intended to visit weren't ideal for a young boy. I'd already sent mindspeech to Morwin; he was on his way. If anyone could calm Barc down, it would be Morwin and the tasks he'd set for the boy.

"I hear you have a pupil in your study," Morwin walked in, smiling.

Barc's eyes grew round at his first sight of an Amterean Dwarf. Morwin's bushy, red eyebrows looked especially bristly today, as if he'd been doing research that delighted him.

One of Morwin's eyebrows lifted as he studied Barc; two of the boy's hands were clasped while the other two fiddled with the pockets in his pants.

"Sir Blevakian," Morwin nodded to Bleek. "Young sir Blevakian," he nodded to Barc. "How much do you know about your home world?" Morwin began.

"I know lots," Barc claimed.

"Ah. Then you know there are giant white cats on the snow-topped peaks of the Kivik Mountain range that are so invisible they can move without leaving tracks?"

"They don't leave tracks? How?" Barc was immediately interested.

"Ah. Well, if you choose to study with me, young one, we will explore all of the Kivik Mountain range, and every other wonder of your home planet." Morwin's eyes gleamed as he considered the information Barc would soak up immediately.

"Pap, I want to stay with Master Morwin," Barc gave his blessing to the arrangement.

"Then you have my permission, and I'll be back as often as possible," Bleek agreed.

Be careful out there, I cautioned Bleek in mindspeech. *With those machines, I have no idea what could happen next.*

"I will," Bleek acknowledged my sending. "Son, give me a hug. The Queen and Master Morwin will take good care of you while I'm gone."

~

BlackWing VII

Berel

Father and I volunteered to go with Kaldill, Caylon, Sal, Bleek, Lafe, Terrett and Yanzi. Those who remained on BlackWing VII had a new objective, now—tracking ships with unscheduled stops. The frightening thing was that once the ASD had begun looking into unscheduled stops for shipments already delivered, they numbered in the thousands across the Alliance.

We desperately needed Quin's help—and Zaria's—to determine whether the crews of those ships had been obsessed. Most ship captains either claimed there was no stop or had a ready excuse.

My concern was that we couldn't believe any of them. That, in turn, increased the heavy load on those investigating. All were concerned about the next mass murder and where it could occur.

That's when Reah, Bel Erland's mother, volunteered to act as Guli in the questioning. She knew the truth from a lie because of her High Demon heritage. I hadn't known there was such a talent until now.

Kooper wanted to question governors and rulers, but was forced to wait (by Alliance Law) until there was sufficient reason to question them.

I'd suggested going to the journalists, feeding them enough information that they carried messages to the population on their world, saying if the politician or ruler of their planet had nothing to hide, they'd welcome the questioning in order to prove their innocence and calm the population.

That plan was implemented quickly. Nobody wanted another massacre, due to hidden poison in their drinking water.

We had a ship of our own, but I believed it to be merely a place for us to sleep and eat, as so many aboard smaller, sleeker BlackWing IX held the ability to fold space.

All of us could mindspeak, and I was more than grateful. Kaldill had carried a glass sphere with two of Quin's black feathers with him when he came on-board. Yanzi said the feathers should be helpful in locating Quin, unless there was too much interference from an unnamed source.

It didn't take much to make the leap; Liron's name was on my mind. He'd created the Orb, which seemed to rule Quin's life. Too many times, it had flung her from one place to another, so the others and I blamed it for Quin's endangerment.

Had we anything from the Orb itself, I believe Kaldill would have hunted it, too, with less than altruistic intentions.

Had I Kaldill's power, I would have considered the same thing.

"We'll get her back," Father spoke softly at my side. "Both of them."

My father, after my mother's death following my birth, had never considered another companion.

Until he'd seen Zaria.

I wanted him to be happy, and Zaria would be the best of all companions for him. In my mind, I could see Father attending state functions with Zaria at his side. The two of them together would be a formidable pair where politics and politicians were concerned.

I realized that family gatherings would be a joy, with Zaria and Quin with us. And, with their other mates, all of whom Father and I liked, it could be even better. I wanted those dinners. Those outings and gatherings.

More than anything.

Those things would help the ache in our hearts—the one caused by the loss of Siriaa. As ill and crippled as it had become before its destruction, we still loved and missed it. It would always be home to us, and one to which we could never return.

We only had our memories, tear-washed and dimming as they were.

～

"Where we go first?" Yanzi turned to Kaldill, who'd set the glass-enclosed feathers aloft and allowed them to float near his seat on the small ship's bridge.

"Goor-Phin. She was there—I can feel it. We must orient ourselves and search from there."

"Very well," Caylon nodded. "Prepare yourselves, I'll fold space with the ship immediately."

~

I never knew of the capabilities Kaldill showed us, once we arrived at the Jordeh Plantation. While the rest of us followed him at a distance, he held Quin's feathers in his left hand while holding the right hand aloft. With fingers widespread, light glowed from his right hand as power was employed.

All about him, images of walls rose. Ghostly furniture appeared atop fine rugs and flagstone floors. When apparitions peopled the spectral spaces, I gasped softly.

None we recognized occupied the kitchen, so Kaldill moved on. Through room after pale and wavering room we wandered, while Kaldill carefully examined every person.

We found Daris Arden occupying what was surely the master's suite. She paced and mouthed words we couldn't hear. Kaldill, with a nod, moved on to the next suite, and the ones after that, until we reached the back of the house.

There, we found Vardil Cayetes and another. I only knew it was Vardil because Kaldill named him. His countenance was much different from the last description I'd read of him.

"In disguise," Caylon whispered softly beside me.

"His valet and assistant, Dorgus," Kaldill spoke softly as he named the second person. All of us stopped still when another walked into the room.

No, the image wasn't one we recognized.

Kaldill stopped breathing for a moment.

Then he cursed—in Elvish.

I didn't know the language, but I understood his tone.

The one who'd walked in—she had irregular features at best, and moved with an awkward gait.

"It changed her," Caylon whispered.

"No," I responded, turning back to the young woman. She looked nothing like my Quin.

"Do not let appearances affect your feelings; this is temporary, to throw us off," Kaldill spoke in Alliance common once more. "This is the one we seek. Memorize her face—you must know it well if you see it again."

Karathia—Past

Zaria

"What's that?" Ilya settled on the side of my bed.

"Just some papers I borrowed," I said. "I was hoping I could get information off them, but no such luck." I refolded the pages and dropped them on the nightstand.

"Want company?"

"Of course I do."

"I was hoping you'd say that." He began removing his boots.

"How are the horses?"

"They're fine. Horel is a pain in the ass."

"He's just bitter because he's not the elite warrior he thought he was."

"He's bitter because he's a horse's ass." Ilya grunted as one boot came off in a slow whoosh.

"Honey, don't insult horses like that," I complained. "Call him what comes *out* of a horse's ass. You know—the stuff flies like so much?"

"Are you saying he's a pile of horseshit?"

"Pretty much."

"It's a good thing I have your bedroom shielded. He's probably attempting to listen in."

"That poor, misguided pile of horseshit," I shook my head as Ilya dropped the second boot on the floor and reached for the buttons on his pants.

"He's not poor. I believe Hegatt has him well-supplied in the money department. You should see his tack and the-um, jewelry he wears."

"I didn't see any jewelry," I began.

"It's not where most can see," Ilya lifted an eyebrow as he stood to drop his trousers.

"Does he have a cock ring?" I gasped.

"It's not a cock ring as cock rings go. It's more like a large piercing. He probably did it to show everybody how high his tolerance for pain is—and to impress the ladies, of course."

"I see," I said, although I wanted to gag. Horel wasn't anybody I'd ever want to bed; I didn't care if his large piercing item was covered in gold and jewels. I figured the only women who'd jump in bed with him were after their own gain or glory.

"Jewelry can only get you so far," Ilya's back muscles rippled as he lifted his shirt over his head.

"Oh, yeah," I whispered, running my hands over those same muscles. "Tell all your Falchani instructors that I really, really like these," I said.

"What, no compliments for me?" He shifted so he was facing me.

"Where do you want me to start?"

"Oh, top to bottom, bottom to top," he grinned.

"Love this," I touched his mouth.

"That's good enough." He grasped my wrist in his hand, kissed my palm and then lowered me to the bed. "Plenty good enough," he mumbled against my mouth.

Cloudsong

Quin

I ducked back into a doorway; Yark suspected he was being followed. That wasn't good for me—especially if he determined *who* was following him. I had no desire to come to Daris' attention; the witch could kill me if she wanted and the Orb allowed it.

I dropped down and made myself as small as possible as Yark's footsteps doubled back. He intended to find the one following behind. Gripping my knees to stop my hands from trembling, I waited for the sturdy, unsympathetic Yark to find my hiding place.

"Oy. Yark. You're needed in her majesty's meeting room," someone called out.

Closing my eyes in silent gratitude, I listened for Yark's footsteps to recede.

Rising on unsteady legs, I peered around the corner to make sure the hallway was clear before venturing out again.

Most of the ancient, crumbling structure was dark at night; if Cloudsong hadn't been a planet pulled back from the brink of death at some point in its existence, I imagined it would be overrun with mice, rats and other animals seeking shelter.

As it was, I'd seen nothing of the sort, including insects. While that was a blessing for Janis, who'd imagined fighting off an army of ants and roaches, there was nothing to invade her food supply.

She kept it tightly sealed in its containers anyway.

What if I wasn't able to save any of them?

What was the Orb's intentions where she and the other servants conscripted by Daris were concerned? Did it intend to let them die— or perhaps bring their deaths?

I understood now that it intended all worlds to die. Deris had servants already on Karathia. Why would anyone bother to transport these when the time came to move there?

I had too many questions and no obvious answers. Yark still held the key I needed. At least on Goor-Phin, the Sirenali had living jungles to run to. Here, there was no safe place to run, once I freed them.

My hope, therefore, lay in those I'd been forced to leave behind. I knew they were searching for me. They wouldn't give up, either, until they found me—alive or dead. I prayed that Kaldill or one of the others would see through the disguise forced upon me by the Orb, else I could die alongside Daris and those who followed or aligned themselves with her and Deris.

A dark chamber beckoned as I slipped from doorway to doorway, hoping not to be seen as I made my way toward the kitchen. It had lights, after all; Daris was forced to fill dark, cracked wall globes with spelled illumination.

Except for bedchambers and suites, nothing else was lit at night. A wise criminal would have left everything else dark so nobody would notice their presence.

In Daris' case, she was too lazy. I knew she was used to being served by others all her life; therefore, she expected someone to do her bidding at all times.

Except when she wielded her power to kill or injure. Deris and she both enjoyed *that*.

Making my way into the empty chamber as carefully as I could, I moved toward the center. In the dimmest of starlight shining through an empty roof, I barely made out what looked to be evidence of fires or blasts scattered throughout.

What had happened here?

It looked to be a place where a battle was fought. Where many had died.

Was that their remains covering the floor in darker patches? All about me, I felt a hush, as if the sky were listening. *Help me*, I pleaded silently, forgetting for a moment that my mindspeech no longer worked.

BlackWing VII

Terrett

Long before the Alliances had developed technology of any kind, the Elf King lived. I doubted I would ever be privy to the Elf King's power, had he and I not been mated to the same woman.

A three-dimensional map hovered above Kaldill's head as he released Quin's feathers.

Instead of floating to the floor, as anyone would expect, they floated upward. I blinked. One went immediately to where we'd seen Quin last—Jaledis. The smaller, more fragile feather hesitated as it searched Kaldill's image, as the areas about it grew in size. I felt as if we were seeing through a focusing glass, as the images became larger and clearer to the eye.

Until it stopped, and the images about it exploded into seeming life.

"Cloudsong," Caylon muttered softly at my back. "Fucking, forsaken Cloudsong."

~

Le-Ath Veronis
Lissa

"There are concealment spells all about the old castle," Kooper barked as he strode angrily through the halls of my palace. As vampire, I could easily keep up with him. Others, not vampire, had a difficult time keeping pace with the angry Director of the ASD.

"The Orb is in charge, now," I reminded him as we made our way toward my study. "It could kill all of them and set those machines free to prey on anything."

"Don't remind me," he hissed and made the turn into my study.

Poor Renée, who stood beside Grant and Heathe outside my study door, remained silent but wore an expression of fear.

I sent mindspeech to Montrose; she'd need his steady hand through this, I imagined. My concern was that Kooper, in the interest of the greater good, would be tempted to blast the whole planet apart —with Quin still on it.

The Orb could shield the machines and still get away with them.

"We can't do anything to Cloudsong without the permission of its Queen," Merrill appeared and spoke level-headed truth.

"Reah," I breathed and slumped bonelessly onto my desk chair.

CHAPTER 16

Karathia—Past
Zaria

I watched Horel and Brill, waiting for any sign of Hegatt's impending attack upon the palace.

I could see in both that they'd visited Hegatt for the past three nights in a row, when they imagined everyone else to be asleep or otherwise occupied.

Marid had completed the ring Hegatt requested, and it was the same one I'd seen in the base of the coffin in Lissa's dungeon.

Essentially, it was a poorly constructed piece of jewelry, but to someone who held power, it was designed as a weapon. Yes, Grey House had been the first to perfect protection spells for objects worn by royalty. Anyone who wasn't authorized would be killed if another took the object and attempted to wear it.

Many crowns across both Alliances were protected in that way.

Marid didn't have the skill or the level of talent Grey House's K'Shoufa jewelers and craftsmen held. This ring could kill anyone who wore it.

Of course, Marid wasn't even aware of the flaws in his design. He'd handed it to Hegatt with a smile while Horel, Brill and Helsa looked on.

Hegatt's plan was to let Helsa wear it first, as Deris' Regent.

The fog surrounding the actual events of the coup was clearing away, revealing painful truths none had recorded.

~

Le-Ath Veronis

Lissa

"Quin could die, and you'd still be no better off," Reah pointed a finger at Kooper. "We don't know what the Orb has planned. Admit that, at least."

Nefrigar, who'd come to support his mate, nodded at Reah's words.

"Look," Kooper attempted to reason with her. "Quin's life—against hundreds and hundreds of millions?"

"It goes deeper than that," Nefrigar interrupted.

"In what way?" Kooper snapped, turning on the Larentii Archivist.

I understood Kooper's concern, but the lesson he hadn't learned yet was, *never get involved in an argument with a Larentii.*

"All worlds lie in Quin's hands," Nefrigar's blue skin darkened and took on the hue of a stormy day. "It was written in that infernal book— the one Liron left at Avii Castle and Halthea destroyed. The Larentii have the only other copy. In it, it explains the method used to save Siriaa from the poison. The same method can be safely employed on all worlds infected with those foul creatures, but it can only be performed by one approved by Liron. In the beginning, the Avii Queen held the ability. She was murdered. Quin remained, although she wasn't allowed to read the book. We understood all along that the Orb had another motive and was far from benign. It holds Quin's life in its clutches. Kill her while destroying those machines and you kill everything else anyway."

No, that hadn't occurred to me. Nefrigar had kept this a secret— and for good reason. Now I understood why the Wise Ones had come to give her life back when it was lost on Siriaa. There was one missing piece, however.

"What does the Orb have that controls her?" I breathed.

Nefrigar grimaced and dropped his gaze. "Something that cannot be removed, lest she die permanently. Together, the Wise Ones brought her body and mind back to life, but they could not remove the device locked in her brain."

"This just gets better and better," Kooper tossed out a hand in angry frustration. "Are you telling me we can't do anything?"

"It is our guess that the Orb will follow Deris and Daris' plan to go to Karathia," Nefrigar replied. "It may set up its base of operations there. I suggest that you warn the King and his allies; war is coming to his doorstep, whether he realizes it or not."

"That's my son on the throne," I frowned at Nefrigar. "What, in your opinion, should we do to prepare for the onslaught?"

"Whatever you wish," Nefrigar shook his head. "Things are moving toward an inevitable conclusion, I believe. What we do from now on may not matter in the least."

~

Karathia

Morid

"He isn't taking us to Cloudsong—for logical reasons," Norn whispered as a bowl of stew was handed to me. "I doubt they'll be gone long. Last night, Kend had a breakthrough, and with the ability Deris and his crowd of allied witches and warlocks hold, I believe they can create the changes in the machines and have them ready for battle in two days."

"Did you say Cloudsong?" I whispered, my food forgotten for a moment. The demise of the House of Belancour had begun the moment Father attempted to manipulate the events surrounding a former King of Cloudsong.

Norn's next words shocked me further. "When they're gone, we're going to get you out of this cage," he added, "and take you to a safe place—or as safe a place as we can find for you."

"You mean I'll be able to stand straight and walk?" I felt tears prick my eyes. My cage wasn't tall enough for me to stand.

"Yes. I hope you've been exercising your legs and arms—they tend to atrophy when kept inactive like this."

"I've done my best," I hung my head.

"My father and I intend to stand with the Royal House of Karathia, after we take you to safety," Norn added.

"Who—Gale is your father?"

"Yes. I was born to him and my mother when he was young," Norn grinned. "Since our ages are not that far apart, many suspect we are brothers." He chuckled, then, and his flash of humor surprised me.

"In a few hours, when Deris and his followers leave, we will come for you."

My mumbled thanks were spoken to his back; Norn had already slipped through the hidden door.

~

Cloudsong

Quin

Ruther Kend may have looked better if he'd passed through Janis' meat grinder. The poor man had worked night and day to deliver what Deris wanted, and had recently found the final problem with the designs he'd been given.

Time was slipping by too fast; I had things to do and no idea how to accomplish all of them.

One thing weighed in my favor, however; Dorgus was occupied in a meeting with Deris, Daris, the Orb and several others, before work began on upgrading the N'il Mo'erti.

Yark's key was a lost cause—he was in the meeting. I had to heal Vardil Cayetes—*the spanner in the works*, as Queen Lissa would say.

The moment I was away from prying eyes, I began to run toward Dorgus and Vardil's shared suite.

◜◝

Karathia—Past

Zaria

One more day remained. I watched Horel as he casually conversed with Wellend and Warlend at the breakfast table, as if he hadn't been given orders to kill them the following day.

I also saw in him that Wallend had been sent to Hegatt's stronghold with the twins while his wife remained at Helsa's palace.

Ilya had already received his orders and left to do Wellend's bidding—spy on his brother and ensure that he was kept safe. This came after Horel told Wellend the lie that Wallend feared for his life and that of his children—brother, nephew and niece to the King as they were.

Neither Ilya nor I failed to notice that Wylend, who'd sent a gift to his older brother as the new King, expressed no such fears. He was happy enough to occupy the summer palace with Lord Morphis and his guards and servants.

Things would change quickly for him within the next two weeks.

I couldn't help thinking of the future, though, and what surely waited to be launched against King Rylend and Prince Bel Erland.

So many loose ends needed tying, and I'd been told not to interfere with the coup.

◜◝

Cloudsong

Quin

For several moments, I watched Vardil Cayetes, whose head drooped onto his breast. He was asleep in the chair in which Dorgus and I had strapped him. At least I knew I could still heal—I'd healed Daris' Sirenali.

They'd likely die when the rest did—I couldn't see that any of them would be useful to Deris on Karathia. That's why I had to do what I'd never have chosen to do before.

Light formed about me as I took a step toward Vardil Cayetes, my known enemy, so I could make him whole again.

～

Karathia—Past

Ilya

Wallend was little more than a pig dressed in a courtier's clothing. I'd only watched him and his children for one full day before coming to that inevitable conclusion. Weakling that he was, Wallend allowed Deris to do whatever he wanted, with Daris looking on in approval.

Together, should the twins be allowed to rule Karathia, they would destroy what they could and then watch Karathia's citizens war among themselves—as long as they didn't make an attempt to take the throne.

I had nothing but contempt for any of them, but still, I watched them from a distance. Perhaps not to keep them safe—I was beginning to see a little of what Zaria could easily understand.

These could not be allowed anywhere near the throne. I think I decided then that if Zaria chose to go against our instructions not to interfere, I would stand with her. Some things were worth giving your life.

This was one of them.

Glad to hear it, a voice sounded in my head. It wasn't Zaria's—it was male. I swallowed with difficulty and began to form my own plan.

～

BlackWing IX

Kellik

Rigo and I had joined Kaldill and the others; he meant to spy on those who'd taken up residence in the old castle on Cloudsong.

Rigo and I could mist in and do a preliminary scout before sending information back to Kaldill. My vampire child and I were ready to go. It had been a very long time since we'd done this sort of reconnaissance; the clothing and equipment had vastly improved in the past several centuries.

Dressed in skin-hugging black leather, we carried ranos pistols, a thin coil of rope capable of holding several times our weight, a grappling hook that folded and a tiny, bright-beamed light. He and I wouldn't need the light to see—we carried it to blind someone should we find it necessary.

"You look like you're prepared for a fight with a ninja," Sal grinned at Rigo, who secured his pistol in its thigh holster.

"Lissa uses that same word at times. I understand it is her native language, but," Rigo began.

"Actually, it's not her native language, although it is one of the languages of old Earth."

"What language?" I asked, curious.

"Japanese," Sal shrugged. "I can get books translated into Alliance common that will explain the Japanese language and culture if you like."

"Of course I would," I said.

"Just get him everything available on old Earth," Rigo said, giving Sal a nod. "He'll have it read and memorized in very little time."

"Shall we?" I deliberately lifted an eyebrow at Rigo.

"Of course, Lord Abenott."

He only used my title when he wanted to laugh at me. "Then we shall go, King Rigo," I replied.

He chuckled, which is what I intended.

Cloudsong
Quin

I will never forget the moment Vardil Cayetes' eyes mirrored a functional mind. That's when V'ili, the Sirenali hunted by the ASD, appeared as if called.

I was elbowed out of the way, as if I presented no threat to each;

they were correct—I merely had no idea what their plan would be once V'ili freed Vardil from his chair restraints.

"They're in a meeting," V'ili hissed. "With Dorgus." I blinked—I'd never heard a Sirenali speak aloud before.

This one could place obsession.

I shrank back as quietly as I could; I had no desire to draw this Sirenali's attention.

"How long?" Vardil's voice was little more than a croak, he hadn't employed it for months.

V'ili echoed my estimation. "We have to get you out of here," V'ili went on. "They want the words to open that coffin."

"They don't work," Vardil hissed, rubbing his wrists where the restraints had chafed. "I've tried. That fool Marid created the spell so only he can open it."

"Perhaps he withheld some of it?"

"It's possible. With that piece of filth, anything is possible. At least he's dead."

"We have his son on Karathia," V'ili muttered. "Come, we must leave before they find you recovered."

"What about Dorgus?"

"You, my friend, can find a valet anywhere. Your life is the one that matters now."

Sinking to my knees in a corner, I realized how things were.

V'ili, originally employed by Cayetes, was merely biding his time with the Arden twins, waiting for Vardil to recover.

I'll admit, if given the choice to serve one or the other, I'd choose Vardil over the twins.

Since the Orb had taken up with them, they'd become doubly dangerous.

Yes, I'd already realized the flaw in my plan. I'd just healed one of the worst criminals the Alliances had ever seen, just to watch him escape with the Sirenali who named himself King of all Sirenali.

He was descended from royalty—yes I saw that in him.

I also saw something else.

Terrett and his brothers didn't know, but V'ili had fathered them.

Even V'ili didn't realize he had sons. He'd dallied with Erithia, never knowing she intended to conceive. Each time, she'd sold their progeny, because she secretly despised V'ili.

I wanted to weep for Terrett and his brothers, none of whom had followed in their parents' footsteps.

Yes, I'd wanted Vardil to cause a stir with Daris and Deris. The tears fell when V'ili folded space, taking Vardil Cayetes away before anyone else was aware.

~

Kellik

Rigo and I—it was as if the universe shifted about us, flinging us from one place to another in as little time as it took to blink.

Whatever had effected the move, it had taken everything inside the ancient castle with it, including two former vampires who were mist.

Disorientation ensued; when finally we got our bearings, we found we'd traveled from one castle to another.

I know this place, Rigo sent mindspeech, his sending thoughtful. *It is the Queen's palace on Karathia. No Queen has stayed here since Helsa Blackmantle-Arden's death.*

Child, I warned.

Bearing down on us were Deris and Daris Arden, and over their heads, a pulsing Orb floated. If I'd been corporeal, my skin would have shivered.

That blazing light knew we were there.

Without my asking, Rigo employed his ability to fold space and flung us far away.

~

Karathia—Present

Quin

Morid, Gale and Norn were gone, in addition to V'ili and Vardil.

Deris had already expressed his fury by destroying an empty wing

239

of the massive Blackmantle home.

Daris was angry enough to destroy another wing, but held back once Deris leveled a nasty look in her direction.

She both worshipped and was afraid of her brother, who held more power.

~

Palace of the King
  Karathia
  Lissa

The moment Rigo and Kell arrived unannounced at the gates of Ry's palace, we knew something had gone wrong.

Kaldill and his crew arrived shortly after, to hear what Rigo had to say.

"I'm sure she was there, we didn't have time to get to her." Rigo held a glass of wine in his hand; only a reserve of steel kept his hand from shaking.

Rylend had seen to his and Kell's needs the moment they were ushered into his study. "The Orb knew we were there—I don't understand how, but it did. It moved everybody from Cloudsong to Karathia. What we didn't see was where the N'il Mo'erti were sent."

"So they're holed up in the Queen's Palace," Erland growled. "Things are happening faster than we anticipated."

"I suggest you call upon your allies, honey," I told Ry. "Do it now. We have no idea how much time we have before they release the N'il Mo'erti on Karathia, and then send them across the Alliances."

~

Karathia—Past
  Zaria

My hands shook only a little as I set the tray of food in front of Wellend. This was the last time he'd sit in his study as King of Karathia.

With the right people about him, he would have been a good King. A just King.

His own family had plotted his death.

His and Warlend's deaths would be recorded in Karathia's history. I wanted to weep for the circumstances that brought us to this point.

I wanted to murder several afterward, for their parts in it.

Only time would tell if anything I'd done would have an impact on the future, and who would eventually sit the throne as the rightful Heir.

Time.

To the Mighty, it could be nothing more than a blink. An irritation. For those of us involved in its everyday workings, it held both hope and disaster.

Even Schrödinger couldn't put time in a box—it was as ethereal as the emptiness between stars and as substantial as the weight of all worlds combined.

So many things depended upon my small nudges and the offering of ideas. Like arranging pieces into a puzzle, it would never become whole unless all were fit into the proper places.

Ilya, I love you, I sent as I nodded to Wellend. *More than you will ever know.*

~

Ilya

Wallend was drinking at a pub near Blackmantle Manor. Even he'd become tired of his son's restless destruction at home. Too many things Deris destroyed were beyond Wallend's ability to set right.

I sat in a corner, nursing a mug of beer that could use improvement in its making when the barkeep slapped a refill in front of Wallend. "Heard yer brother's on the throne, now," the barkeep growled.

Wallend, who'd had too much ale already, chose to argue.

"My brother is not the rightful King. My son, by right according to the last Q'elindi's prophecy, will be King."

241

"I heard yer son is nothing but a useless whelp who likes fire too much fer his own good. Can't be a King if the palace is burned to the ground."

"Filth!" Wallend's spell went awry, knocking bottles and crockery off the shelves behind the bar instead of hitting the barkeep as intended. The scent of fermented alcohol followed the nerve-twisting crash of glass shards and chunks of pottery spilling in crunches and tinkles across a stone floor.

Before I could hold up a hand to stop it, the barkeep sent a Fourth-level blast against a drunken Prince, whose body slammed against the wall near the door and lay there, unmoving.

What followed that day will be burned into my memory; not because it happened, but because I never stopped any of it.

The barkeep had allies, I discovered, and they arrived at the bar in moments. Wallend, already dead, was stripped of his clothing and his body mounted on a pike outside the bar before a mob of at least a hundred gathered to attack Blackmantle Manor.

Hegatt had enemies, it appeared, and if what I feared were true, Deris had fanned the flames of discontent in the surrounding villages by his penchant for harming others. Someone, somewhere, had let it slip that Deris' father and grandfather thought him the rightful heir to the throne. If my guess were correct, Deris himself may have said something.

The people were striking back. What concerned me most, however, was who showed up at the last to lead the charge against Blackmantle Manor.

In disguise, most wouldn't recognize him.

I recognized him easily, as I'd been born during his reign.

Wylend Arden had come to destroy his younger brother Wallend and Wallend's eldest child.

No, I didn't see Lord Morphis anywhere, but that didn't surprise me. It would be easy enough for Wylend to take time away from his lover—time enough to lead the charge against this branch of the family tree.

In ten days' time, Wylend would lead a charge of a different kind—against those usurpers intending to take the throne.

By that time, his eldest brother would be dead.

The Heir's ring hadn't come to him. Did that precipitate this act of violence, or had it been fermenting in Wylend's mind for longer than that?

Had Zaria seen it, and not told me?

That's when her mental voice sounded in my head. *Ilya, I love you,* she sent. *More than you will ever know.*

Could that be a lie as well? I no longer knew what to think.

Yes, the plan I'd made was now less significant than the dust beneath my feet. Whether Wallend deserved death or not, it shouldn't have been delivered in this way, by his brother, who held no place in court. Only the King and his Regent could force Wallend to account for crimes committed.

Wylend had taken matters into his own hands. While he hadn't delivered the death blow himself, he'd likely orchestrated it.

Deris and Daris hadn't reached their majority and remained at Blackmantle Manor, while a mob surged in their direction. Deris had probably been foolish with his words regarding a prophecy he'd only heard once, but this was not justice.

Justice.

It hung upon the tip of a pin. A shift in any direction and it would fall. Once justice fell, only chaos would remain—with murder in its wake.

As despicable as I found Deris Arden, Karathian law prohibited this attack upon him and his sister. Yes, I understood what the future held and argued with myself while precious time passed. With a sigh, I let the argument go.

Deris Arden, I sent, *you and your sister are in danger.* Pulling his father's body off its pike with power, I employed more power to send it to Blackmantle Manor.

This is what awaits you if you stay, I continued.

Your choice is disappointing. The voice was new to me—and female.

~

Karathia—Present

Quin

The adjustments to the N'il Mo'erti must have been minor ones—they were accomplished in little more than a day. I didn't understand how that was possible until one of Deris' loyal warlocks spoke about it at dinner.

"Good thing those machines learn from one another," he grinned and bit into one of Janis' rolls. "Easy enough to tell one and let it tell a hundred more. I think we should keep the cook alive," he spoke around another mouthful. "Good bread."

Would the kitchen crew survive with Janis?

That would be something, at least. For now, too, Dorgus was still alive and still acting as Vardil Cayetes.

I wondered when the twins would learn that Vardil would soon retake his criminal empire. Would his war be with the twins instead of the Alliances?

I had no answers to that question; I only had guilt and shame for what I'd done.

Without Vardil, I was no longer needed to assist Dorgus, who found me repulsive anyway. I offered to help Janis, who'd welcomed me into the kitchen.

She was the only one who knew of Vardil's escape—with the assistance of V'ili. I couldn't bear to tell her the initial mistake was mine. Had I not healed Vardil, he'd still be here. Janis assumed he'd recovered on his own.

The Orb—had chosen to ignore Vardil's escape. I fetched and carried for the servants in the dining hall while fretting about that.

That's when I recalled that the Orb had marked all for death; all, not just Vardil Cayetes. Through Deris and Daris and the deadly machines they held, entire worlds would die in invasions of N'il Mo'erti.

Even Vardil's strongholds would fall if the N'il Mo'erti came. It no longer mattered that he could hide behind Sirenali, or have V'ili place obsession for him. The twins had Sirenali of their own, plus machines not susceptible to any obsession.

"We have after-dinner entertainment," Deris appeared in the dining hall with Dorgus, whose face was purpling with bruises. Dorgus also wore heavy chains—placed there by Daris, who arrived shortly after her brother did.

I went still.

Deris would experiment with his newly repaired machines.

Dorgus would be the target.

Brushing tears away, I shuffled toward the kitchen for another bottle of wine.

Karathia—Past

Zaria

We were forced to watch as the bodies of King and Regent were burned in the castle courtyard. My focus wasn't on the makeshift pyre, or on Hegatt, who stood with arms crossed as he waited for the fire to consume it.

My focus was on Helsa, who held a book in her hand.

No, it wasn't the book that appeared whenever a legitimate heir took the throne. This book was one of her own making. She would force the castle staff to believe that she would rightfully ascend the throne once the bodies on the pyre were gone.

I waited for that moment, with full understanding of what would happen. Nearly a week had passed and word of Wallend's death had reached the palace. Helsa barely acknowledged the loss of her youngest son. Word also had it that Blackmantle Manor, Hegatt's home, had been reduced to ash.

For me, there was no word from Ilya and Deris and Daris had disappeared, if the rumors were correct. Hegatt and Helsa likely had mindspeech from them; they seemed unconcerned by their absence, so they were in a safe place.

Helsa couldn't hide that information from me; I merely didn't wish to take it from her, yet. Deris wouldn't inherit the throne anyway until he reached his majority at twenty-two. Helsa intended to rule until then. Her fantasy would be interrupted soon enough.

In the interim, many had come to pledge their loyalty to Helsa; they feared their homes and families would be targeted if they didn't. Hegatt and his daughter had reputations on Karathia, and neither were good.

I wondered how many of these citizens intended to honor their vows to Helsa and oppose Wylend Arden when he arrived to take the throne. My guess is that their loyalty would lie with whomever came out on top, without their involvement.

The wood of the pyre fell inward with a crash of high-flying sparks, while white-hot coals burned in the depths of thick tree trunks. The crackle of the flames roared a song as smoke drifted and eddied through the courtyard.

I watched, unfeeling, as Helsa finished writing and closed the book she held.

Hegatt nodded to his daughter and both left the courtyard, calling for wine to be served in the Queen Regent's study.

~

Karathia

King's Palace

Lissa

What are they waiting for? I didn't voice my question aloud or send it to anyone—the thought was private as I didn't want to engender fear.

Bel Erland wore the uniform of a Commander in the King's army, his Falchani swords strapped to his back. Drake and Drew had trained him, just as they'd trained Rylend. Gavril arrived, then; I understood that he'd left Tybus in charge of the Campiaan Alliance.

Tory had come as well. These were Ry's brothers and they would stand with him, no matter what the outcome.

Then, the strangest thing happened.

A contingent from Grey House arrived, led by my daughter Nissa and her mates Toff and Trikleer.

Never in written history had Grey House wizards allied with the Royal House of Karathia. It helped a great deal that Ry was related to Grey House, now.

"Mom," Nissa made her way to me and wrapped her arms about my shoulders. I hugged her back and kissed her cheek.

"What are we going to do?" She pulled away, her eyes searching my face for an answer.

"Baby, this is a problem. If they order all those things to attack, we won't know where they're attacking from and spells sent toward the flying bursts probably won't be going in the proper direction. It's the way these things are made. Not only do they have ranos technology, they can send the blasts in loops before they ever reach a target."

"Meanwhile, we could be sending deadly spells toward villages and homes," Nissa shook her head.

"Sit down with me," I led her toward a small chamber outside Ry's throne room. "I need something to drink. We'll discuss this and you can decide whether you want to stay."

"We're here, Mom. To the bitter end." My daughter's mouth was set —much like mine could be. If circumstances were different, the resemblance would have made me smile.

Karathia—Past

Ilya

I hadn't expected to be punished.

Not like this. I'd been informed of my poor choice—and what I should have done instead. I realized how true it was when it was presented to me.

I'd been moved, too—in time.

Presently, I occupied a time six days past—well, six days may as well have been six thousand years.

Zaria was lost to me and I wept.

CHAPTER 17

*Z*aria

Hegatt made sure that all who occupied the palace were in the throne room to witness Helsa's taking of the throne. A page stood close by; the ring Marid crafted now lay on the pillow the boy held.

Many had stayed to kneel at Helsa's feet after she sat the throne.

I waited.

As did Wylend's army.

~

Karathia—Present

Quin

Deris insisted that all attend Dorgus' public execution.

No, I didn't realize what he had in mind. I thought Dorgus' death would be swift.

It wasn't.

The Orb circled Deris' head like an evil crown as spell after spell was leveled at Dorgus. After Dorgus' initial shrieks when small, carefully aimed fires burned his flesh, Daris muted them. They were disturbing her enjoyment of Deris' artistry at torture.

Most of us closed our eyes after that; we had no desire to witness the silent torture of a man whose main crime was allowing his heart to rule his head. That's why I opened my eyes after a while and took Dorgus' life with the talent I held.

None would save his life; therefore, I spared him further torture. Dorgus' body slumped, lifeless, while Deris cursed him, kicked his body and set it aflame again. He hadn't gotten to employ one of his death machines at the last; Dorgus died before Deris could unleash his full fury.

Unless a powerful witch or warlock came—one stronger than Deris—Dorgus' ash would forever stain the courtyard of the Queen's Palace.

I sent up a silent prayer, too, that Dorgus' next life would be easier. My mistakes, considerable as they were, were piling up and I feared I would never be allowed to ask forgiveness from those I'd harmed or offended.

Karathia

King's Palace

Lissa

"Mom, I think we should shield the palace first; I've got eyes in the surrounding villages. We won't fire until they're under attack."

My son, King of Karathia, had spoken. Erland, his father, nodded his agreement. "They will attack those around us—when they determine we're using all our capability to keep the palace safe," Erland said. "Once they begin the attack on the rest of Karathia, then and only then we start firing back."

"We don't have enough firepower to protect every life," Ry turned away to gaze at a painting hanging on a nearby wall. He'd replaced what had hung there during Wylend's reign—a rendering of Wylend's coronation, with a wide beam of light falling on Wylend's image as he lowered his head to accept the crown.

A landscape hung there now, of a large pond with reeds and grasses growing about it. There, a young woman and a boy could be seen skipping rocks on the water.

This was one of Ry's favorite memories of Reah and Gavril; he'd had it painted by a well-regarded artist after Gavril's death.

I considered that for a moment—Gavril had been dead for a time. He'd been granted his life again, not as a favor to him, but to those about him who'd deserved such a gift. Rylend was reliving a memory, gazing upon that painting. I folded away to give him a few moments of peace.

~

Karathia—Past
Zaria

I considered the differences in Wellend's court when he heard grievances, and Helsa's court, as she waited to receive the ring and the crown before sitting the throne.

Wellend had heard everyone, dressed poorly or well. In Helsa's court, only those dressed to Hegatt's standards were allowed in the throne room. All others waited in the courtyard, where the ash from the pyre had left burn marks on the stones.

"It has been recorded in the book," Hegatt, as Regent, announced. "Helsa Blackmantle-Arden will act as Queen of Karathia until her eldest son reaches his majority." He lifted the ring from the velvet pillow, allowing the page to step back. "This is the ring signifying her rule, and will pass to Deris when he is crowned."

Hegatt held it aloft, for all to see. They didn't know, as Bekzi, Gerrett and I did, that it was crafted to inferior standards; the wizard who'd made it long gone with Hegatt's money in his pockets.

I waited, my breathing shallow.

Helsa couldn't hold back the greedy giggle as Hegatt lifted her hand to place the ring. Behind her, shining golden in the light from a high window, stood the throne of Karathia.

My breaths stopped. The ring circled Helsa's finger, but had not yet touched flesh. I wanted to giggle too—from hysteria.

People always think there'll be a moment of joy when someone receives their comeuppance.

Not in this case.

Helsa shrieked when the ring was seated; Hegatt was blown backward by the ensuing blast. Everyone inside the throne room witnessed Helsa's torturous death as she fell to the floor, writhing and screaming as the ring killed her slowly.

I couldn't bear it for long and gave her death, to spare her further pain.

～

Karathia—Present

Quin

The Orb had forgotten me—or so I'd thought.

Until Daris appeared in the kitchen, grinning at Janis before turning that unholy expression in my direction while the Orb bobbed over her head.

It knew.

It knew I'd healed Vardil.

Morid's cage, empty of its previous occupant, waited for me.

No, the Orb wouldn't kill me. Not yet, anyway. Things were coming clear and I cursed myself for being such a fool.

I was a hostage and had been all along. The Orb knew its enemies cared for me. It intended to use that—and me—as bait. Unless the Karathian throne was handed to Deris Arden, it would torture me. It would rule Deris and his sister Regent while the Alliances fell. Worlds outside the Alliances would then fall one by one, until nothing was left.

I wasn't the puppet the Orb created in the beginning, but it still intended to use me to ensure its plans came to fruition. It would torture me if that didn't happen.

Worse, it could hand me to Deris to torture.

I'd already seen his handiwork and it terrified me. Dragging out a death with waiting was torture enough. Adding pain until life left me was so much worse.

My shoulders slumping while Daris tossed pain spells at my back, I was marched through the palace until I came to the storeroom that housed Morid's cage.

Once I was locked inside, Daris leveled one last spell against me, which bent me over in pain. She laughed as she and the Orb left the storeroom; I huddled in a corner of the uncomfortable cage and considered my fate.

Don't let Bel and the others see this, I prayed. *Let them make the right decisions. I accept my punishment. Let them live.*

～

Karathia—Past

Zaria

Wylend's attack came after Hegatt crawled to his daughter's side. She was dead—none would bring this one back to life.

Hegatt knew better than to take the ring from her finger and wear it himself. Instead, all of us watched, horrified as he regained his feet awkwardly, shaking still from the force of the blast. After removing the ring from Helsa's blackened and mangled hand with power, he sent it and her book elsewhere, using up the last of his strength.

The boom against the outside gates of the palace came then, announcing Wylend's arrival.

"I am Regent," Hegatt's voice, meant to be a shout, nevertheless echoed through the throne room. Limping along, he turned and sat on the throne.

If I hadn't held a shield about Bekzi and Gerrett, they'd have been blown back like all the others when Hegatt's body exploded.

Karathia

 King's Palace

 Lissa

"We have a message," Ry's tone informed me that something unexpected—and terrible—had happened.

"What?" I demanded.

My son's face looked as if he'd dealt with a thousand years of intense pain when he handed the folded paper to me.

Yes, I fully believed the note to be from Deris or Daris when I opened it to read.

Liron had finally revealed his hand—by signing the message at the bottom.

Images flitted across the surface of the paper. I'd seen Kaldill accomplish something similar, but this was nothing the Elf King would ever consider.

"Call all of Quin's mates. Immediately," I snapped at Corolan, who waited by the door to Ry's private study. "We need them here. Now."

This would kill Bel Erland.

All the images unfolding across the message depicted Quin in her new guise, and all of them involved torture.

Bel Erland

Even Bleek turned his head away after seeing the first few images. No matter what we decided, I felt Quin's life was over. Liron would never let her live, even if we capitulated and allowed Deris to take the throne.

Quin—that would be the last thing she'd ever want.

Dad and Granddad's faces were pale and worn—*surely they weren't considering this.*

"Dad?" I walked toward him.

"Baby boy?" He hadn't called me that in ages. Not since I'd grown a

253

CONNIE SUTTLE

full set of teeth. I was wrapped in his arms quickly—I knew he loved me. Mom arrived, and she hugged us both. "We're not giving them the throne," I mumbled against Dad's shoulder. "If you don't want to go with me, I'll understand."

"Where are you going?" Dad's eyes were misty as he and Mom pulled away.

"We're waiting on them to attack us. Well, I'm not waiting anymore. Liron intends to kill us, no matter what. I'm going to attack the Queen's Palace and everybody in it. Quin's being tortured. At least we may gain her a swift, clean death."

～

Lissa

I offered transportation to Ry's army—which now included all of Quin's mates. Kaldill—I'd never seen the Elf King dressed for battle before.

Instead of fine fabrics, Kaldill was dressed in shades of green, the colors blending and changing with their surroundings. Kaldill, with the power he held, could walk unseen past anyone. He held no weapons—he'd fight using only his talents and the experiences of who knew how many lifetimes.

I'd heard from Ildevar Wyyld, too.

He was ready to prepare all worlds for the onslaught if Liron won this battle. I waited to see what else he'd packed inside that Orb—or *who* else he'd packed inside it.

Quin's glass spheres gained a new perspective and respect—Liron had devised them. All of them, except the few she'd taken away with her, lay in the bowels of Avii Castle.

Did some of them contain sleeping rogues?

I felt ill.

All along, our doom lay no farther than the glass castle and what was hidden inside it. Where were the Three? Had they no concern for any of this? I admit; the choices lying ahead of us terrified me.

~

Karathia—Past

Zaria

Wylend Arden never saw Helsa's body—a handful of his allies hidden in the crowd removed her before he strode into the throne room as if he'd owned it all along. Behind him were Erland Morphis, Gale and Norn.

Except he called those two by different names. "Corolan, will you dispose of this ash—here and in the courtyard?" Wylend asked, turning to blond-haired Gale.

"Without a doubt, my King," Corolan grinned before attending to the task. In moments, Hegatt's ash lifted from the marble floor and hung in midair as he considered what to do with it.

Before he caused it to disappear, he turned toward me.

And winked.

~

Karathia

King's Palace

Lissa

"Ready?" Erland asked. Commanders, Generals, Captains and others filled Ry's throne room. Outside in the courtyard, others waited to be transported to the Queen's Palace.

"Kell?" I cast a puzzled glance at him and Rigo.

"It is my belief that no Sirenali can place obsession on a very old vampire," Kell flashed a smile. "We go, Lady Queen, to do whatever we can."

"Good. If you find Quin, mist her out of there, all right?"

"As you command, my beautiful Queen," Kell bowed.

"Lord Abenott, that is my wife," Rigo muttered beside Kell.

"Duly noted, King Rigo," Kell straightened, still grinning. "Duly noted."

"We go," Bel Erland nodded to me. I transported all of them to the Queen's Palace, which had stood empty for thousands of years.

Bel Erland

All our deaths were assured when the massive line of N'il Mo'erti assembled outside the gate of the Queen's Palace. We couldn't fold space farther than that; something stopped Gran from getting us any closer.

I assumed it could only be Liron, protecting himself and the ones inside the palace.

The machines that opposed us were faceless enemies, instructed to fire if attacked. Looking down the line, I watched Bleek and Lafe pull blades from scabbards at their backs.

They had no power, yet they were willing to fight anyway. Berel stood with them, a single blade gripped tightly in his fist.

Terrett stood next to Berel; I'd never seen him in his other form, before. He looked deadly against humanoids. We didn't face humanoids.

We all appeared weak against this army of machines. Anyone with power would realize this gathering of N'il Mo'erti was only for show. These were expendable. The real army lay elsewhere, ready to strike when we cast the first blow against the ones we could see. It was a standoff, and I knew it.

"Leave now, or she dies."

Liron, tall, white-winged and angry, appeared before us; Quin, looking small, wingless and weak, struggled in his grasp.

She bore evidence of burns across her body, although her face had been restored. Liron wanted to leave no doubt to any of us that he held her captive and at his mercy.

Be brave baby, I sent to her.

My mindspeech bounced right back inside my skull. He'd done the same to her—cut off her mindspeech so nobody could reach her.

There would be no messages of love between us before we died—

and we would surely die. Gran—I'd seen it in her face. Liron had some sort of power backing him, and I had no idea what it could be.

Deris and Daris appeared, then, while the Orb—Liron's hiding place—floated above their heads.

They were Liron's puppets, now. He no longer needed Quin to do his bidding—that much was obvious.

"No arguments?" Liron cackled.

"Raise your weapons," Deris commanded. Every N'il Mo'erti at his back lifted its guns.

"It's a pleasant day to die," Bleek announced, dipping his head to Liron in the traditional, Blevakian way.

At any other time, it would have been a pleasant day. Puffy clouds floated past on an unseen breeze; fall had come to Karathia while I'd been occupied with other things.

"On my command," Deris raised his right arm. When it fell, the battle would begin.

In slow motion, I watched Deris' arm descend while he laughed.

"Stand down," a voice shouted, and followed those words with others I failed to understand.

Deris' arm dropped. Quin shrieked in pain as Liron flung her to the stones at his feet.

Unable to move, I blinked at the scene unfolding before us.

Karathia

Queen's Palace

Lissa

Every N'il Mo'erti's weapon dropped to its metal, mechanical side. "Raise your weapons," Daris shouted at them.

He even leveled spelled blasts against two, who remained unmoving.

What the hell just happened? Winkler sent. He'd come; I merely didn't realize it until then.

I think it's more like who the hell just happened, I responded. Liron was furious, that much was certain. I imagined that Quin suffered broken bones, he'd thrown her so forcefully against the stones of the courtyard. I hoped she'd remain unconscious—if she woke, the pain would be excruciating.

Deris and Daris, faced with an angry army of witches and warlocks, began to back away, looking to hide behind N'il Mo'erti that no longer followed their commands.

Or Liron's.

Their Karathian allies either cowered inside the Queen's palace or had folded space to get away when things began to turn against them.

"Show yourself!" Liron shouted, his wings unfurling at his back. "I wish to see my enemy, who has chosen to die first!"

"You look just like an angel. Except for the nasty grimace. You should work on that," Zaria appeared before the rogue god. With Black hair crackling about her, she still looked small and insignificant against Liron's might.

"You are nothing, Q'elindi," Liron snarled at her.

"Maybe not." All of us stepped back for a moment when she changed. This way, her height was nearly that of Liron's.

Corinnelar, the Larentii had arrived.

Liron knew her, now.

"Come closer and I kill the girl," Liron hissed.

"Really?" Zaria barely lowered her eyes to Quin, who'd wakened and now huddled in pain, weeping at Liron's feet.

"Once she is dead, I care not what you do, Larentii. I will see the worlds die."

"Then I'll save you the trouble on this one."

Yes, my legs refused to hold me up when Corinnelar held out a hand and reduced Quin's body to a pile of pale ash.

Bel Erland

"No!" My shout was echoed by Bleek, Lafe and the others. If Rigo hadn't appeared at my side to hold me back, I would have run toward what little remained of my love.

That would have been a mistake; Liron would have killed me with half a thought.

Deris and Daris turned to run inside the castle, but something stopped them. Yes, I'd heard it was done before, but this time, it appeared even more humorous—to all except Quin's mates and loved ones.

Daris shrieked inside her invisible ball, running faster and faster, only to make the ball rotate with her until she fell. Her ball continued to rotate for a moment, flinging her about inside it. Deris discovered his cage fast enough; he stopped running and sat down to pout, much like a spoiled child.

Light formed about Liron—his anger was rising.

Zaria didn't seem to care. For me, it didn't matter that she was Larentii. I intended to kill her the first chance I got, for murdering Quin.

Holding out a hand, Zaria *Pulled* something from Quin's ash. From where I stood, it looked like a bubble ball with fragile spikes. The object settled onto Zaria's outstretched hand.

"So this is it—how you knew where Quin was and forced her to do your bidding. You're a colossal asshole, you know that?" Zaria accused Liron. The object she held winked out of existence in a flurry of sparks.

"You no longer have any hold on Quin without that," she shook a finger at Liron.

"She's dead. It doesn't matter anyway," Liron pointed out. Yes, I could see he wanted to kill her too—but something held him back.

"Ah, how little you know," Zaria laughed. "Remember when we met before, Liron? When I told you that only a few had the power to bring someone back from the dead, and that you weren't one of those few?"

"As you are not, either," Liron insisted. "Larentii or not, I grow tired of this conversation with you. You threatened to kill Siriaa, and it died. I will have no mercy."

Zaria laughed. Rigo was forced to hold on tighter as my fists clenched. I never wanted to kill anyone so much in my life.

"Your own people killed Siriaa," Zaria chuckled, waggling her finger at Liron. "With the help of a foolish wizard you employed to hide Fyris and the poison it contained from all others. That's how Siriaa died. I used what I saw in you to get you to leave Earth. The plan you came up with set the destruction in motion. I had nothing to do with it."

Down the line, I heard Berel gasp. Somehow, Zaria had forced Liron's hand; he'd acted and the result was Siriaa's destruction. I imagined that Berel now wanted to kill Zaria as much as I did.

"I do not accept this blame—it is all your fault," Liron snapped.

"You know, I'm really tired of listening to you," she stated flatly. "I have other, more important things to do, and none of them include listening to a delusional rogue."

"What?" Liron's voice sounded like thunder.

"Things like this." Zaria the Larentii held out a hand while her entire body began to glow with blinding light. Even Liron took a step backward and hid his eyes with a wing.

The rest of us gaped as Quin's ash stirred, rose in the air and reformed. Bones became visible, and then were surrounded by organs, muscle and flesh.

Quin fell with a sigh once she landed on her feet, her hair long and blonde, with streaks of gold, silver and copper whipping about her face. The three metallic colors in her hair matched the bands on the ends of lovely, white feathers. She was naked—until Zaria clothed her.

Reaching out, Liron's hand grasped for Quin, who disappeared before he could touch her.

"Nope," Zaria said. "Not even if you say please."

"Then I kill you," Liron pulled power to him. He intended to blast all of us—not just Zaria. I could see it easily in his face.

His light—and power—flickered.

Eyes opening wider, he tried again. This effort was weaker. Less.

The Orb moved over his head.

Quin appeared next to me.

"Destroy the Orb," she whispered and nearly fell.

By that time, Bleek and Berel had reached us; Bleek's arms went around Quin while Berel moved in front of them, his blade held steady before us.

Kill the Orb! Zaria's voice startled me from a near-trance.

Mustering the blasting spell Granddad taught me, I launched it against the Orb the moment a thousand Larentii appeared.

CHAPTER 18

*K*arathia
　　　Queen's Palace
Terrett

Nobody understood why the N'il Mo'erti failed to heed Deris' command. They'd been prepared to fire at us. Perhaps we could have destroyed some of them, but there were others waiting to kill us from another location.

Until Zaria arrived and became a Larentii.

I watched Quin die and then live again. Whatever Liron employed to control Quin was now gone—we'd all watched as Zaria destroyed it.

Liron—I could see he wanted to shrink into himself the moment Bel Erland launched the spell that destroyed his Orb.

It had been his hiding place for years, but Bel destroyed it in a blast of blinding light. Quin sagged against Bel Erland afterward, and he was more than happy to lift her in his arms.

Why have the Larentii come? Berel sent mindspeech.

At least a thousand had appeared randomly throughout our crowd. Liron knew they'd come. He was fearful as a result.

Two Larentii waded through our army to stand beside Zaria.

"Who are you?" Liron feigned contempt. He was terrified by now.

Why was a god terrified of the Larentii?

"I am Valegar, son of Nefrigar, Archivist for the Larentii," the blond Larentii spoke.

"I am Kalenegar, son of Ferrigar, Head of the Larentii Council," the red-haired Larentii spoke. "This is Corinnelar, our mate," Valegar nodded toward Zaria.

She had another name? I was astounded.

"My father was killed by a rogue god," Kalenegar said. "I know exactly what happens when a Larentii dies," he added.

It appeared that Liron did, too. He made himself smaller.

"What do you want?" Liron asked.

"Whatever Corinnelar wants," Kalenegar said. "But first we wish to inform you that all the glass spheres at Avii Castle have been removed. They now rest upon the Larentii homeworld, where you cannot siphon the power they hold."

Liron went completely still.

As did I.

Lissa

"What are you cheering for?" Charles appeared at my side with no warning, causing me to jump.

"What the hell are you talking about?" I hissed, elbowing him in the ribs.

No, it wasn't wise to elbow Wisdom in the ribs, but really, he had it coming. Besides, you didn't cheer for a *what*, you cheered for a *who*. I wanted to follow up my first question with a *"Where the hell have you been?"* but I didn't. I figured he already knew what I was thinking—Wisdom was like that.

"No, it's a what. What should Zaria do with Liron?"

"Oh. Now I get it, yuk, yuk," I muttered. "Well, I'd like to see his particles scattered, but he'd have to be truly corporeal to do that."

"It can be arranged," Charles shrugged. "We owe Zaria—Corinnelar —whatever name she wants to use," he said.

"Then why are you asking me instead of her?"

"Because you're going to have to deal with your own problem in very short order. I thought I'd give you a pleasant experience before we get to the hard stuff."

"You can't get harder than this," I insisted.

"You say that now," Charles waggled a finger, much like Zaria had at Liron.

His words troubled me—they were a warning. I had no idea what he meant and I didn't like getting blindsided.

"I'll send a message to Zaria. At least she'll listen, unlike that asshat Ilya."

Charles disappeared. I think the entire army went to its knees when Zaria held out a hand and reduced Liron to winking sparks that died within seconds.

~

Avii Castle
  Berel
None of us saw Zaria again for weeks. Speculation was that she was on the Larentii homeworld. Quin chose to stay with Bel Erland on Karathia, but she'd been visited by all her mates—except one.

Justis waited for her at Avii Castle, so I chose to wait with him. Deep within the bowels of the glass behemoth, no more glass spheres remained. Queen Lissa had misted inside the cavern and come out again, shaking her head.

Not even the tiniest marble remained.

She'd been visited by both her Larentii mates, or so I'd heard, and appeared afterward more thoughtful than before. I wished I'd been invited to that meeting, but not even her other mates attended.

Deris and Daris were captives inside power light cages in King Rylend's dungeon, awaiting a day of judgement. I had no idea when that day would come, but I'd already sent mindspeech to Bel Erland, asking to attend. He responded, saying all who desired could do so.

The whole thing seemed anticlimactic to me in some ways, and still I pondered how the N'il Mo'erti had been rendered powerless.

I believe that question lay on many minds, with no ready answers available. What I do know is this; all those machines disappeared when the Larentii left Karathia. I assumed they did something with them, but I couldn't guess as to what that might be.

There was a sadness in Quin, too, that I imagined was due to her temporary death. I, like all the others, skirted that issue. She was alive now and that's all we wanted.

"If you had wings," Justis turned toward me as we stood on the balcony outside his suite, "I'd ask you to fly with me around the castle."

"What color wings should I have?" I asked, smiling at the king.

"Blue—the scholar's color," he said without hesitation. "You deserve them."

~

Le-Ath Veronis

Lissa

Seldom did outsiders receive royal commands to appear at hearings conducted by the Karathian court. Included in my invitation was a guest list of other invitees. The list was rather long and included my father, my grandfather Wylend, and several others connected to Wylend's court.

It did involve family though—this hearing, so I supposed anyone with connections to Deris and Daris were commanded to come, although a few of the names puzzled me.

Quin's presence was required; all her mates were strongly advised to attend as well. Quin would testify against Deris and Daris—I had little doubt as to that. She'd been forced into their operation by Liron, disguised as the Orb.

I hadn't spoken to her since the incident on Karathia—she'd been busy reuniting with her mates, although she chose to spend most of her time on Karathia.

Zaria—Corinnelar—I had no idea where she was. When I asked my Larentii mates, they didn't hazard a guess, either. I assumed she was with Valegar and Kalenegar; they'd come to help her on Karathia, so it made sense.

Edden Charkisul asked often whether I'd heard anything from her. The answer was always no—with an apology. He'd been invited to attend the hearing as well.

~

Karathia

Bel Erland

Valegar had asked for some time before we passed judgment on Deris and Daris. My father was happy to allow it.

"Tea?" Corolan set a cup of my favorite at my elbow while I sifted through questions Dad and I wanted to ask of the twins.

Their ultimate fate depended upon the answers.

"Thanks, Corolan," I smiled at him. He'd watched after me so many times when I was small. Sang songs to me when I went to bed and helped me filch food from the kitchens when I was hungry.

He'd stayed with Dad when he took the throne after Wylend's abdication, while Garek, Wylend's other mate, chose to go with Wylend.

Both had been with Wylend from the beginning, although I had no idea of their history before Wylend took the throne.

"You're going to learn a lot today," Corolan sighed. "I trust you not to be hasty in your judgments."

"They're filth," I shook my head at Corolan. "Whatever Dad decides to do with them, I'll support."

"I doubt that's the only thing you'll see or hear today that will affect things going forward."

"What do you mean by that?"

"Nothing, perhaps. Perhaps everything." He shrugged and folded space.

"Son, we have an addition to the hearing," Dad poked his head inside my study.

"Who?" I blinked at Dad, expecting the name of some ally or courtier currently in favor.

"Morid of Belancour," he said.

~

Karathia—King's Palace
Nefrigar, Chief Archivist
Larentii Archives

Hearings at any royal court seldom begin on time. This one was no different. Valegar and I had come, as the outcome of this particular hearing could affect a great many things.

I couldn't help noting that the Lyristolyi drug played a role in the events scheduled for discussion and somewhere, I feared that more of it was available, as it had been to Dorgus, Vardil Cayetes' assistant.

Dorgus' violent death had been reported; I merely waited for official word and an accurate description.

"All rise for the King and Crown Prince," Corolan announced. All attendees rose, including Valegar and me. After all, it was wise to follow court protocol, as things were generally made easier with compliance.

Steps echoed on marble floors as King Rylend and Prince Bel Erland made their way to the throne. Rylend would sit the throne; Bel Erland sat on the step at his father's feet.

Nearby, Corolan and Erland Morphis had chairs, in case the King or Prince needed anything.

The rule of law on Karathia is that none sit the throne except the King. In his absence, should he ask someone to stand in for him, the King exchanges the throne for a replica.

On this day, I determined we'd learn why that was.

Father, Valegar sent mindspeech.

267

Corinnelar had arrived, bringing two others with her. While she chose to be Zaria today, we understood she could be either or both if she wanted.

The two with her—I imagined we'd learn their identities in good time. "All are present, my King," Corolan turned toward Rylend, who'd taken a seat on the throne.

"Please, be seated," Rylend lifted a hand. All present took their seats.

That's when the coffin arrived; Lissa had arranged for the thing to be removed from her dungeon for this hearing. The Blevakian, with his son sitting beside him, frowned deeply at the elegantly carved burial box.

"Bring the prisoners," Rylend said, once the coffin was in place before the throne. Deris and Daris wore surprised looks when their powerlight cages appeared next to the coffin.

For so long, they'd attempted to open it and get what was inside. Today, perhaps, all would see what it held in its depths.

Terrett

Morrett and Gerrett sat with me in the balcony placed above the throne room. From there, we could see and hear everything easily.

Gerrett had been absent for weeks; Morrett and I learned only that morning that he'd spent time with Zaria.

What troubled him—and Zaria—was Ilya's absence. Nobody had seen him.

"This hearing will now begin," Corolan announced from the floor beneath us. All of us turned toward the events below.

Quin

Except for the weight of my guilt, I felt good. Better than good, actually. I was healthy, had all my memories and still loved all my mates.

Only one thing stood between us, and it was of my own making. Today, I intended to tell those present that I'd released Vardil Cayetes, healthy and whole, to trouble the Alliances.

It also worried me that I could be accused of aiding a known criminal for my actions. I was concerned that the Royal House of Karathia would no longer wish to be allied with me, following my announcement.

Therefore, I laced my fingers together to stop their trembling as Zaria came forward. Did I blame her for my temporary death?

Not at all. I'd not have blamed her if she'd left me dead. I considered that she likely knew what I'd done and had chosen to allow me to tell the truth of it.

It shamed me, and only hours separated it from those I cared for.

"May it please your majesties," Zaria began, "I wish to hear Wylend Arden tell of the coup against King Warlend, and how he came to the throne of Karathia."

Bel Erland

Why does she want to hear that—we already know it, I sent to Dad.

Maybe there are some here who need to hear it for the first time, Dad replied. *I'll allow it.* "Very well," he spoke aloud. "The court calls Wylend Arden, former King of Karathia to come forward and speak as requested."

Wylend strode toward the center of the room with confidence. I'd heard this story from him; Gran heard it much later, but it was the same story.

Wylend nodded to all present and began his tale.

"You say," Zaria stated as Wylend finished the tale, "That Warlend was King when the coup happened?"

"He was."

"Why do you lie?" Zaria asked him.

My breath stopped. Dad leaned forward, as if he hadn't heard clearly the first time. From the corner of my eye. Grampa Erland rose from his seat; after all, he and Wylend still spent time together. Grampa had helped Wylend when he took the palace away from those who'd killed Warlend.

"I do not lie," Wylend hissed. His words hit me in the gut—no idea how I knew it, but I did. He was lying and Zaria had caught him at it.

"Wellend was King, wasn't he? Warlend abdicated in favor of his son. You were there, were you not, when Warlend made this announcement?"

Zaria waved an arm and a marble-topped table appeared between her and the glass-topped coffin. Papers were lined up evenly across the top of that table. Zaria lifted one of them, glanced at it briefly, then set it down again.

Deris and Daris, whose cages held them mute, were nodding enthusiastically.

What is happening? I asked Dad.

I have no idea, he replied.

"Would you like a chair?" Zaria asked Wylend, who was beginning to appear uncomfortable.

"Yes," Wylend snapped. He was angry; anyone could see it. "I wish to remind you that I am not on trial here," he added.

"But we must hear the truth before Deris and Daris' fate can be decided," Zaria said. "Back to the question at hand—did you or did you not witness the abdication of your father in favor of Wellend, his eldest son? Remember, I am Q'elindi as well as the Vhanaraszh. I can see the lies, Wylend Arden."

I don't think I heard anyone breathing in the throne room by that time. Dad's shoulders stiffened. If Wellend were King, what did that mean? For me, things were going in a direction I didn't expect, and I wasn't sure I liked it.

"Yes," Wylend gripped the arms of the chair that had been brought in with power. "Warlend abdicated on his birthday, leaving Wellend to take the throne. This filth," he hissed, turning and pointing to Deris, "Was denied the heirship—both by my father,

Warlend Arden and by the Heir's ring. When Wellend pulled the ring from his finger, it disappeared. It never went to Deris or anyone else in that room."

"Including you?" Zaria asked softly.

"Yes, may the gods damn it," Wylend muttered.

"Let's move forward, then," Zaria said. "Wellend took the throne. How quickly did Helsa and Hegatt, her father, take the palace after Wellend was named King?"

"Less than a month," Wylend hung his head. "Hegatt was so sure the last Q'elindi's prophecy named Deris the King Karathia needed, that he did everything in his power to give him that chair." Wylend pointed toward the throne.

"Deris wasn't old enough," he continued, "so Hegatt decided to place Helsa there until Deris reached his majority. There was just one hitch—instead of killing Warlend, like he intended, he had to kill Wellend instead, in order to take the throne."

"What did you do during the time Hegatt and Helsa took over?" Zaria asked.

"Nothing. When I heard of the coup, I put an army together to take back the throne."

"Nothing?"

Wylend didn't speak.

"Do you mean to tell me that you didn't have an army ready before that time? That one of your trusted warlocks never ran a pub in the small village near Blackmantle Manor, where Wallend and his two children had gone to stay safe?"

"Narr was a trusted friend, that's true," Wylend admitted.

"And he was a warlock strong enough to take Wallend down, isn't that right?"

"Why are you asking these blasted questions?" Wylend erupted. "You already know the answers."

"But the others here don't," Zaria said. "After Narr leveled a spell blast against Wallend, killing him, he notified you. You came in disguise, didn't you, to march against Blackmantle Manor, kill Wallend's heirs and burn the manor to the ground."

"I never killed them," Wylend stood and flung a hand toward Deris and Daris. "You see them there, don't you?"

"Only because they were warned of your coming. All you had to do was take them and keep them imprisoned until you took the throne, and then pass judgment. Yet you did not. You intended murder, didn't you, Wylend Arden?"

"There is no way I'd let that insane bastard sit the throne," Wylend shouted, flinging a hand in Deris' direction. "He hurt people, just to make his sister laugh."

"I fully understand that, yet you went about this in the wrong way, did you not?"

"I served as a good and just King. My intentions notwithstanding, I never killed either of them. You see them standing there, do you not, with murders stacked against them to their hairlines and beyond?"

"Did you kill Helsa or Hegatt?"

"I never saw either body. Both were dead when I walked into the palace."

"So this was a bloodless coup on your part, if you don't count Wallend, that is."

"Yes. I walked into the fucking palace and everybody there went to their knees. End of story."

"Why did you lie about Wellend being King?"

Zaria's voice had gone soft.

"Because of the fucking Q'elindi and the fucking prophecy. That he'd father one who'd be the ruler Karathia waited for. He was weak and childless with two wives, because," Wylend didn't finish.

"Because you created the spell that left him sterile when he married his first wife," Zaria said.

I'd only imagined the stillness in the room before. Now it was more silent than a tomb. Wylend Arden was guilty of fratricide and of treason against the Crown Prince and the throne of Karathia.

"Then who would have taken the throne?" Wylend snapped. "The Heir's ring disappeared that night. It didn't come to me or Deris. Or Helsa or Daris, for that matter. It's gone forever," he added. "There wasn't anyone to take the throne after Wellend and Warlend died. So I took it."

"You say the ring's gone forever?" Zaria asked.

"It never reappeared. I always assumed it made its way back to its maker."

"Do you know who that was?"

"No. I only know it came from Grey House."

"Did you know the throne was also crafted by Grey House?"

Dad's and my eyes went straight to the throne upon which he sat. We'd never asked that question. We knew, however, that the throne was far older than the Heir's ring.

"So the ring disappeared when there was no Heir for it to choose, yet the throne remained. Can you explain that?"

"I cannot."

"Perhaps I can, then." Zaria sighed before reaching into the bosom of her silk tunic and extracting the bauble on the end of a necklace.

With power, she removed it from the chain and set it on the table beside her.

I knew it from written descriptions.

Zaria held the Heir's ring.

"Do you not recall that Warlend asked all servants to come to the dining hall to witness his abdication in favor of Wellend?" Zaria's gaze leveled on Wylend once more.

"Helsa had so many servants, some lasting as little as a day, that I paid them no mind," Wylend stuttered.

"I was there," Zaria said. "The ring came to me."

Lissa

"What the hell is this supposed to mean for our son?" Erland demanded. Already he'd distanced himself farther from Wylend, who wore a lost look as he stood beside a window in the palace library.

"I doubt it means anything," I said. "I don't believe for a nanosecond that Zaria intends to take the throne away from Ry."

Charles had been right, of course. This was a problem for me, because I'd just learned my grandfather was guilty of having one brother murdered and committing treason against the other.

Ry had called a short recess; I imagined it was to allow him time to digest what he'd just learned.

"Wallend was a prick," Erland picked up the thread of our discussion.

"Honey, pricks are everywhere. It doesn't mean you get to murder them anytime you want," I pointed out. I think what irritated Erland most was that Wylend had done his misdeeds right under Erland's nose and Erland hadn't seen it.

"His children were criminals—even before they reached their majority," Erland went on.

"And that will be dealt with soon, I'm sure," I said dryly. "Honey, you loved Wylend so it was difficult to see those things in him. You saw only good, and that's what he wanted you to see."

"Fuck." Erland was far from happy. Wylend always did have a dual-sided personality; it had appeared before, when he'd alienated Reah.

At least he was sorry afterward for that one.

This—he wasn't sorry at all. He'd gotten what he wanted—the throne of Karathia. I had a feeling there was more to this story and Zaria was waiting to tell it.

Quin

"From Zaria," a note was placed in my hands by a white-gloved servant.

I was afraid to open it. What if she called me out just as she'd called out the former King of Karathia? Would I have to sit in the chair next, while answering questions that would surely destroy me?

With shaking hands, I unfolded the paper to read.

Quinnie B, she wrote, *people make mistakes. You meant to do a good deed and I name you blameless in this. Never fear, we will catch Master Cayetes—together.*

Z.

Wiping tears away, I tucked the note in a pocket. "Dearest," Kaldill suddenly stood before me, a beautiful, white silk handkerchief in his hand. I accepted it gratefully.

"She told you, didn't she?" I dabbed my eyes.

"She did, but it was something I'd already guessed. Don't fret, my love. Cayetes will not elude us forever. Janis and the other servants are asking after you," he added. "Janis had to be told twice that you're the Avii Queen—with feathers and everything."

"Can I see her? I wish I could hire her. She's such a wonderful cook," I wiped more tears.

"Zaria tells me that there may be a solution to the poison problem, but she will only discuss it with you," Kaldill smiled.

"I love you so much," I wept.

"And I you." Kaldill lifted my face and kissed away remaining tears.

Ilya

For thousands upon thousands of years, I wandered Karathia, operating a Blacksmith's shop here and there to buy food and lodging. When the time of my actual birth came and went, I realized that a second version of me was out there, learning from the Falchani and playing at being a warrior.

I won't say I didn't learn things through the years, because I did.

Mostly what I learned was what not to do the next time.

Yes, all it would have taken to prevent so many deaths was to go to Blackmantle Manor myself, place Deris and Daris in restraints—I held sufficient power to do so—then take them to Wylend Arden after he became King. Their fate would likely be the same, but so many people wouldn't have died in the interim.

I'd feel responsible for all those deaths, even if they hadn't been pointed out to me by someone few had ever met.

Sitting at a pub table while the Mighty Heart measured you and found you wanting is far from a comfortable experience.

My punishment was this; she'd left me in the past, to work my way forward in time and learn whatever lessons came my way. By this time, I had a far greater respect for Zaria Keppler than anyone could ever imagine.

I sat in the back row of the upper balcony, watching the proceedings as she leveled accusation after accusation against Wylend Arden. She'd known all along he wasn't innocent, as he'd claimed.

If only I'd followed her lead, I wouldn't have been left to wander aimlessly throughout Karathia for millennia, under an assumed name.

She held the Heir's ring—all the more reason for me to have followed her lead.

Rafe Blacksmith, people called me through the centuries. Time had weathered my face and callused my hands. My parents would no longer recognize the son they'd raised. They'd be ashamed if they knew what I'd done.

"Time to begin again," Corolan announced. There was a gleam in his eye—I could see it, even as far away as I was from him.

Zaria

"Q'elindi," Rylend Morphis dipped his head to me as I took my place next to the table I'd brought in. We were done with Wylend Arden. Time to turn to Deris and Daris.

"Terrett," I turned my eyes upward to the balcony where he and his brothers sat. "Will you join me, please?"

Terrett rose and made his way to the steps leading downward to the throne room floor.

"It's time," I smiled at him.

"Time for what?" Rylend asked.

"Time for Terrett to open the coffin," I said.

CHAPTER 19

errett
 For decades, I served Vardil Cayetes, before he gave me to Marid of Belancour. Marid knew I was mute. He thought me mostly deaf and stupid as well. He paid it no mind that I was listening on the day he spoke the spelled words to seal the coffin belonging to the twins.

Yes, I knew what they were.

Zaria was asking me to reveal that secret—and the other one I kept as well.

Yes, I'd received a gift from one powerful beyond measure. I would use it now.

"When Marid of Belancour spoke the words of the spell he employed to seal this coffin," I croaked, "He cared not that I was listening. My tongue had been removed, you see, by the one my mother sold me to when I was young. I was passed from one criminal to the next, until Marid died and I was imprisoned. There, the unlikeliest person rescued me." I turned toward Quin.

"Sometime afterward, I was given a great gift and told that I would know when the time was right to employ it. I was given speech, and I am using it now."

Turning toward the coffin, I spoke a child's rhyme from Marid's early years. A gasp went through the crowd when the top half of the coffin rose and moved aside on its own.

There, lying in the bottom half on red satin, lay a book and a ring.

"Recognize those things?" Zaria turned toward Deris and Daris. With a wave of her hand, she released their invisible cages, although their restraints remained intact.

"Where are the bones of our father?" Deris hissed.

"Oh, don't pretend you cared for him or anyone else in your family," Zaria snapped. "That won't play to a Q'elindi. Or a Larentii."

She drew herself up to her full height as the Larentii she could become, while her skin became the blue of a summer sky and her hair turned from black to nearly white.

"I don't give a donkey's shit what you think you are," Deris shouted. "I'm the rightful King, here, and I demand justice."

"Shut up," Zaria said pleasantly. Deris' mouth closed as swiftly as a trap on a hare's leg. The blessing came when he couldn't open it again, no matter how hard he tried.

"This book," Zaria *Pulled* it from the coffin with power, "was written by Helsa, who had no claim to the throne. It is invalid." The book flopped open with a rising of dust upon the table next to Zaria. "This ring," the ring followed the book, settling on the book's open pages, "was designed as a new piece, designating the rightful ruler of Karathia. It was designed by Marid of Belancour and paid for by Hegatt Blackmantle. Helsa was supposed to wear it until Deris reached his majority, at which time she would step aside and allow him to take the throne. Now you may speak," Zaria turned to Deris.

"Give it to me. It's mine," he shouted.

"Shall I give it to you?" Zaria lifted the ring and examined it carefully. "Do you wish to place it upon your finger for all here to see?" Zaria extended the ring on the palm of her hand.

"No," Deris whispered, shaking his head.

"Someone told you what happened to your mother, didn't they?" Zaria accused. "You wouldn't place this ring on your finger if King

Rylend offered you the throne in exchange. Would you?" Zaria walked closer, still holding the ring.

"Get it away," Deris whispered. "I won't wear it."

"Then why did you demand it? What about the throne, Deris Arden? If King Rylend rises, will you agree to sit on his chair?"

Deris' restraints kept him from stepping back, otherwise he would have. I didn't understand—what would be the harm in sitting the throne?

"Would you care to enlighten these people here, as to why you refuse to sit on King Rylend's throne?" Zaria as a Larentii stood tall and stern as she studied Deris Arden.

"It will kill all except the rightful ruler," Deris hung his head.

"So, you know that, too, do you? And yet you wish to be King of Karathia?"

"I can get another throne," he said, staring at his shoes.

"Karathia deserves a better King than you can ever imagine yourself to be," Zaria huffed. "King Rylend, I am done with these two. They aren't worth the sand in a fisherman's shoes."

Zaria

King Rylend rose, then, and walked toward me. "Do I have your blessing, then, to keep the throne?" he asked.

"You don't need my blessing," I said. "That blessing came from another."

"Who?" Rylend asked. He thought he was asking a rhetorical question at the beginning. He was about to learn better.

"Father?" I turned toward the crowd. They'd used many names through the years, most recently Gale and Norn. They came forward, allowing their disguises to fall away.

I was told not to interfere with the coup. I was never told not to hand out advice. Part of that advice was to change Horel and Brill's likeness to resemble Wellend and Warlend when the coup happened.

The bodies Hegatt and Helsa burned in the palace courtyard were those of their own loyal servants.

Wellend came to me first; he smiled as his arms folded around me. Warlend beamed as the crowd gasped. Wylend Arden whimpered before disappearing from the throne room. His father never approved of his taking the throne. Wellend, the King, gave permission for his brother to hold it in his stead.

"We have our books," Wellend and Warlend's volumes appeared in their hands. "I abdicate to you, Rylend Morphis. However, I have written in here," Wellend tapped the book he held, "that Zaria will keep the Heir's ring. Should there ever be one given the throne who should not have it, Zaria will assert her claim, as is her right."

Terrett

I turned toward my brothers, who still sat in the balcony above. Far behind them, I saw a man walk toward the exit before he folded space.

Ilya Ironsmith had been here all along. Turning toward Zaria, I saw her stiffen and pull away from Wellend's embrace.

She knew.

Le-Ath Veronis
Lissa

"Where are they now?" I asked Erland.

"At the Queen's Palace—they still own it," Erland shrugged. "I read the book for myself—Wellend was quite thorough when he handed everything to Ry. He can't come back and take the throne from him."

"He wouldn't. Didn't you see the look on his face when he hugged Zaria? He knows what she's capable of. She's the one he'd prefer to see on the throne, but he let her decide."

"I still can't believe all those things about Wylend," he muttered.

"You can't?" I squeaked. "He's my fucking grandfather. I feel like an idiot."

"How would it have been—if Zaria hadn't been caught up in the Lyristolyi drug and Wellend had fathered his child? What would Karathia be like with her sitting the throne?"

"I think the entire court would be afraid to look at her wrong," I said.

For the first time in days, Erland laughed.

~

Avii Castle

Quin

"My love," Justis' hand stroked my feathers as I settled my head in a comfortable hollow of his shoulder.

"I missed you so much," I whispered. "So many terrible things happened, and I dreamed about your strong arms and black feathers."

"Black feathers?"

"Justis, that is how I see you in my dreams—with the black feathers you were born with. Red is beautiful, but I fell in love with a man whose black feathers stretched wider than any other's."

"Ah. I understand, now," he said. "Liron changed my feathers, so I'd become King."

"Please, never mention him again," I begged. He was silent for a while. "I hear we still have work to do, tracking Vardil Cayetes," Justis said, breaking the silence.

"We do. Zaria says she'll help, but Vardil has V'ili with him," I yawned.

"You never told me what happened to Deris and Daris—or that infernal coffin," Justis said.

"The twins were stripped of power and sent to the prison planet," I said. "The coffin—Zaria separated its particles. I was glad—if it were kept, I'd always see Barc inside it," I whispered. "That is a terrible memory to have."

"Then go to sleep and have good dreams," Justis soothed.

"Tomorrow, we will fly over the tour boats and drop flowers if you want."

"That sounds like fun."

It did.

~

Lissa

"These are the ones for Quin," Zaria appeared with a crate in her arms.

"Huh?" I rose from my seat behind the desk in my study as she set the crate on my desk. Inside it, thousands of marble-sized glass spheres were stacked neatly.

"These glass spheres—they don't hold power stored by Liron," she said. "They're safe to use."

"For what?" I still didn't understand.

"These are what the Avii Queen used to keep the poison at bay in Fyris," Zaria shrugged wearily. "If you recall," she went on, "Quin has an uncanny ability to call things to her. Think on that."

"I have questions," I said before she turned away to leave.

"What's that?"

"Vardil Cayetes—and V'ili?"

"I said I'd help Quin hunt them. I intend to keep my word. I doubt Ilya will join us. She'll need another guard if she goes out again." I could tell that Ilya's defection troubled her greatly.

"We still haven't found the kidnap victims," my shoulders sagged in response. "We've shut down several drakus seed farms, but there are still people missing, not to mention the growing concern about the reappearance of the Lyristolyi drug."

"V'ili knew where all the victims were," Zaria sighed. "So he and Cayetes have probably moved them. The drugs—we'll find them." She was resolved—determined on those things. "I take it you got no worthwhile information from Deris and Daris before their sentencing?" she asked. She'd left with Wellend and Warlend before Ry and his Council made those decisions.

"Nothing we could use, as it turns out. Whatever they gave us was no longer any good."

"I thought so. Terrett is V'ili's child—as are Gerrett and Morrett. I saw that in Quin. She recognized the kinship in V'ili. Any similarities end there."

"The N'il Mo'erti?" I asked the question I really wanted answered.

"Oh. They're uh—on Tiralia. Where they originated."

"What happened to these? What made them stop working?" I forged ahead. I could see she was tired and beyond depressed, but I needed answers.

"Hegatt bought the plans from a noble on Hraede," Zaria shrugged. "Hegatt carried them with him, even when he slept. He slept soundly one night."

"You altered them, didn't you?"

"Yeah. I gave the machines a command word. All I had to do was say it and they'd deactivate. They can't reactivate unless I say it again. I will never, ever, say it again."

She disappeared before I could call her back.

Zaria

"Dearest?" Valegar sat on the sand beside me. I'd chosen the seashore on a deserted world to lie naked and soak up sunlight to feed myself. I hadn't felt like eating normal food since the hearings.

Somewhere, Wylend Arden still held his power, as did his son, Brenten. "They should have exiled him at the very least," I muttered.

"My love, stop fretting. That is over," Valegar soothed.

"Ilya was at the hearing," I said, closing my eyes. "The minute I became Larentii, he got up and left."

"I know." Valegar was just as upset as I was about that. "The others stayed. Edden Charkisul is begging to see you, as are Gerrett, Caylon and Bekzi."

"Val, I feel so tired," I mumbled.

"I know. This has not been easy for you, my love. Will you not let them care for you? I believe they'd like nothing better."

"I'll think about it," I said.

EPILOGUE

KELL

"**W**hat's this?" I waved the piece of paper at Rigo. Ever since I'd come from the shadows and met Rigo's Queen, I'd gotten more correspondence than I ever had before becoming vampire.

"It's a wedding invitation," Rigo said. "If you'd read it, you'd see for yourself."

"I don't want to attend a wedding."

"What you want doesn't matter. My Queen requests it; therefore, you will go. I hear there may not be a ceremony, however. Rumor has it that Miss Lexsi will refuse the arranged marriage to her High Demon intended. Perhaps there is another reason Lissa wants you to be there."

"I hope not. Will there be cake?"

I'd gotten a taste for sweets, once I could eat normal food again.

"There will certainly be cake, Lord Abenott," Rigo grinned.

"Then what shall I wear, King Rigo?" I asked.

The End